PRAISE FOR A

Recipe for Second Chances

"As a reader and a writer, I am always over the moon when I find a new author with a refreshing, wonderful new voice. Such is the case with *Recipe for Second Chances*—I couldn't turn the pages fast enough. When I got to the last page, I felt sad that the story was over. I wanted more. To me that is the mark of a really good writer."

—Fern Michaels, author of 153 (and counting) *New York Times* bestselling novels

Praise for Ali's Cookbooks

"Ali Rosen is saving our dinner parties one dish at a time."

—Carla Hall, chef and television host

"It's a necessary and *delicious* addition to any collection!"

—Kwame Onwuachi, James Beard Award–winning chef, *Top Chef* judge, and executive producer of *Food & Wine* magazine

"Ali's got us and I'm so glad that she does."

—Dorie Greenspan, author of *Baking with Dorie* and *Everyday Dorie*

"I want to give Ali Rosen a big high five for writing this book."

—Pati Jinich, James Beard Award–winning and Emmy-nominated host of *Pati's Mexican Table*

Recipe for Second Chances

Other Titles by Ali Rosen

Cookbooks

Modern Freezer Meals
Bring It!
15 Minute Meals (coming 2024)

Recipe for Second Chances

ALI ROSEN

 Montlake

Published by Montlake, Seattle

www.apub.com

Amazon, the Amazon logo, and Montlake are trademarks of Amazon.com, Inc., or its affiliates.

ISBN-13: 9781662513701 (paperback)
ISBN-13: 9781662513695 (digital)

Cover design and illustration by Sarah Horgan
Cover image: © alaver / Shutterstock; © Annadomenika / Shutterstock; © 1494 / Shutterstock

Printed in the United States of America

To Daniel.
I like you, I lust you, I love you.

Things could be the same if things were different.
But things are the way you made them.
—*The Awful Truth*

I think you know how to love better than any of us.
That's why you find it all so painful.
—*Fleabag*

You know I love you more than my luggage.
—*Steel Magnolias*

CHAPTER ONE
JUNE, NINE YEARS AGO

"Can we order yet?" I was hungry and flagging from the wait.

"Yeah, sure, Stella, of course. Let's start, and he can order more whenever he arrives."

I could tell that Luca was trying to placate me. I kind of adored the small power that our group of friends held over a new boyfriend who was desperate to be liked. It would have been endearing if I wasn't so tired and anxious from a day surrounded by food but never actually sitting down for a meal.

So Subrata's new boyfriend was *not* my problem. It was Friday night and I was ready to eat. And drink. And this dark, divey, all-you-can-eat-and-drink sushi spot on the Lower East Side was the place to make that happen quickly.

Except there was one kink in the plan: one of Luca's friends was late, and I was done pretending I cared enough to keep putting my night on hold.

I started penciling in selections for everyone on the flimsy little sheets they gave us, writing in more drinks than was probably necessary.

"Remember, the all-you-can-eat deal does not include overordering. Anything you do not eat you have to pay for," said the waitress, in a dull and practiced tone, when she saw my order for the table.

I narrowed my eyes at her, offended by her doubts.

I was about to assure her of our certain gluttony when a voice chimed in: "I'm here, I'm here. Don't worry, I could eat all of this."

I looked up and saw a man standing right behind our waitress, grinning at us all. Luca and his other friend stood up and gave him a hug, so presumably this was our dinner's missing musketeer.

"Everyone, this is Samuel," Luca explained. "He actually suggested this spot, so despite his lateness you have him to thank for the overabundance of food this evening."

This guy did not bode well for the quality of the restaurant we were eating in. He was wearing the squarest outfit I could imagine—khakis (was he eighty-five?) and a red polo shirt. He was cute, in kind of a dorky way, although I had to admit that his smug grin, framed by coffee-colored hair and eyes, was kind of hot. He was broad shouldered and probably average height. I also couldn't see his shoes from my vantage point, but I figured that probably wasn't a loss, based on the rest of his outfit. Luca had mentioned that his friend who grew up in the city had picked this spot, but surely anyone who grew up in New York City wouldn't be wearing khakis out on a Friday night?

"So nice to see you again, Samuel," Subrata said, standing up and giving him a hug. I guess Subrata was sucking up to Luca's friends as much as he was to hers. Nauseating. "These are my friends—Elena, Catalina, and Stella."

"Like, 'Steeeeelllaaaaaa'?" he asked, winking at me and widening his grin.

"Yeah, I've definitely never heard that one before," I said dryly.

"But never said by someone who was such a keen look-alike for Brando?" he quipped back.

I cocked my head at him. "So, movie over the play?"

"Not necessarily, but come on. Anyone yelling 'Stella!' at you is imagining that they are Marlon Brando."

"They probably think I'm going to hand them a beer. That's usually the reference that wins over Tennessee Williams, but you never know."

"Do people really ask you for beers?"

"You think if your name was Heineken they wouldn't?"

He laughed. "Touché."

He sat down across from me, watching me, quizzically, with interest. The depth of his gaze was penetrating, and I felt an absurd desire to cover myself up somehow, my stomach tightening. It was as though x-ray vision was cracking me open and a magnifying glass was examining all my little quips and tricks. *You think you're so cute, Stella, with your beer jokes and surface-level literary references. I bet he can see right through your coded armor of self-reliant bullshit.*

"So you guys all went to boarding school together? Didn't you miss being at home?" he asked, like a tractor beam trying to pull all my most notable life decisions from my core.

I couldn't tell if my discomfort with the attention was of his doing or my own. I shook off the quiet, unsettled feeling and replaced it with nonchalance.

"I missed my parents, but I'm more comfortable taking control of my own life. I wanted to go. And there's a community and friendships and teachers who become like your own little family while you're there."

The blasé stock explanation bounced right off him.

"That's not the same as your actual family, though," he countered, smirking a bit.

"No. But someone doesn't have to be in a room with you to support you."

"Tell that to my overprotective mother," he whispered, letting his eyes go comically large.

It made me sputter an involuntary laugh, fueling a sudden intimacy between us.

"Right, well, I guess I figured out early on that I'm better off when I don't have other people's expectations and needs making me anxious," I said quickly, then closed my mouth instantly once it had come out, surprised at the ease of admitting something so personal to him.

Jesus. What is wrong with me tonight? Just blurting out every possible thing that came to my mind. It must have been because he was dressed like a middle-aged, off-duty shrink, making me feel at ease while spilling my guts.

But my word vomit didn't seem to put him off in the slightest. His lip curled up into a knowing smile, as though the selfishness on the surface of that statement wasn't as important as the vulnerability of it. I felt caught off guard. Naked underneath his gaze.

"Well, even if you don't *need* them in the room with you, it must be nice to have your friends back together again."

His observation was more accurate than an arrow in the center of a bull's-eye. After boarding school, college had flung us all apart. I was across an ocean in Scotland, and the other three were scattered across the US—Cat in California and Elena and Subrata on the East Coast. So this summer was supposed to be our time together: four soul sisters in New York, living in bunk beds with plastic flooring beneath our feet and fluorescent lighting in our faces. It felt paradoxically freeing to be so close again. But I didn't want to admit any of this to him.

I needed to change the subject, or I was going to get pulled in by the undertow that was brimming to the surface. I put my hand on Elena's shoulder and wove her into the conversation, seamlessly, trying to get her take on the pros and cons of boarding school—as though that was what he was asking about, and not delving into a personal exploration of my uncanny ability to push other people away, with a preternatural confidence masking my insecurities.

It was amazing to watch the way he brought out little nuggets of gold from every one of my friends as he got to know them. He had the kind of confidence that felt like the rudder steering the conversation—bringing people into it, asking questions, and keeping everyone lively, always sharing an opinion on whatever topic was going.

The evening sizzled with laughter and stories and conviviality. He enthusiastically gave advice to Cat about how to showcase her ideas to her team leader in her management consultancy internship after she'd admitted shyly it was her dream to get a job offer there after graduation. (*How* that could be anyone's dream I did not know, but Cat's strategic brain seemed to meld in perfectly, and Samuel didn't question her boring job for a minute.) They joked about growing up in the city, and I honestly learned more about her boyfriend back on the West Coast than she'd ever let me pry out of her.

He let Elena regale him with stories about how much she'd already shifted the sales strategy at the start-up she was working for. And he somehow was able to tease Subrata about how much time she spent with Luca in a way that seemed much less whiny than when I did it.

But despite his uncanny ability to weave everyone's stories into a cohesive narrative throughout dinner, I couldn't help but get the feeling that Samuel's attention was always latently on me. He always brought it back to me, always seemed to catch my eye whenever his had been off mine for too long. I kept feeling my cheeks inexplicably flush, like a physical ramification of his gaze that I wanted to tamper down and ignore.

We all decided to head to a bar after dinner—our two-hour time limit on our table came too quickly for the evening to end.

"Can we go somewhere where I can watch the Yankees game? They're playing the Sox, and I want to see the last innings," Samuel said as we all stepped outside.

"Oh boo, come on, the Yankees?" I said teasingly. I had probably had one more sake bomb than was necessary.

"I grew up in New York. I'm supposed to root against my home team?"

"No, it's just that the Yankees suck and are terrible."

"Okay, well, by any normal measure, like actually winning games, they are in fact not terrible at all. Aren't you from North Carolina? Why do you care?"

He definitely had been listening when I mentioned *that* offhandedly during dinner.

"I went to high school outside of Boston."

"Oh no."

"What?"

"Please tell me that doesn't mean you're a Red Sox fan."

I tilted my head at him as if daring him to ask me again.

"You think that my fandom is truly terrible?" he said, laughing. "Please look in a mirror."

"'Fandom' is a strong word." I was hedging, but it was true. "I grew up in a decidedly nonsports family. I'm just saying that living in Boston for four years has seeped a Yankees hatred into my bloodstream."

"Wow. I was going to ask you out on a date, but now this? If you're a Red Sox fan, I don't think I can."

His comment made me mentally stumble for a moment, and I had to catch myself to stop from looking so shocked. What kind of guy just comes right out and says that? No playing hard to get, no extra flirting, just a blatant admission that he was going to ask me out?

I had obviously noticed his flirtatious vibe from all his low-level teasing throughout the evening, but my instinct with men was always to undersell my expectations. It would have been easy to write it off as banter. But now here he was just openly saying he was going to ask me out.

That level of confidence in a guy with such terrible taste in clothing was disarming. It was almost . . . earnest?

"I'm not really dating right now," I said, truthfully, and with as much of a casual air as I could muster.

"Oh, well then, thank goodness you're a Red Sox fan. I wouldn't want to waste a perfectly good breakfast at Sarabeth's on someone who thinks Boston is even remotely comparable to New York."

"Okay, seriously? Are you an Upper West Side grandma? Sarabeth's?"

"Seriously? Don't knock pancakes."

I looked at him incredulously.

"Please, I would never knock *pancakes*. It's just I don't need to eat pancakes in a stuffy setting surrounded by teenage girls. Give me Veselka or some other downtown diner food any day."

He laughed, and I could almost see the wheels spinning in his head. "Fine, then, how about this. If the Red Sox win tonight, you can treat me to a meal at Veselka. And I know they're open twenty-four hours a day, so you can't even pretend you don't have time." *Damn it, how did he already know what my immediate excuse would be?* "And if the Yankees win, I'll take you on a date to Sarabeth's."

I was already a little drunk, and I didn't quite know what to make of this situation. He was so sincere and straightforward. How could someone simply say exactly what he wanted without any means of hedging or protecting himself?

He had enough of a sardonic tilt, but he was mostly too available for me to be interested. I didn't even live in the country most of the time. And since I'd just watched my sister's marriage implode, my care-free summer plans did *not* include a boy my age who took women on breakfast dates.

"I already told you I'm not dating," I finally said.

"Friendly sports-bet-related outing, then?" he countered with a smirk, his eyes shooting down quickly before meeting mine again.

I could feel my fingers and toes tingle. I ignored it.

We had arrived at a bar, and all our friends started to go inside. I shook my head and followed them in.

It's a good rule of thumb that if you feel drunk before you walk into a bar, you probably should just order water, but I was too young and dumb to follow such logic.

To be fair, we weren't even legally allowed to drink, so I'm not sure I could be fully blamed. Three beers later the bar was loud, people were cheering for the Yankees (who were clearly winning by quite the margin), and my head hurt. I sat down in a booth, put my head to the side, and closed my eyes, waiting for the feeling to pass.

I felt someone sit down next to me.

"Sleeping in a bar definitely seems like the most fun way to experience it."

It was Samuel, of course.

He'd given me some space after my date deflection. He stood with his friends watching the game, joking around, not seemingly fazed by anything. There were a few times I felt his eyes on me, and I had to deliberately not look toward him. But that tingly feeling hadn't gone away.

"Leave me alone. I'm dehydrated and tired and my friends don't want to go to bed yet, so I'm just resting my eyes."

"'Resting your eyes,' huh?"

"Yes."

"Not drunk." The amusement reverberated in his voice.

"Not drunk at all," I replied as soberly as possible.

I opened my eyes so I could glower at him. He chuckled.

"So you're just resting your eyes and also dehydrated, and it has nothing to do with alcohol consumption. Sounds very logical to me."

I sat up, with the sort of drunken epiphany I usually later regretted. "I wish humans were like frogs. They can absorb water through their bodies, like magical osmosis. I wish I could just go home, stand in the shower, and soak up all the water so that tomorrow I'd feel like a normal person."

Samuel looked at me with more affection than I could have thought possible for someone who had only known me for a few hours. His expression was somehow both mocking and tender as his lips hitched into a small smile.

"All right, Kermit, I can't solve your osmosis dilemma, but I certainly can walk you home if your friends aren't ready to leave yet. Come on," he said, holding out his hand to me with a confidence and assurance that made me think there was no point in arguing.

I *did* want to go home and lie down. I never was cut out for late nights.

So I took his hand and let him pull me up.

We were only a ten-minute walk from my building. It was that kind of early-summer night where there's heat in the air but it isn't yet muggy and it makes you want to stay outside just a little bit longer.

I finally got a good look at his shoes—beat-up loafers. Fitting.

We talked about our summer jobs and fall college plans, keeping things light and breezy.

He was incredibly easy to talk to. He was the kind of guy who would pepper you with questions, but not in a way that made you defensive. He easily got out of me that, yes, interning at a recipe website was a string of long days that consisted of endless nonsense tasks for people.

It was like he couldn't stop himself from being interested and wanting to view me from every possible angle, drinking in each tidbit he could find while being delicate enough that he could carefully chip below the surface, allowing anxieties and insecurities to surface without judgment. He had a curiosity and attentiveness that was alluring, and he didn't dodge any questions when I asked him right back.

I liked having his conversation all to myself, although I adored the level of insight he brought to the topic of my friends.

"I don't think I've ever seen such a tiny person talk so much shit about grown men. Elena is going to have all of those idiots working for her in a few years," he said, and I couldn't help but smile at the image.

"So, so true."

"I also have to say, Subrata has been so great for Luca. She is quiet, but she always says the most incisive things once the rest of us are finished babbling on. And I've really never met a woman more put together. I think basically everything she owns is like linen or silk—"

"Subrata does have a way of making us all feel like our wardrobes are too filled with an excess of colors, wrinkles, and stains. But she somehow manages to be elegant without coming off like an asshole."

"You should put that on a T-shirt."

I snorted, enjoying his teasing. I was a bit disappointed that we were almost back to my place. But before we could cross the final block, I realized something.

"You didn't really drink a lot tonight," I said, more as a statement than a question.

"I have my driving test tomorrow."

I stopped and looked at him with big eyes. "What do you mean you have your driving test?"

"What else could that mean? I'm trying to get my driver's license."

"But you're a fully grown adult."

"Am I?" He looked down at his clothes, pretending to be shocked by what he saw.

I gave him a little push.

"You know what I'm saying. How do you not have your driver's license already?"

He looked at me with what I was now sensing was his trademark smirk.

"I grew up in the city. I never had to drive. It just felt like it was time to get it. So I'm borrowing a car and taking my test."

He wasn't embarrassed. It was amazing to watch someone who seemed to have such comfort in his own skin. Maybe the outfit belied some internal age where he was really two decades older at heart, and it was coming out through his clothing.

Most people well into college probably wouldn't have wanted to admit so openly that they were only now completing a rite of passage typically reserved for people in the middle of high school. But that clearly wasn't Samuel.

He was somehow both a high-energy, constantly in motion, brain whirring kind of person while also being a completely at ease, steady in himself person. He wasn't looking to impress me through anything other than being totally and utterly himself.

"Well, Sam—"

"Samuel."

"Oh, we haven't reached that stage?"

"It's not a stage. My mother named me Samuel, and she hates when anyone calls me Sam, so that's what I go by."

I nodded. Another strange confession. A mama's boy who couldn't drive. And we were just coming right out with it. Okay.

"Okay, Saaaamuel," I said, letting the drunkenness come back a little more strongly than it had been for the previous ten minutes. "Good luck on your driving test. Thank you for walking me home."

We had reached my building. I stood there in front of him, a few inches deeper into his personal space than would be considered friendly. I was wearing heels, and as a result we were basically the same height. I wondered what I looked like in that moment—my long dark hair was probably a mess and my makeup a little worse for wear.

But he was looking at my eyes intently, without shifting or looking away for even a second, as though he was searching for answers to all his questions about me, and if he could look long enough, he was bound to find them.

I was filled with my own questions and wants, and we were like two little magnets, imperceptibly moving toward each other. It was undeniable that something was sparking between us.

Maybe I was just drunk, but the fervor of this attraction was disquieting, inexorable in its nature.

He smelled like the ocean mixed with herbs.

The tingling had come back. It had moved from my fingers and toes all the way to my center. Heat rose within me, and I tried to tamp it down, but it wasn't going to budge.

The shadows danced along the sharp cut of his jaw, and I could see the small bristling of stubble emerging on his face from the long day. I was close enough to feel him breathing. I wondered if he could sense my own heart racing.

My lips parted ever so slightly. I wondered if he was going to kiss me.

I expected that he was going to kiss me.

He wanted to go on a date with me. He'd asked me almost as soon as he'd met me. He had walked me home, alone.

Clearly he was going to kiss me.

But then, just as suddenly, the moment was over. He put a hand on my shoulder and turned away. My whole body clenched with disappointment.

As he walked, he turned around and said, "The Yankees won, by the way. So I'll call you about when we're going to Sarabeth's."

He didn't even ask for my number.

Little did I know that with Samuel, he'd always be one step ahead of me—in ways both good and bad.

Chapter Two

Wednesday, present day

"I'm sorry, Signora Park, but it appears your bag did not get on the plane with you."

I stare at this sheepish, disheveled beanpole of a man and try to keep my face as sunny as possible. This, despite feeling like I've been run over by a truck due to a night "sleeping" in the middle seat of a middle row of an international flight, where the child behind me kept kicking and the mother next to him kept apologizing so profusely that I couldn't help but say, "It's totally fine," over and over again.

But the man in front of me has nothing to do with either the bag mishandling or the seat destruction. So I take a deep breath and try to will away my rising anxiety before responding.

"Do you know why my bag did not get on the plane?"

I'm gesticulating too much, like an overtired charades player.

"I am afraid I do not have the why." He looks forlorn, and I almost find myself saying *It's totally fine*—again—but the déjà vu is too extreme. "But, I can tell you that the next flight from New York lands here at *le quindici*, fifteen o'clock, and your bag is *al momento* on this plane."

I look up at the giant industrial clock looming over the airport terminal. It is barely past nine a.m. here in Rome. That makes it three a.m. at home, and I am definitely feeling a little loopy because of it. My typical early-to-bed, at-least-eight-hours-of-sleep kind of self is not programmed for jet lag. It's the worthy price of travel—usually—when you have a bag of clothes to change into after a strange night on a plane. But just knowing that my bag is delayed makes me feel even more in need of a shower. Do I smell? Probably, at this point. I am kicking myself for packing my makeup bag in my suitcase. Although, to be fair, I needed the room in my backpack so I could bring those cookies I baked before I left. Still the right trade-off.

"So," I say slowly, trying to focus on the cookies instead of the looming luggage crisis. "What will happen to my bag then?"

"Ah, we will deliver it to you. Here in Roma."

My heart sinks. Of course. This was going to become impossible.

"But I'm staying in Umbria, I'm afraid."

"Ah, well, *si*, that will make it *slightly* more delayed then," he replies, genuinely deflated.

I nod, trying to breathe and convince myself that I can *definitely* be a person who lives spontaneously enough to not have a suitcase in a foreign country.

"Okay, Stella, I've got the car keys whenever you're ready."

Elena is walking toward me, looking like a ray of sunshine. How does she do that? I have never met anyone else who could sleep so little and genuinely be as perky as her without any undertones of annoying or annoyance. And having known her for fifteen years, I've seen her with every possible tone. Maybe it has to do with her small stature— she just doesn't need to store up as much energy—or something. She is projecting confidence in our trip, even though it was clear an hour ago that my bag was probably not on the same trajectory that we were.

"Thank you," I sigh. "It appears we will indeed be leaving without my bag."

"Well then," she says, pulling my backpack off my back and lightening my load to nothing. "I guess that means it's time to go?"

I nod and slide a piece of paper with my phone number and address back across the desk to my bereft baggage handler.

"You'll call us when you have an estimate on her bag?" she asks.

"Yes, and signora, luckily you will be at a hotel, so at least someone will always be there to collect it upon arrival!"

"Yes, how lucky for us," Elena says, in a voice so chirpy you wouldn't pick up on the slight edge of sarcasm unless you really knew her.

I'm so tired that her expression makes me giggle. If my bag is going to be lost, then I might as well find the humor in it. And having Elena here means I can try to more effectively ignore the anxiety my lost luggage would normally cause.

Her efficiency always makes me feel cocooned. We are both straightforward, rational people who agree on the need for GSD—or "getting shit done." It is our shorthand for moving forward and keeping the world in order when other people might whine or stall or overcomplicate things.

Elena is like me in that sense, and in so many smaller ways. In the many years since we'd first met as scared southerners in a sea of kids at boarding school outside Boston, we'd grown up and found our place among other students who genuinely wanted to be at school, and it became an extension of home for both of us. That total earnestness hidden beneath an armor of competence has bonded us for life.

It also means that by this point, we wordlessly know when it is time to pick up the other's slack—and in this instance, my slack is definitely an inability to be at my best when deprived of sleep and trying to keep my cool over problems I cannot control.

As we leave, I turn and wave at my sad baggage man. He gives me an unconvincing thumbs-up. It certainly isn't an auspicious start to the trip.

Elena soon has me in our bright-red, very old-looking Fiat, bopping along to some hideous Italian pop music playlist she has acquired just to torture me. The car is a manual, and I'm not actually convinced she really knows how to drive it, but there's no point in saying anything as she starts to get the hang of it while we're exiting the airport.

"You can wear something of mine for the dinner tonight," she declares, staring straight ahead with one hand on the wheel as we make our way along the ring road around Rome that will take us north toward the Umbrian countryside.

"Yeah right, any of your dresses will be so short on me that I'll look like a teenager still wearing her childhood clothes after a growth spurt."

"A growing teenager is not such a bad look," she says with a wiggle of her eyebrows. "You never know what excitement we might need at this wedding."

I snort, and she grins softly even as she keeps her eyes on the road.

I don't want to ask her if there is something specific she is referring to or if she's just trying to make light of my unfortunate bag situation. It seems unlikely that Elena can't read the nervousness on my face; there is no way my perceptive friend doesn't remember that this wedding might hold some awkwardness for me, even if I haven't spoken about it for almost a decade. I put up a strong facade whenever anxiety swirls through me—my go-to is to always whistle a happy tune and try to push away the bad. But even if I don't mention it to my friends enough, Elena has always clocked it, even if she sometimes gingerly steps around it when I need her to not bring it up.

That's what a best friend is for, really: to ignore when necessary while still chiseling away at even the sturdiest of walls we've built up around ourselves. I may not always say it out loud, but I know she's ready to listen whenever I'm ready.

Twenty minutes into the drive, right when the adrenaline of losing my bag is wearing off and I can feel the internal slump start to hit my jet-lagged brain, my phone rings. It's my sister, Sophie. *Why is she calling?*

"Soph?" I say, a tinge of nervousness in my tone. She's on a trip in California with her new boyfriend, Bassem, and it's almost one a.m. there. It's been ten years since her divorce, but I can't help but always be on guard whenever she has a new man in her life.

"Stella! I hope you and Elena had an easy flight"—I look over to see Elena, turning the music all the way down and watching me as much as she can out of the corner of her eye—"and I'm sure you're super jet lagged, but I just *had* to call you!" I can't help but brace for whatever bad news is coming next. "I'm engaged!"

What? I look down at my phone, like my jet lag fog has somehow gotten me on a call with the wrong person and I merely imagined it was Sophie.

"You've been dating him for like three months, Soph," I finally reply, and her silence fills the now music-less car.

"So?"

"*So?*"

"When you know, you know," she says matter-of-factly.

"Says the divorced woman," I retort.

I hear a sharp intake of breath from Elena next to me, but I turn my body away from her and look out the window.

"I just mean . . ."

I don't want to hurt Sophie's feelings, but I'm her sister and I owe her the truth. *I* was the person who had to watch as the happy-go-lucky yin to my orderly yang turned sad and skittish for years after Charlie left. I can't let that happen to her again.

"I just mean that Bassem seems like a lovely guy, but after everything you've been through, maybe you should be a little more cautious this time around. You have plenty of time to get engaged once you've known him a little longer."

Sophie doesn't respond, and for a minute I think maybe she's hung up. But then she speaks, and her voice is softer now.

"Listen, Stella, I know my divorce was hard for you, and I'll always appreciate how much you were there for me. You were so young and so close to Charlie—"

"This isn't about me—" I scoff.

"And I get that my mess imprinted on you in a more permanent way." She is just barreling on, ignoring my protestations. "But I'm okay. It took me a few years to get past it—"

"More than just *a few years*—"

"And now I know." She's on a roll. "I know that this is the right choice for me. Charlie wasn't, and you and I never talk about it, and that's fine because it was a long time ago. But it's water under the bridge. This is a good thing, Stella. I thought you'd be happy for me. I thought you liked Bassem?"

"Of course I like Bassem," I say testily, like she is completely missing the point. "This is about *you*. And what happens to *you* when a marriage doesn't work. And recognizing that maybe you can't handle that as well as some people."

"Gee, what a vote of confidence."

"It's not confidence! I'm just trying to protect you!" I say a little more loudly than I intended.

I can feel Elena's opinions silently seeping off her, but I keep deliberately not catching her eye.

"I don't need your protection, Stella. I'm almost forty years old. I wanted your support."

Her voice is strained, and I hate that this conversation has taken such a turn. But obviously she doesn't get it if she thinks she can jump without a parachute. As her personal parachute for the last decade, I know better.

"Sorry for loving you enough to be honest," I finally grumble.

"Well," she says with a new sharpness, "I hope you've got some better enthusiasm in reserve for Subrata's wedding this weekend, because she deserves better. And so do I. I'll call you later."

The background noise of her California seaside evening cuts out, and I cringe at the thought of being cut out as well. I probably could have handled that better.

Okay, I *definitely* could have handled that better.

Maybe I'm just tired, and this is one too many weddings to think about. But at least the one Elena and I are driving toward is built on a long-term partnership between two strong, capable people. This thing with Sophie is too risky, too poorly thought out. Yes, she's been back to a more peaceful, upbeat version of herself for the last few years, but she's also been avoiding dating. Being supportive doesn't mean ignoring red flags.

I put my phone away, decisively glad that I didn't let excitement and emotion overshadow precedent and realistic caution. If I give her a few days, she'll understand.

Elena is watching the road, the silence tentative. She is deeply familiar with everything that happened to Sophie—she saw it all unfold.

But while she's listened for years about my worries for Sophie, we've never really discussed how her experiences affected me. I was a stalwart for Sophie, but I could've let Elena and my other friends be a stalwart for me. Maybe now, with Elena overhearing my conversation with Sophie and with the specter of facing my own past failed romances hanging like heavy humidity in the air in front of me, this might be the time to metabolize my anxieties with my friend.

But I push the thought aside. I need to be focused on Subrata this weekend.

We drive the rest of the way without mentioning Sophie or my bag again. I am clearly the queen of avoiding discussing an actual problem, and today is not going to be an exception. I'm in Italy, for crying out loud—I need to get out of my own head and let nothing stop me from having fun while I'm here. And I'm afraid once I open that box it'll be impossible to push it all down. I'm a mess, but at least I *know* I'm a mess. That has to count for something, right? I can handle my own mess.

I turn the volume back up, and Elena smiles, accepting my decision to whistle a happy tune instead. The Italian pop segues into nineties R&B, then into Adele, slowly inviting us to sing louder and more obnoxiously as we go along.

We have to turn down ABBA's "Take a Chance on Me" as we pull into the long driveway of our hotel. After coming off the highway and up some hairpin turns around small towns, I feel like the narrow stone road is welcoming us into a new universe. We are suddenly swaddled beneath a dome of wisteria that winds its way up a long pergola. The gnarled, tough vines twist up and around, in contrast to the delicate shocks of purple that hang from the sides and above in every direction.

I immediately roll down the window to breathe in the elegant perfume of my favorite flower. A light, lazy breeze blows through the window as we finally reach the end of the path and turn into the entrance of Villa Amati.

It looks like a small palace, with brick battlements rising grandly on the top of the building and decorative flairs of warmly painted ceramic lining the walls. Every window is a beautiful bay with wooden shutters flung open. Low bushes with blooming flowers line the gravel walkway leading to the giant fortresslike door (which has clearly had automatic sliding glass installed in this century, after a renovation). The stress of the morning and anticipation of what's to come could not possibly hold in this setting.

"You made it."

I hear a soft voice behind me and turn to see Subrata, fresh faced and lovely, her skin glowing and her chic black bob perfectly in place. She gives me a warm hug, and I can feel the softness of her impeccable linen shirtdress pressing neatly against my crumpled, disheveled form.

"I am a little embarrassed by how disgusting your wedding venue is. How are you possibly coping?" I tease.

Subrata rolls her eyes at me. "Yes, yes, I could not possibly bear this without your wit and charm to get me through."

"Well, thank goodness we've arrived then," I drolly shoot back.

I take her hand in mine and look down at the simple ring on her dainty finger.

She is the perfect picture of a calm and ready bride. She and Luca somehow made that leap from college sweethearts to bona fide adult partners.

But this wedding would certainly be the ultimate test for them—they are both cool cucumbers from cultures that are decidedly louder. I don't know how you combine a large family of Indians and an even larger family of Italians into a small(ish), understated wedding in the hills of Umbria, but I certainly know that they are going to try. Perhaps they chose the remote locale in hopes of reducing their families' pushy needs and guest lists. Either way, with an interior designer and a wine importer planning a wedding in such a naturally beautiful setting, I am hoping it won't be anything other than perfect.

"Did you two pack in the same bag?" Subrata asks, clearly confused, as Elena pulls her bag behind her after handing the car keys to the valet.

I shake my head.

"Sadly, no. I am without my luggage."

"What do you mean?"

Subrata's eyes dart quickly from me to Elena and back again, as though her two most reliable friends must have some kind of answer for arriving under the cloud of a conundrum.

I shrug as Elena regales Subrata with the full story from the morning.

"Well, I have extra things you can wear if you want," she suggests in solidarity.

"Oh yeah, not only are you and Elena able to star in a convention of five-foot-tall people, but you definitely want my boobs stretching out everything you own the weekend of your wedding. Perfect plan."

"Obviously I wasn't suggesting something with stretch."

She raises an eyebrow at me as though I should have known better than to even suggest it.

"I have a maxi dress that I think will fit her," Elena offers, ignoring me completely and focusing on getting Subrata on board with her plan. "It might be a bit more 'tea length' on her, but it will at least look appropriate. We'll see what happens tomorrow, but at least for the sangeet on Friday, she should have her bag already."

It doesn't seem like my opinion (or sarcasm) are wanted in this situation, apparently. I'm just window dressing for their conversation. Very smelly and disheveled window dressing who at least has one trick up her sleeve.

"I was smart enough to pack freshly baked cookies into my carry-on." I whip out the bag of cookies from my backpack like a shiny object of distraction and toss them over to Subrata. "Goodness knows we need them more than clothing or toothpaste or other totally useless suitcase items."

"Oooh, are these the hazelnut ones you were telling me about?" she asks, distraction accomplished, already stuffing one into her mouth.

Elena snatches one before Subrata can take them away and looks triumphant.

"Oh, well done, stealing from the *bride*," Subrata sniffs.

"Oh, I'm sorry," Elena says sarcastically, "is it going to be like this all week? Because I need a drink if we're getting 'brided' already."

"Only when it comes to Stella's cookies. Everything else I'm very relaxed about."

She takes a large bite of a cookie and smiles serenely. I actually believe her. But before Elena can object, I pull out another bag of cookies and hand them over to her. Elena's eyes go wide.

Please, like I would ever only bring *one bag*.

"Yeah, I think this recipe is the keeper version," I reply, going back to Subrata's original question. "The secret is in adding a little bit of miso paste to enhance the earthiness of the hazelnuts. Well, that and a lot of sugar. They're going to run in the magazine in the fall."

Subrata nods, and I can see the gears turning in her head.

"Speaking of work—what happened with that meeting?" she asks me, deftly switching the topic to the other unpleasant subject I've been hoping they'd forget about.

"I don't want to talk about it," I huff out, starting to feel the energy that ABBA and cookies provided earlier draining out of me and jet lag rearing back in to take its place. "It was as expected."

"So they gave Reid the promotion?"

"Yes," I mutter, trying to squash my irritation. "They gave Reid the promotion. Like I said, as expected."

Elena and Subrata exchange a look, and I can see they're going to drop it. They know I'm not going to delve into my feelings, especially if they're of the unpleasant variety.

I'd imagined it would be a long shot to go for this promotion at work. Associate editor to editor at a food magazine in an era when most magazines are shrinking is always a big jump and a hurdle to climb. But at the very least I was hoping it would at least go to someone other than Reid.

At a food publication, you'd think that the better recipes and prose would win out. I've always thought that if I keep my head down, go above and beyond at my job, and maintain positive relationships with everyone both senior to and below me, I will be recognized.

But that conversation with my boss about the not-happening promotion was possibly even more mortifying than I could have imagined. Yoli explained how Reid had emailed all the senior editors, mentioning his every success and win for years. He constantly asked others around him to mention his good work to every boss imaginable.

When it came time to pick a new editor, there was one person who had been touting his leadership skills for years and another who had been diligently doing the work for everyone else without complaint.

Why wouldn't they want to go with Reid? And why wouldn't they want the one person everyone could count on to turn around assignments quickly and without errors to stay in that role for a few more years?

I had applied for the role hoping that my work would speak for itself, but I should have been the one speaking up for myself. Yoli is also a GSD kind of person—she gets shit done faster and more efficiently (and with three kids) than anyone else I know. But the decision wasn't hers.

I cried in her office, just a little, until I could pull myself back together. I cried for the first time ever in front of a boss. I had bit the side of my cheek so hard trying to stop it at first that I made the inside of my mouth bleed. I quickly wiped the tears away as soon as they started falling, but the look on Yoli's face made me break a bit inside.

"You and I both know you're the better writer and leader, Stella," she said with earnestness. "But this time, flash won out. You're going to have to get better at exploding some fireworks in their faces."

Her voice is still ringing in my ears as I stand there with Elena and Subrata. I might need a bit more flash in my professional life, but no one is going to dim my star here. I am dependable and fun, and I am going to support my friend no matter what shambles I've left my work and now personal life in at home. This is not the time to suddenly turn into a whiny, emotional basket case.

I barely get any vacation anyway, so if I'm only going to be in Italy for a measly five days, I'm going to make it count. I mentally push the voice over the cliff of my memory and smile at my friends.

"So—*molto bene!*" I exclaim loudly, clapping my hands together. "Let's check into this dump!"

CHAPTER THREE

After collapsing into my fluffy dream of a hotel bed like I'd never seen one before and taking an exceptionally long nap, I am finally standing under the shower and feeling like a new woman. I have washed every inch, but I am still lazily languishing with my face under the water, letting the heat pour over me. It's doing its best to erase the last week of job headaches and the entire morning of bag disasters and sisterly confrontations to get my pulsing, anxious undercurrent under control. This is where I excel—I don't need anyone else to pull me through it. Mind over matter and let it wash away. The smell of fancy soaps and the chic Italian marble surrounding me are certainly doing a lot to get me into a new mindset.

I step out of the shower and pile my hair back on top of my head—without any products of my own, I am just going to have to try and make a messy bun look like it is purposeful. Although I can't decide whether the clementine and bergamot shampoo is making my hair give off an eau of Italian countryside or if I'm just now one whiff away from smelling like an unfortunately floral tea bag.

I wrap a bathrobe around myself and look at my sad, dirty plane clothes. Sighing, I pick up my underwear. This is the true downside of losing my luggage—I can borrow all the ill-fitting clothes I like, but I definitely cannot borrow anyone's underwear. I wash it out in the sink and wring out as much water as I can. I look at my watch—it's almost four p.m., and dinner is not until eight. I peek out into the room and see Elena napping, sprawled out like a starfish across the bed, totally out like a light. She really can sleep anywhere at any time.

I am not going to take her clothes without asking. And I don't want to sit inside while she sleeps. It would be totally fine to wander around a country hotel in my robe, right? I could be going to the spa or the pool. No one has to know my bathing suit is probably somewhere in the back of a car in Rome. If I'm lucky.

I put on some hotel slippers, walk outside, and meander my way along a path that leads to the pool. Giant trees shade most of the walkway, and their ancient roots play in stark contrast with the perfectly trimmed hedges and neatly lined rows of flowers that delineate the path. Little nooks are tucked in everywhere—a hammock over here next to a small pond; a bench next to a gate brimming with more wisteria; a set of tables in the distance near the pool, shaded by umbrellas the color of a sunset. The poolside tables seem to still have a few stragglers enjoying the last bits of sunshine, chatting animatedly—it looks like an older couple and a younger one. My skin starts prickling a bit before my brain realizes.

Fuck.

The younger man turns a bit to point back toward the hotel, and I dive behind the wisteria-covered gate. I catch my breath and peek out again.

There he is. The broad back with his sloping shoulders should have given him away instantly. He always had such a particular stance. It's been so many years since I've seen him, but even from far away and with just a glimpse of his side, it's clear that Samuel Gordon is indeed in attendance at this wedding.

I hadn't dared to ask Subrata, but I knew in my gut that this punch was coming. I've stopped myself from imagining this scene too much, but when I have, I've certainly never imagined it with me in a bathrobe and no makeup or even underwear on. This feels like a classic Stella tale if there ever was one. Lack of underwear couldn't possibly lead to something sexy and interesting: only a collision disaster.

I can't see him close enough to tell if his telltale smirk is still there or if his dark eyes are boring into the person he's talking to. His hair still has that adorably mussed wavy texture. I can see him fidgeting a bit, though. It isn't out of boredom; it was never out of boredom (he wouldn't stay in a conversation that was boring him). But I can't help but smile as I watch his impossible energy burn through him, even from this far away. I try to picture him close up, wondering if I could still tell when his brain is going ten times as fast as everyone else's around him. It always made him seem a little bit on the move, even when he was standing completely still.

I watch him from behind my wisteria curtain, and I can feel my insides slowly lurching as I stare. For almost a decade now, I have never allowed myself to think about Samuel for more than a passing moment without instantly, and intentionally, pushing him out of my mind.

I can't think about him—about that summer, when things were good, or that fall, when it suddenly and definitively wasn't—without being reminded that he had burrowed his way into my core and I was never able to fully extricate him.

I wish I could replace that lurch with annoyance; it was his choice, after all, that we don't speak anymore. I'd always known deep down that I was too complicated for him, but he deliberately didn't see it. Until one day he did.

I have every right to be annoyed with him.

But I'm not. Any reminder of him has always made me physically miss him, even if I then curse my traitorous body for not shoving him aside. So why would seeing him in the flesh be any easier? He isn't simply a memory today. He is thirty feet away, looking put together—and, frankly, very sexy—while I hide like a coward. This is . . . not the ideal reaction, to say the least. If anyone saw me, I don't think I could possibly look more pitiful.

So how is he just *standing there*? How does he exist and suddenly zap me back to being twenty years old without doing anything other than talking to some old couple, while I stare at him like a crazy lurker fluttering behind a sea of flowers?

I hear the woman next to him laugh, and it shakes me out of my spiral. I haven't really focused on her, but she is pretty. She's tall, with a cascade of brown curly hair, and that laugh is so loud and contagious that I feel annoyed at how much I instantly like her. Her arm is linked in his, and she could not possibly look any more comfortable standing next to him. They clearly are at ease in each other's presence. My stomach starts to ache.

I knew Luca and Samuel had stayed close friends after college, so there was always a world where we were bound to bump into one another. But I never asked after him, and Subrata only thought we'd gone out a couple of times and then lost touch. I'd deliberately kept so much of it close to the chest at the time that I doubt at this point she even remembers we were briefly connected. He's like this giant black box that I've always known exists but haven't really known any of the current details about. It's seemed better that way.

But standing here now, with no up-to-speed accounting of who this man is today, just seems really, incredibly wrong. This memory of a person is a real person, someone who has lived nine years without being a part of my life and has not ached for me whenever he allows himself to think of me (if he ever thinks of me). He has a girlfriend and the same shoulders, and I am just an idiot in a bathrobe without underwear because my single hand-washed pair is drying on the towel rod of my hotel room.

I look down at my feet, covered only by flimsy hotel slippers, as I crouch down behind the gate as awkwardly as possible. I'm a mess right now—hair sticking out, pulling my robe in as much as possible so I don't flash anyone, hunched over so this small decorative gate doesn't give me away as the most pathetic human in existence. This is not the chic Italian version of myself I was picturing for this weekend. This is like that woman's crazy aunt who can't put her clothes on properly.

I have to get out of here. I don't care what Samuel Gordon thinks of me anymore, but I certainly don't need *anyone* to see me like this. I don't know what I was thinking, leaving my room in the first place.

I stand up and turn around quickly. I walk as fast as I can without running or tripping or having my robe fly open. I don't look back. I can't look back.

CHAPTER FOUR

JULY, NINE YEARS AGO

"Do you want to just stay here? I mean, we're going to the same place tomorrow." Marc lifted one eyebrow up suggestively. He had nothing covering him except a thin bedsheet, and he looked pretty good in it.

"Thank you, but nah," I replied breezily. "I'd rather have all my stuff. I can easily grab a cab now and see you tomorrow at the office." He looked at me with acceptance—not necessarily upset that I was going home, but perhaps hoping for another round before we went into work in the morning. Yet the idea of real sleep and some time alone was probably making him feel the same way I did. I kissed him on the forehead—nimble, perfunctory—and walked out of the room.

The hot muggy summer air hit me as I left the building—I quickly hailed a cab and jumped in. Marc was probably too old for me, and he definitely shouldn't have been hitting on interns, but he worked in the photo department, so it wasn't like he was a boss of mine in any dimension. The good news about men who asked out interns was that they had no agenda beyond the summer. Unlike some people.

I looked at my phone. Of course. I had a new voice mail from Samuel.

"So you know, cagey, noncommittal text messages are really fun, but every time I leave you a voice mail, the implication is that I am actually trying to talk to you and not converse with a robot. I'm glad to know that you're alive, although since I can't confirm without voice recognition that it is *actually you* sending those text messages, I'm going to have to assume that Luca gave me a fake number and is just seeing how long he can troll me. I'm onto you, Luca. If you are in fact Stella Park, and you did in fact lose a bet where the honor of baseball and pancakes were at stake, then I'm going to let you know that I am making a reservation for Saturday, and I expect you to be there. I'm going out on a limb and saying eleven o'clock. And then if Luca shows up, I'll have to strangle him and get your real number out of him."

I smiled and leaned back into the seat. What was with this guy?

He clearly was not getting the hint that we were not looking for the same thing. It wasn't his fault—I hadn't exactly shared with him my summer determination to ignore men for anything but physical release.

Other than Samuel's deliberate obliviousness, my time in New York was generally shaping up exactly the way I'd planned it—I needed a *break*. I'd crossed an ocean to go to college, thinking my parents and my beloved decade-older sister, Sophie, were safe and boring and didn't need anything from me. But by Christmas I arrived home, and Soph had just moved back in with my parents, emotionally bruised from the sudden implosion of her marriage only six months after their offbeat, gorgeous, hazy, hot summer wedding.

Charlie, the older-brother figure who'd been ruffling my hair since I was nine years old, was suddenly a ghost. Charlie's long-standing love for Sophie had been as much a given in my life as having ten fingers and ten toes. Until it wasn't. The echoes of my speech from that summer festivity—my ode to their example of youthful, pure love—ate at me every night while I rubbed her back and she cried herself to sleep.

Going back to school after the break had felt like abandoning a lost puppy. But our late-night phone calls drifted off as winter turned into spring and Sophie hardened to her circumstance. She was done giving a fuck. And after watching her pull herself back up, so was I.

Sophie had made the mistake of falling in love young, before she was strong enough to weather abandonment. I felt lucky to have had a vantage point of male disappointment so young. I promised myself I'd spend the summer enjoying being an untethered college student without a care in the world.

"We really have a duty to our future, more boring selves to use men the same way they're always so casual about using us," I'd said when I shared my plan with my roommates during our first weekend back together.

"Absolutely. And what did our mothers fight for if not for our sexual freedom?" Elena chimed in, always ready to back me up even as she lazily sprawled out over one of our couches, her tiny legs barely covering the entire length.

Subrata and Cat were more skeptical. They sat together like a wall of dubiousness, Subrata in one of her typically chic beige dresses and Cat still in her uptight work button-downs, both shockingly without a hair out of place despite the late hour and the growing number of drinks.

"You think your mother burned her bra so that her daughter could hook up with a bunch of dudes?" Cat asked, her lanky frame doubling over and laughing at the absurdity of it all.

"Well, I'm sure she didn't think of it that way *at the time*," I said.

"And probably wouldn't want to think about it now either," Elena chimed in.

"Right," I concurred. "No sharing this part of the summer plan with my mother. *But* yes, I am here to have fun, and men are dumb and it's the summer, so that's my plan."

"Makes absolute perfect, logical, total sense to me," Elena said, self-seriously.

Subrata and Cat just shook their heads, hiding smiles. They were both lost causes anyway, smugly enjoying their recent boyfriends without any thought to the future.

They didn't have Charlie in the back of their heads asking for permission to marry their sister; they didn't have tearstained vows of forever to reminisce on; they didn't have to listen to silent sobs late at night when their sister thought no one else was still awake.

Men might *think* they know their own feelings, but men in their twenties are capricious creatures, and I didn't need to give any unformed zygote the chance to disappoint himself or (and especially) me. At this age they're good for one thing, and that's what I was going to spend the summer making the most of. I couldn't care less that Charlie was a liar.

But I did have to respond to Samuel. It had been two weeks since the sushi and the baseball and the walking home without kissing.

He infuriatingly only called and left voice mails, and every time I texted back he insisted on responding only through voice mails. He didn't give up, and he didn't even seem fazed.

I was really not in the mood for a guy who was this earnest and interested. My season of friendship and revelry was not going to include *dates*. The entire point of summer was to be ephemeral.

But—his voice mails made me feel just the smallest amount of giddiness. They always made me laugh. And maybe—just maybe—I also felt a niggling sense of irritation that a guy who was trying so hard to get me out on a date hadn't tried at all to kiss me. A date with Samuel would be fun; it was impossible to imagine him not being fun.

But definitely not a breakfast date. There was no making out on breakfast dates.

Stella: I'm not a Luca troll. I just really don't want to wake up early for mediocre pancakes on a weekend. How about we do dinner instead? We can go somewhere casual.

I sent the missive off into the universe. I immediately saw him typing back.

Samuel: Dinner it is. Let's say Saturday. And since I want pancakes and you want dinner I'm going to let you win—unlike the Red Sox—and say let's do Veselka. 24-hour dream spot. You can pick any time you want.

I smiled and typed back. Deal.

Samuel: Why don't you ever answer the phone?

Stella: Why do you insist on calling like an old man?

Samuel: I would think it would show my dedication to the cause.

Stella: Have you ever heard of playing hard to get?

Samuel: Not my style.

Stella: Have you ever heard of modern technology?

Samuel: Some things are just better with tone and context attached.

Stella: Like someone could misinterpret, "What day should we eat pancakes"?

Samuel: No, but what if I'm sad because I failed my driving test?

I paused the rapid-fire texting. Well, that sucked for him. I had failed my own driving test—I may or may not have backed up into a parked police car, which led to outright cackling from the tester and an automatic failure despite having done everything else right. Hitting a car, even in a minor way, is apparently a bridge too far for a driving test.

I wondered what had happened during Samuel's test. I looked at the phone.

Fuck it. I dialed his number.

"Oh, so you do have a voice box?" he said gleefully when he answered the phone after one ring, before I'd had the chance to change my mind and hang up.

"Obviously I do. I just wanted to say sorry about your driving test. That sucks, and I failed mine the first time, and I wanted a lot of sympathy at the time—many, *many* years ago—so for that reason and that reason only, I am calling you back."

"But I didn't fail my driving test. Bummer about yours, though."

I sat up as the cab went over a bump.

"You just said you failed."

"No, see, that text message really messed with the context and sarcasm of what I was saying. I was saying what *if* I was sad because I failed my driving test. That's the problem with kids these days and their text messages."

I rolled my eyes, even though he couldn't see me. What a dork.

"Okay, well then, the sympathy call was apparently unwarranted. Won't make that mistake again. See you Saturday. Let's say seven o'clock."

"Oh, you're giving me the early shift then?"

He really didn't miss a beat. But in this instance, other men had nothing to do with it.

"I don't know if you noticed, but I'm not exactly a late-night person on my best of days," I said honestly. "I'm giving you the only dinner shift, and that's all I'm good for."

"I would imagine you're good for a whole host of things."

I could hear the smile in his voice. The flirting, the sarcasm, and the earnestness of him all blended together to make him intriguing and exasperating enough to agree to a date of any kind.

"I am indeed. See you Saturday."

CHAPTER FIVE
WEDNESDAY, PRESENT DAY

The restaurant's garden is decorated impeccably and with abundance. There are small white lights strung up everywhere and low candles on each table. Vines with small flowers bursting out snake their way up every wall and gate. Our hotel is outside Norcia, but this dinner is right in the center of everything.

Norcia is an ancient town with Roman ruins and Renaissance structures that exists like a flat island in a sea of more mountainous towns. It has survived countless strong earthquakes, including two particularly devastating ones a few years back. You can still see some buildings across town in disrepair and chunks of structures missing.

But in the intervening years, as the town has rebuilt, it has also taken on a magical air of rebirth. Old buildings mixed in with new patches. The enthusiasm of seeing tourists streaming through again is palpable. You can still see the remnants, but it's clear this town has been through such a long history that even natural devastation can't remove its charm. Parts of the restaurant's back wall have crumbled, but it now has an air of bohemian clutter where plants have taken root in the fractures.

The wedding, like all Indian weddings, is taking place over a number of days, but this first night is a casual dinner with the guests who arrived this morning. I'm still surprised by the number of seats—I guess when you're coming all the way to Italy, you take the extra few days. Some of Luca's family still live in Italy, but the vast majority of the guests are coming from the US, just like us.

I look down self-consciously as we walk in. Elena and I are certainly not well matched to share clothes. Calling it "tea length" didn't really change the fact that this dress just looks like it was meant to be worn by someone seven inches shorter. My hair is up in a topknot, and my makeup is more minimal than I would have liked—beyond our heights, Elena and I have completely different coloring, so we couldn't exactly mix and match everything. At least my underwear had dried by the time I put it back on.

"Let us marvel at the little victories," Elena said earlier when I went to check on it.

"Are we counting dry, semiclean underwear as a victory? Because that's a little sad."

"Hey, I already ate all the cookies, and you somehow managed to get your hair into even more of a rat's nest than it was earlier, so I would say dry, semiclean underwear is about as good as it's going to get here," she said, tossing over the dress. I scrambled to catch it and changed into it and the underwear. "See." She was staring at the space between the dress and my ankles. "You look great."

I rolled my eyes but gave her a little twirl. No use moping over something I couldn't control.

But now, standing here at the party, it's a little harder to brush it all off. I hate to admit it, but I'm still shaken by my sighting earlier this afternoon, and I would have liked to wear my exterior like armor—sleek hair, sharp makeup, and a casual-but-chic dress to work like a battering ram against any internal flutterings. Instead it feels like every private self-doubt and anxiety is oozing out of me, cracking through my ankles and concealer-free face.

A waiter walks by with a tray of bright-orange Aperol spritzes, and I quickly grab one. I hold Elena's hand for a comfort she doesn't seem to mind that I need, and we say hello to Subrata's family as they see us.

Her mother is practically glowing in a copper-colored draped sari. Her father and brother look sharp in their suits. We gush appropriately at the lights and the setting and then continue onto our admiration of the hotel and all *its* many attributes.

It's nice to see her parents so at ease—that's what a wedding should be, after all. Two families coming together with comforting certainty that their children have made a choice that will keep them cherished long after the parents can try to ensure it. I can't help but feel a pang for my sister at the thought.

But the moment passes as Subrata's parents quickly get caught up in the sea of new guests congratulating them, and as we turn around, I bump straight into someone. I look up to quickly apologize, and there is Samuel.

All the air goes sharply out of my chest. The hum of the crowd suddenly dims around me, and despite all the years since we've been eye to eye, the familiar pull of him is so strong I feel statically jolted.

"Hi," he says simply with a docile smile, still so familiar that it almost hurts to be this close to it, save for a few crinkles at the sides of his eyes.

But even though I've pictured that smile so many times, today I can't read it. That mask I've wished for myself seems to exist on the surface of his face—cool, calm, and collected, without a hint of emotion betraying him. I wonder if his insides have needed containment like mine.

Probably not.

The calm on his face is probably because he *is* calm. I need to channel some of that energy and get over myself. This isn't a big deal. This is what I do best—external calm in the face of a storm, even if below the surface every inch of me is sloshing around. I am merely a faint memory to him from almost a decade in the past. I can't stop myself from fidgeting with the small ring on my pinkie finger to try and distract my stomach from continuing its free fall.

"Hi."

It's the lamest-possible response, but I think standing in front of Samuel has made it impossible to get words from my brain out of my mouth. Apparently, the only thing my mouth is capable of is being a fickle friend, since it automatically curves upward unprompted until somehow I'm practically beaming. I can't help it—his presence is tugging on me from the inside out.

We stand, staring, without saying anything else for just a moment. It's probably imperceptible to anyone else, that spark inexplicably broiling between us again, hot honey drizzled on my insides. He is looking so straight into me that I feel like he's taken root inside my brain and is able to poke around my thoughts. So, one thing about him certainly hasn't changed.

"Nice to see you again, Samuel." I hear Elena pipe up beside me, and I immediately brush every semblance of feeling off my face.

It breaks the reverie, and when I look back at Samuel, I see that whatever I've been imagining clearly is not happening. I wonder if Elena has clocked my nerves—she knows about Samuel that summer, *sort of*. I know at the time I thought if I minimized him to my friends and kept it breezy, then that could keep *me* breezy. He couldn't hurt me if I didn't actually care. But I was never sure if Elena actually bought it.

Samuel is no longer looking at me and instead is giving her a friendly nod.

"How've you been, Elena? What's new?"

She launches into an explanation of her job in tech, and I stop listening after a minute. Suddenly I'm like an explorer given a moment to investigate. His hair is a bit longer than how he used to wear it, but it still has that slight wave that I always wanted to get my hands into. He has filled out more—in a good way; he's grown into himself as he's aged—and his suit is tailored perfectly. I wonder if that means he wears a suit to work every day. No ring—yet.

He catches me staring, and I immediately snap my head back toward Elena, pretending to be intensely interested in an explanation that I could have given myself in my sleep.

"That's really great," he says back to Elena, with such genuine enthusiasm. "I'm glad things have been going so well for you. What about you, Stella?"

His attention is back on me, but the placid expression has also returned. I'm willing that spark from a few moments ago to exist. But I really am pathetic—I must have imagined it because it is truly, *truly* not anywhere even in the vicinity. It seems I don't garner quite the same enthusiasm as Elena, apparently.

"Oh, I'm fine, thanks. Working at a magazine, writing recipes, investigating ingredients, saving lives, you know."

He looks nonplussed, so I can't really stop myself from continuing. My nervous energy is propelling me forward, like a train wreck in slow motion.

"Just kidding. I mean, not kidding about the magazine, but the saving lives part. Because obviously, food writing doesn't do that. But I do think it gives people really valuable information about how to cook and improve their cooking, so in that regard I guess it really does *contribute* to people's lives, even if it isn't saving them."

I can feel Elena's eyes on me, probably wondering what the hell I'm saying. To be fair, I also don't really know what the hell I'm saying, so I shouldn't be surprised that I'm confusing her. I smooth out my dress with my hands, trying to think of some way to save myself from the torture of this conversation.

"At any rate," I try to finish, "it's been great, and I love being in New York full time, and I'm happy where I am. So it's good. I've been good. I'm good."

I stop. This has to stop. I need to make it stop.

"What about you? Whatcha been up to?"

I say it with such fake casualness, as though I am not staring at his hands and remembering them on my body. As though I could think about *anything* else—there is nowhere to look at him without resurrecting some memory.

Why is it like this? Why hasn't a single frame of the moments we spent together disappeared or even dulled now that he's standing right in front of me? How lamentable is my life that I haven't lost even one drop of him from my mind after so much time? Have I really been alone for so long that I'm having this kind of reaction to a guy from so many years ago whom I didn't even date for *that* long?

I finally decide it's better just to sort of look to the side of him to stop myself from spiraling even more. I can't tell if he's pretending not to notice my total floundering or if he genuinely doesn't care enough to notice.

"I've been fine, thanks. I . . . I'm in New York too. Working at a law firm that I'm enjoying for now."

I nod my head with such fervor it probably looks like he has found the cure for cancer. I didn't realize he was back in New York. I'd heard he'd gone to Chicago for law school, and I always sort of assumed he'd stayed there once he graduated. It struck me as sort of absurd now to have imagined that he would stay there when he was such a New Yorker to his core—but it was easier to believe he was still there, away from me in some cold midwestern stock photograph that I never wanted to give real edges to.

There is a gaping chasm of conversation now between us. What has your life been like for *nine years*? What have you been doing? Is your family well? Do you still do that thing where you get totally lost in whatever you're reading and even if someone is speaking right in your ear you just legitimately can't even hear them? Who have you been sleeping with? Do you think about me late at night when you are feeling lonely and unsatisfied? Can you not articulate that feeling to anyone else in your life because you never really told any of your friends about this sort-of relationship you had with a person who might have been your favorite person if you both hadn't been young and stupid?

Or maybe that's just me.

"Well, that's great—who would've thought we'd all end up in New York?" Elena replies, grabbing onto the conversation and hoisting it up when it must otherwise seem dead to anyone else watching.

We both nod back at her blankly. But as I'm trying to think of something else to say, I see Samuel's girlfriend walk up to our group. She's wearing a belted burgundy dress with white Converse sneakers, and I'm so jealous that she can manage to look so cool and still be comfortable at the same time. *She* is effortless and vibrant, while I'm standing in a too-short dress with wet hair thrown into a bun. This just keeps getting better.

"Samuel, I think they're encouraging everyone to sit down," she says quietly, and he looks at her with the same blank stare he was giving me.

She laughs. "Okay, okay, obviously that's a total sham reason for being compliant. I mostly don't want to miss out on eating all those breadsticks."

She winks at him and then turns to us with a smile that seems to contain some hidden secret pocket of joy just for us.

"Hi, I'm Hadley, so nice to meet you guys."

We shake hands and introduce ourselves, and she couldn't have reacted less to my name if she'd been trying to. Guess he talked about me en route to this trip as much as I talked about him. At least now I know how little he cares about seeing me again. If only my neuroses would make this ancient history feel less relevant to the present.

"Can you believe this gorgeous garden?" Hadley continues, sweeping her arms around at the scene. "Between the lights and the aperitifs, I feel like I'm in a movie and Sophia Loren's going to come out and bat her eyelashes at me any moment now."

She's practically glowing.

I chuckle. I like her. How could I not? Her enthusiasm is infectious.

But then she looks back at the other side of the room. "Well, we're sitting over here, Samuel—want to join me? Ooh, now they're putting out bread with some prosciutto-looking meat on it. That is definitely calling my name."

She grabs his hand and waves goodbye to us, and just like that he's wandering away, with a slight look back to give his own small, tentative wave.

I deflate. All these years, and that's how I said hello? By babbling like an idiot about my job? But if Elena notices, she isn't saying anything about it.

"Come on, let's find our table."

She leads me along the rows, looking at the names on every seat while we move farther and farther away from where we were standing.

We find our seats and sit down. I watch as Subrata and Luca flit around the room, like two lightning bugs drawn together and lighting up the space as they move through it effortlessly. They are so exceptionally happy and in their element—two self-possessed introverts managing to be at the center of attention because it is about each other and they are taking a leap together that feels like the natural next stage.

She looks beautiful and calm, and my heart beats with so much joy for her in this moment, even if the thought of that leap terrifies *me*. To take such a monumental step with clarity and ease seems like the greatest gift. Subrata is always so cool and collected, but she never shrinks herself or hides from seizing what's hers. She will always quietly but assertively grab onto what is right for her. She did that with Luca, and she did it at the interior design firm where she is so beloved. I can be brash and sarcastic, but I could never just ask for the things I actually want. It is such a contrast.

I am so in awe of my incredible friend tonight—and every night, really. But I take a sip of the drink that's in front of me and try to relax a bit at that thought. What a pleasure to be able to join in your friend's happiest moments.

I turn to see Cat, newly arrived, as she plops herself down on the seat next to me. I instantly, giddily, bowl her over with a giant hug. Cat travels so much for work that instead of flying in with us from New York, she's come directly from some meandering multileg trip from the project she's working on.

She looks exhausted, in that hidden way that only Cat can look—never complaining, never letting anyone see when she's flagging, and only those of us who've known her for the last fifteen years can spot the tells. Cat's mom passed away three years ago, after a long illness. Sometimes it still seems like the whole world is achingly on her shoulders. That GSD side of my brain wants to scoop up my old friend and ply her with her own bag of cookies before letting her take a nap in one of those gorgeous beds back at our hotel. I want her to get the vacation she deserves right now.

I resolve to be more focused on making sure she is okay and stop focusing on stupid ghosts of boyfriends past. *This* is what matters. I'm here for my friends. I'm here to celebrate Subrata. I'm here to help slowly dig Cat out of her yearslong weariness. I'm here to give Elena the fun weekend she needs.

I turn and say hello to the other people at our table, friends from various stages in Subrata's life. I go big on regaling the whole table (but most importantly Cat) with my tales of lost suitcases, hand-washed underwear, and too-small dresses. When I get a belly laugh out of Cat, I know the weekend is off to a good start. Everyone is light, bright, and happy with that mixture that only jet lag, a beautiful location, and a steady stream of alcohol can provide.

Platters upon platters of cured meats quickly disappear, followed by a salad of roasted artichokes, followed by a ravioli with a creamy truffle sauce, followed by a lamb chop with an Umbrian pesto. Everyone gushes over the food—it is mountainous and never ending, a salty, savory parade of spring produce and aged ingredients. It is satiating down to my bones.

And even though I hate that I'm even thinking about it, I can't bring myself to look over at Samuel to see if he and Hadley are having as much fun as we are. I want to believe his eyes are on me, that I am radiating and laughing and performing for someone who is watching.

He was always so good at watching me.

But that was such a long time ago.

CHAPTER SIX

JULY, NINE YEARS AGO

I crossed the street toward Veselka and its auburn-and-yellow awning. The sun was setting, and the neon *Open 24 Hours* sign glowed back through the hazy air. A sandwich board outside the restaurant declared *Borscht Is Back* in neat, flowing cursive. I walked in, and the air-conditioning clobbered me immediately, right as I saw Samuel.

He was leaning against a stool, but not necessarily trying to sit down at the counter. I bet he wanted a real table. He beamed when he spotted me. It was impossible not to smile back at that. I couldn't help but notice the polo shirt and khaki combination was still in full force, but for some reason this time it was endearing.

"I wasn't totally convinced you were going to show up after avoiding me for so long," he said, wagging his finger at me while still grinning in a languid, teasing sort of way.

It was clear he was never in doubt that he would actually get me to go out with him. Patience did not seem to be a problem for Samuel. I almost got the impression that he was enjoying that I'd made him work for it. Strength from me only made him seem more convinced that he'd chosen an equal match to spar with.

"I was told there would be pancakes," I responded slyly.

"No, *I* was told there would be pancakes, since you rejected my original choice of locale. So now *you* have to provide the pancakes, at the very least."

A waitress beckoned us over to a table that had just been cleared, and I walked in front of him. I could feel his eyes on my back, and when I turned around, he didn't make any effort to conceal that he'd been checking me out. So much for wondering whether he'd *wanted* to kiss me when we were in front of my apartment. He was looking at me like pancakes were not the dessert he had in mind.

Even with my forward nature, I still liked to hide behind some subtlety. Samuel evidently did not do subtlety—what you see is what you get. He'd made it clear as day from the moment I met him that he wanted to take me out, and there was no hiding his delight to have me standing across from him. It didn't feel inappropriate or uncomfortable—merely honest and direct. It was disarming to have that out in the open. No games, no hot and cold, just appreciation mixed with a dose of desire.

"I feel highly confident in my choices," I said with a pointed stare as we sat down. I picked up a menu.

"All your choices?" he replied with a hint of a taunt.

"In food, definitely. In my personal life I'm not so sure."

He laughed and put his hands dramatically over his heart as though I had wounded him.

"Well," he said slowly, "we'll just have to make you sure. What do we have to order here?"

"Obviously after all that, we need to get some pancakes," I said, staring down at the menu. "You can't come here without getting their latkes or pierogi, so we'll need to order some of those. We probably need to get some blintzes too. How hungry are you?"

He stared at me. "I think I might be in love."

"All it takes is for a girl to eat a pierogi? You have some low standards."

"Maybe I'm not meeting the right women," he said pointedly.

"You should have just sat at the counter at Veselka, waiting on a diner stool for some seventy-five-year-old Ukrainian woman to eat you under the table. It wouldn't have been so hard."

"True. I've been going about this all wrong."

He waved the waitress over and proceeded to order a mountain of food. I normally hated when guys ordered for me, but he ordered based on everything I'd suggested without any hesitation. He was trusting my judgment while also taking the lead. It was sexy.

Our conversation was in sync in a way I hadn't ever experienced with a person I'd just met. It was like two best friends catching up, only instead we had everything to share from the start. He talked about growing up in the city with immigrant parents who had the typical high standards for everything academic but none whatsoever for helping his mom cook or clean.

He was fascinated by my growing up in the South with engineer parents who made everything into a debate. I loved trying to shift his view of North Carolina, from vast countryside to cities that just happened to be a fair bit smaller than the one he was used to. He had never traveled farther south than Washington, DC, so it was like trying to explain away everything he had seen in movies and normalize a whole different part of the country. He had so many questions about what it was like, whether I liked growing up within driving distance of mountains, whether I couldn't stand the cold after living in the heat for so long. It amused me how many scenarios he could imagine.

"How has it been going from your spacious college life to sharing a tiny room in New York City with your three best friends?" he asked.

I couldn't help but grin at the thought.

"It's been amazing, actually."

"Amazing? Smashed together in a glorified dorm room?"

"Yeah, but we're used to that from boarding school," I said, a satisfied smile on my lips at just the thought of all of us getting the chance to be together again. "Friends you live with in high school are more like sisters anyway. I'm used to sharing bathroom space with Cat's blow-dryers and closet space with Subrata's unending colorless, perfect clothes. Elena and I have always eaten each other's food without asking, but Elena *also* always bakes me cake just because. Subrata teaches me how to not look like a homeless slob, and Cat makes sure I'm organized enough to function. I've hated being so far away from those three."

"So why did you want to go abroad for college?" he asked.

"After boarding school it just felt like I needed a more dramatic change. I'd already gone away from home and lived with roommates and rolled out of bed to class. I didn't travel much as a kid, but I have loved every minute of it that I've been able to. So yeah, of course I miss my friends and family, but I really wanted to immerse myself in another culture by living it. So I did."

"And your parents just let you." It was a statement, not a question.

"My parents have always been pretty great about treating me like an adult and believing me when I said I needed something—they didn't want me to go away to boarding school, either, but they understood that I was ready to be more independent, and they said okay. They've always let me take care of myself more than I think other kids wanted or needed. Maybe it came with having a sister who was ten years older."

He shook his head. "My mother always let me do everything my own way, but I cannot imagine her having allowed me to leave five seconds earlier than I was supposed to. But then again, I'm the oldest. She is so cautious with me."

He said it with such a fondness that I almost wanted to grab his hand. He paused, clearly thinking through our conversation. He was a good listener.

"Your parents must really love you to have seen you as yourself at such a young age."

It was such a perfect way of articulating how I viewed my parents. I had always been that weird kid who genuinely *liked* my parents. They had their issues, and they could be impossible in an argument. But it was the big thing most people got wrong about why I went to boarding school. I didn't leave because I wanted to get away—I was able to leave because I felt secure enough at home to do it. I knew my parents had my back and that my sister was like a bonus protector. Distance wasn't going to change that. I *wanted* my parents to have high expectations, and I wanted to be able to fulfill them.

Sure, maybe sometimes it made me a little more hesitant to deviate or take a risk, or even let people in, but the freedom I had was worth so much more than that. I felt more secure the more control I had over my life.

I wondered if he understood this because he grew up with similar parents. Maybe they were more cautious, but his security in their belief in him seemed to be pretty deeply rooted.

"Yes, that's exactly it," I replied, unable to contain my emotions on this particular topic. "Even when I was little and wanted to do stupid shit like dye my hair or take up skateboarding, my mom was always first in line to let me try what I needed to try out—and either get it out of my system or move me forward. I think it was the best kind of reverse psychology, since it made rebelling feel unnecessary."

"So you're saying your mom let you dye your hair as a kid so that you wouldn't become a little punk later in real life?"

I had to laugh. He was probably right about that. My mom was always a few steps ahead of me.

"But if *your* mom didn't let you do that kind of stuff, why aren't you rebelling now?" I asked.

"I was never the rebelling kind," he said dismissively. "They weren't super strict on anything other than grades, so maybe I just never felt hamstrung. I know my mom certainly heard me throwing up from drinking a few times in high school, because one time I came out of the bathroom and she'd left some aspirin next to my bed. But I wasn't exactly staying out late every night either."

"Those khakis haven't seen a whole host of trouble?" I teased.

He barked out a laugh and looked down at his pants.

"No, can't say that they have."

We smiled at each other, goofily, like we had somehow cracked the code of innermost nerd secrets to being nonrebellious, nonexciting teenagers. He shared information about himself freely, and without any attempts to make himself sound cooler or more interesting when the situation didn't merit it. It was the thing that actually *made him* cool and interesting. He just was who he was. He made me feel warm, like I could tell him anything about myself and he would understand it.

Well, almost anything—I didn't get the sense that he was dating as casually as I was. I didn't get the sense that he *could* do anything casually. He wasn't like me in that one particular sense. He asked for what he wanted and ignored anything that wasn't good enough or was just fine for now. He barreled right in, whereas I was on a meandering journey to avoid anything that could turn out to not be easy.

That thought pierced through the warmth and made me sit back, a little warier of giving him the intimacy he seemed to have drawn out of me without any effort. Was this how it had started for Sophie? Lured in by charm at a young age and convinced she'd known so instinctively? I pictured her and Charlie sitting across the table from each other when they were my age, at ease with their ribbing and so optimistic about their future. Ten years was a long time to believe in a fairy tale, only to have it pulled out from under you. And who was I compared to Sophie? If my beautiful, composed sister wasn't enough, how could I, an anxious bulldozer, ever be?

That front-row example had made young love seem foolish, no matter whatever else Samuel had in mind. One banter-filled evening didn't have to be more than that.

Our food came all at once, and it was suddenly like we were presented with a smorgasbord of carbs and perfection all laid out with no frills on heavy ceramic white plates with a burgundy trim. Steaming cheese and meat pierogi sat to one side, crispy potato latkes piled high on another plate, and our fluffy stack of pancakes—blueberry, we had decided—had been plopped in the middle of the table, ready to be devoured by all takers.

We attacked everything with ferocity, only punctuated by Samuel's undying admiration for every bite he took. I couldn't help but feel thrilled that he loved food as much as I did. I had worried a bit that maybe he was fussy, or a snob about presentation or decor. Growing up in the city as he had, I imagined his standards might be a little different from mine. But he was a snob in the same way that I was—fully committed to the best version of a food, no matter what surrounded you.

When we finished, we looked at the empty plates.

"We're definitely ordering dessert, right?" he finally asked.

I couldn't stop myself from letting my face break out into a huge grin.

"I like their desserts, but I was thinking we could walk for a bit to this gelato shop I love. I think I need to move before consuming anything else."

He nodded and made a motion to the waitress to bring us the bill. I hadn't meant to cut the evening off, but on the other hand he didn't seem to have taken it that way. He was just decisive—our next decision had been made, so it was time to move toward it.

Our waitress hadn't even set the bill down before he handed over his card, and I protested immediately once I saw what he was doing.

"Wasn't I supposed to be taking you out, since the Yankees won?"

"No, that was the opposite of this plan. Since you didn't even give me the dignity of taking you to the spot where I wanted to go, you're going to have to let me pay for our first date."

"Date." There was that word again. So adult and serious.

I didn't want to have to delve further into defining what he saw this evening as, but I knew if I let him pay, it certainly wouldn't help my case. And come on, chivalry could take a very important back seat to equality, thank you very much.

"We'll split it," I said with finality, handing my card over to the waitress.

I could see the protest on the tip of his tongue, but I was surprised when he swallowed it and nodded.

"Okay," he said, his tone light but his eyes boring into me again, clearly seeing my need to be taken at my own word. "But I get to pay for the gelato."

"I accept," I said, pleasantly, pleased to have ended that line of questioning.

We lingered for a bit after our bill came back as we chatted about our coursework and what classes we had planned for the fall. We got up and started walking, and the conversation continued to flow.

"Why are you taking a political science course if you're interning at a food website?" he asked, trying to put another piece of the puzzle into place, like a detective who needed all the facts at his disposal.

I shot back, "Why are you taking one if you're interning at a corporate law firm?"

"Fair enough," he said, tilting his head. "I guess I just wondered whether journalism courses might be more up your alley."

"I like politics. I find it interesting, even if I don't think I have the stomach to make a career out of it. And I think writing is writing, for the most part. That's the most important thing I can learn for any future job anyway."

He nodded his head in agreement while his enthusiasm burst out. "I have always said that to people. The best way to learn how to write and communicate is just to keep doing it. It doesn't matter what you're writing about—just practice."

"Exactly."

We arrived at the gelato shop, and I ordered myself a cone—chocolate and raspberry—and he ordered a single scoop of chocolate in a cup. We walked in companionable silence for a few minutes. I was a bit surprised by how much I wanted to watch him lick his spoon. The thought made me blush, but it also made me think of one other pressing topic. As we approached my building, I had to ask the one question that was irking me.

"Why didn't you kiss me the other night?" I said, stopping and turning toward him.

He paused and looked at me, but he didn't say anything for a moment.

To break the silence, I continued: "You know, when you walked me home?"

He gave me a light smile.

"I knew what you meant; I was just thinking of how to respond."

"Oh."

I waited. Had I read this whole thing wrong? Maybe after spending an evening with me, he'd been hoping he could just drop me off and say good night.

"I didn't know you thought I was going to kiss you," he said quietly.

I could read his nervousness now, and it was almost jarring after spending the evening with someone for whom being nervous didn't even seem possible. I didn't know how to respond.

But finally he spoke up again. "You'd drank a lot. I don't typically kiss women for the first time in that kind of scenario."

I stood there a little dumbfounded. I'd never known any man to avoid kissing someone a touch tipsy. Maybe not *sleep* with them, but not kissing seemed like an overly cautious act of chivalry.

I couldn't think of a response.

"I didn't think you noticed how hard it was for me not to kiss you, though," he said finally with a small grin. "I tried to walk away before I stopped having the ability to be a good guy."

He was looking at me with an intensity I hadn't seen before. His eyes filled with sincerity mixed with lust, and I found myself suddenly short of breath. The muggy heat had been making my skin prickle all night, and I suddenly felt damp and warm all over. Anticipation hung in the air. He didn't move, he just watched me, waiting to see what I would do next, his eyes boring into me, but with that hint of apprehension that was clearly stopping him from moving any closer.

I suddenly needed to remove all that distance and anticipation from between us.

"What about tonight?" I asked, slowly shifting ever so slightly more toward him, so that the rest of him was periphery and all my eyes could really focus on were his dark eyes and the freckles that splattered across his nose so lightly that you would have to be standing this close to even notice them.

Without my heels on, I was a few inches shorter than him, but I was more aware of his expansiveness compared to my slight frame the closer I stood to him. His breath hitched. I got the sense that for all the bravado and security in himself, he wasn't quite as sure what to do with this moment.

I leaned in and kissed him, softly, biting his bottom lip. He tasted like the last hints of chocolate gelato. He kissed me back slowly and with so much tenderness that I almost pulled away. He was testing, seeing, finding where my comfort level was, even after I'd been so up front with my questions and my invasion of his personal space.

I pulled him closer and knotted my fingers gently into his wavy hair and kissed him more deeply. With that, something in him snapped, and he wrapped his hand tightly around my waist.

He pushed me back up against a side wall around the corner from my building's entrance. He kissed me with an urgency that made my whole body clench, and I found myself pushing up against him and moving my tongue deeper into him as I felt myself losing it. All night he'd been attentive to my words, but now I could tell all that attention was on me in a different way.

He started kissing my neck, and I tilted my head back and tried to breathe. We'd gone from casually standing to practically mauling each other within seconds, and I was so turned on I probably would have taken off my clothes on the street if he'd asked me to.

One hand was still around my waist, but the other was behind my upper back, stopping me from getting scratched up by the brick wall that he was pushing me so hard against. It was a touch of softness amid the chaos, and I liked it. I could feel him firm against my jeans, and I found myself tipping my hips into him, like I could get closer to him through my clothes if I only tried hard enough. I nibbled on his earlobe, and he moaned softly but pulled back.

He put one hand out against the wall and stood a few inches away from me, breathing heavily and trying to compose himself. I put my arms around him and my hands in the back pockets of his pants and pulled his waist back toward mine. I wasn't ready to stop yet. My body was not going to let me stop yet. I was keyed up and impulsive and trying desperately to remember whether all my roommates had plans tonight.

"Come upstairs with me," I said, dipping my head to look him straight in the eyes as he attempted to look down and away from me.

I could see that his attempts to calm himself down were not exactly working. He didn't resist when I pulled him back toward me, and I leaned back against the wall, holding his head with both of my hands and pulling him in for another kiss.

It was slower this time, less insistent, even though I'd pulled him forward enough that he was fully against me. There wasn't even the smallest crack of space between us, and I felt the heat of him all over me. I was vibrating with want.

He put his hand on my cheek and moved his head back, just slightly, to look me in the eyes.

"I think it's pretty obvious that I appreciate the invitation," he said with a smirk, his body so firmly pressed against mine that I could feel the innuendo from his words. "But I'm going to have to decline—otherwise I would lose all the good guy points I accrued the last time I was standing outside this building."

I raised my eyebrows at him.

"No one is keeping score. It doesn't mean anything if you come upstairs right now."

He stepped back a fraction, and I knew the moment had broken.

"It certainly does mean something to me."

His words lingered in the air between us, but he didn't let the sentiment sit for too long.

"I had an exceptionally good time tonight," he said, leaning forward and whispering it in my ear like a dirty secret.

It sent a shiver down my whole body, and I found myself aching to have him press against me again, to feel his weight on me against the wall. But it was clear he wasn't going to change his mind.

A prickle of frustration crept in that he was engaging in some bullshit emotional gallantry for what obviously could only ever be a summer fling. His sincerity radiated off him, and I wanted to be turned off by it. But standing there in front of him, I couldn't feel anything other than a deep desire to have him stop toying with me, throw me over his shoulder, and carry me upstairs. I momentarily contemplated whether I could just drag him with me.

But he clearly had more willpower than my horny little weak body possessed. He kissed my cheek.

"I would really, really like to take you out again."

"If I let you continue this dating charade, will you let me drag you upstairs next time?" I asked, honestly.

He closed his eyes and shook his head, dismissing me with so much gentleness that it made my insides melt, and I felt utterly charmed.

"I'd probably do anything to keep you from calling this a 'dating charade,' when all I want is to get you to agree to go out to dinner with me for the next five nights in a row."

"So upstairs we go then?" I said, taunting him and pulling him back toward me, wiggling my eyebrows suggestively.

He wasn't going to be swayed.

"You might have been put on this earth to test my fortitude, I swear to God."

He kissed me again, but I knew it was a good night gesture rather than a continuation. He put his hand behind my back and steered me to the entrance of my building.

"I'm serious, Stella. You say how high and I'll jump. You decide when you want to go out again, and I'm there. Just don't make me leave you twenty voice mails in the meantime, because I'm obviously not above doing that."

He kissed me quickly one more time for good measure and then turned and started walking away down the street. I watched him walk, staring at his perfect butt in those stupid khakis, until he turned a corner and was gone.

Chapter Seven
Thursday, present day

I wake up Thursday morning to banging at the door and bright light streaming in through the small crack in the heavy green velvet curtains that I've closed as tightly as possible. The rooms at the hotel are like a masculine balance between the history surrounding us and the expected modern touches. The stone walls are flanked by leather chairs and thin metal desks. I slowly sit up against my bed's large, plush gray fabric headboard while rubbing my eyes.

"Come on, if I'm driving you two goobers, you have to actually get up," Cat shouts through the heavy wooden door.

"We are up!" Elena hollers back from the bed next to me.

No one could be less categorized as "up" than Elena right now—she's facedown on her pillow with the sheets pulled up to her ears. I chuckle as I pull the comforter off me and stand up.

"You are obviously not up." Cat's voice is exasperated but still amused. At least that's a good sign. I hope she got some sleep last night after such a long trip by herself. "You know everyone's leaving at eleven so we can be in Spoleto for lunch. I wouldn't have thought you'd need a ten-thirty wake-up call."

I look at the clock next to me. *Technically*, 10:28. Cat is so corporate sometimes it is unbelievable. She's had the same job since college, always goes to bed on time, and somehow I've never had to hold her hair back when she vomits. Elena and I are always three sheets to the wind before we notice that Cat has gone to bed.

But, to be honest, we are probably lucky she knows us well enough to bang on our door. This is the one day before the wedding stuff really kicks in when Subrata and Luca actually get to explore a town for the afternoon. Elena and I are usually on top of our shit, but with the suitcase debacle already front of mind, I do not want to do anything other than be the dependable sidekick Subrata knows and loves. I swing my feet over onto the cold floor and throw on one of Elena's sweatshirts. I lug open the heavy door.

"Thank you for waking us up," I simper begrudgingly.

Cat looks pleased that I am admitting to our dereliction of duty.

"No problem," she replies, in a way that indicates it is indeed at least a little bit of a problem. "I'm grabbing some breakfast. Want me to get you something so you don't get hangry before lunch?" I nod, gratefully. "Okay. I'll see you guys outside in twenty-five minutes then."

I love how she's trying to inject a time construct into our brains despite openly admitting that that would be five minutes earlier than the agreed-upon leaving time. It is no wonder Cat, Elena, Subrata, and I have all stuck together for so long—we are all completely comfortable pushing each other to be better versions of ourselves with no artifice or fluff. We are so similar in our genuine love for one another and desire to only be around down-to-earth but sharp people. But we each have our own specific strengths that counter the others' weaknesses.

Growing up in New York gave Cat an innate confidence that went along with her intelligence. She was totally comfortable being the dorky math nerd she was inside, but she was also collected, observant, and dependable. Sometimes Elena and I especially needed that kind of a nudge (such as we clearly did this morning). But at the same time, we brought out Cat's goofier side and let her relax, always trying to convince her to take a weekend off from work before she even realized she was burning out.

Subrata, on the other hand, could mother us all, even as we encouraged her to ignore her own mother's nitpicking. Our strength as a group is in those incremental nudges forward when one of our team is lagging. We can all walk our way up the mountain, but everyone needs a friend to hand over a bottle of water or suggest a rest now and then. We are stronger together.

Elena tosses some real clothes in my direction—a white V-neck shirt and a flowy cerulean skirt that once again would have to be interpreted as "tea length." She hands me a straw hat as the final touch.

"How are you faring on your underwear and bra situation?"

"Don't ask. I really hope my bag comes today."

Elena nods at me optimistically, but I'm still nervous. I can't imagine another night without a shield of properly fitting clothes. Maybe there will be some cute shops in Spoleto.

I quickly shower and once again go through Elena's makeup to see what I can do for myself. My hair has dried, but it's still unruly, so I'm keeping it in its current topknot. A lip stain and some eyeliner will have to do. At least the dark circles under my eyes from jet lag and lack of concealer will be covered by the sunglasses I mercifully kept in my backpack on the flight.

"10:59!" I exclaim gleefully to Cat as we saunter up to the lobby, where she's already waiting for the valet to bring her car around.

"Never doubted you for a moment," she says with a hint of a smile.

Subrata and Luca amble into the lobby arm in arm, followed by Luca's friend James and one of Subrata's cousins, Anjana. Samuel and Hadley aren't far behind. I guess everyone is going to be impressively punctual today.

Mercifully, Cat's car comes around first, so I hop right into the back with a wave at everyone, keeping my eyes from looking directly at Samuel. Although looking down and seeing beat-up loafers doesn't help keep my insides from fluttering as much as I hoped avoiding eye contact would.

My eyes shift over to Hadley's shoes to avoid looking at any other part of Samuel's body. She has on simple gray sneakers and, looking up, I can see she's keeping it casual with jeans and a T-shirt, with her hair wrapped in a voluminous bun. She looks like a tall, chic California surfer girl who just woke up, threw on some clothes, and still manages to look like casual perfection.

But she returns my wave with gusto, so I have to smile at her.

I shut the door, and we are on our way—Cat driving, Elena fiddling with the radio, and me closing my eyes in the back, trying to get my stomach to settle down before we join back up with the group upon arrival.

Walking around Spoleto is like stepping into an old Italian advertisement bursting with color. Little cafés dot the streets and are already filling up. The shops and houses are all painted with faded versions of sunset hues—hazy blue, orangey salmon, marigold, and dusty pinks. They all have large rounded black-and-blue shutters and equally archlike stone entrances where large wooden doors are nestled. Streetlamps jut out from the sides of buildings with misty, globe-shaped balls attached to twirling wrought iron.

Since we've arrived a little earlier than the others, I quickly dart into a gelateria that's won awards for the best pistachio gelato in all of Italy (who am I to argue with such proclamations?) and purchase two extra cones for my unwilling coconspirators, and we walk toward the spot everyone's agreed to meet in. It's hard to feel anything but bliss while licking a perfect cone of gelato with the sun beaming down on my face. That combination of flecks of pistachio with cream is the ultimate salty-sweet jolt I needed to stave off any residual jet lag.

When we reach the meeting point, I sit down on a marble step in front of a building painted the brightest canary yellow, with a stately wooden door flanked by iron doorknobs so large and ornate I doubt they could actually be used to open anything. I finish the gelato, wolf down the cone, and have to stop myself from licking my fingers.

Subrata, Luca, James, and Anjana make their way toward us, and I can see Samuel and Hadley not far behind. I stand up and blot my mouth with a napkin, but I can still feel my fingers are a little sticky from the gelato, like a toddler with a poorly held secret from her parents.

We all make our way up a winding series of cobblestone staircases. Samuel and Luca take the lead, and I hang all the way in the back, taking in the sights so I won't have to join whatever very enthusiastic conversation Elena and Hadley seem to be having.

Some of the staircases are narrow, with small stones nestled together, forming cascading steps between two ancient-looking stone walls with small ferns and moss crackling out of the sides. Others are wide, with larger stones, smoothed out over millions of steps over hundreds of years.

When we get to the top, the view out over the city is beautiful—curved terra-cotta tiles line the roofs of old buildings and meld into newer ones as you look farther and farther out, until the hills turn green in the distance.

We all stop when Subrata decrees we have reached the restaurant, a casual little spot on the giant plaza. She's organized a long table shaded by the building, facing out onto the Romanesque cathedral, the frontal view an exquisite mix of rose windows, dramatic arches, and a gargantuan golden mosaic at the top.

Small children race toy cars on the herringbone-patterned stones, while a few buildings down, a group of old men sit on a set of steps together, smoking cigarettes and gesticulating wildly.

I sit at one end of the table and see Samuel sit on the same side, all the way at the other end. It makes my skin prickle—is he deliberately sitting as far away from me as he possibly can in a group of fewer than ten people? Or am I just desperate to believe I'm causing him as much discomfort as he's causing me? I *feel* his eyes on me, but every time I steal a glance at him, he is definitively not looking my way.

Elena sits next to me and Hadley next to her, a solid buffer between myself and distraction. Anjana plops herself across from me, and we both immediately order a Campari spritz and catch up on everything we've both been doing since we last saw each other. I am thrilled to have a distraction.

The mood at the table is convivial throughout the meal. A dried-sausage and prosciutto plate gives way to briny sardines, which give way to truffle-covered gnocchi topped with a plethora of herbs. Richness cut with acidity, herbaceousness and cool breezes at every turn. A simple ricotta and lemon fettuccine topped with sharp pecorino is the perfect counterpoint.

I am not driving, and apparently Anjana isn't, either, so we both order a Cynar and soda. "How can we digest all the pasta without another digestif?" we exclaim to the waiter, giddily. Meat, carbs, sunshine, and lingering music coming from across the plaza have stirred us up, and soon our dessert—some sort of chocolate cake with walnuts—arrives. It's dense in that fudgey way a flourless concoction can be, like it has molded itself into the perfection of pure chocolate. The crunch of the walnuts is a counterweight, drawing me deeper into the flavor.

I haven't been inspired by food like this in a long time, despite spending so much time *thinking* about food. The atmosphere at work has sucked so much of the joy out of thinking about recipes, but I find myself taking little notes on my phone for recipe experimentation when I get home. The realization jolts me.

I've always felt like I have the perfect job for a creative who happens to also be a bit left-brained. Recipes are an intriguing puzzle every single time. Today's fettucine is the perfect example. The tartness of the lemon paired with the smooth pasta and pillowy ricotta is the no-brainer part. But the trickier puzzle piece—the one that is necessary to connect the rest of the puzzle to the whole—is the light grating of pecorino on top. That tang, that edge, that cutting spice works in tangent with the lemon to give the dish its power. Lemon alone wouldn't have been enough. Pecorino alone wouldn't have been enough. The dish is so simple, but it has to fit together perfectly to work. These little moments, these exciting eurekas, are the elation I normally get in my job.

And I've always believed that my ability to sense those nuances is my particular superpower. Everyone knows when something tastes good, but intuiting the *why*, and how we get there, is a skill. I love being the person whom colleagues come to with a spoon and say, "What's missing from this?" Or when someone brings in a pastry from a bakery and asks, "What's the ingredient here that's making this so much better than everything else?"

But creativity has a hard time flourishing without enough inputs. Every plant needs to revive its soil to thrive, not just a base level of water and sun. I've needed this reset—I need some inspiration and to get out of the rut my conversation with my boss has left me in. In this moment, I can't help but feel grateful. The warmth of the sun is cutting in as it moves through the sky, and it's paired with exquisite food to parse and appreciate. It's rejuvenating.

Not to mention the additional benefit of being with friends. Anjana and I are on fire, laughing and joking and riling each other up. There's so much lightness in the air.

I have so much to focus on right here that I'm able to quell the small part of me that's deliberately ignoring the other side of the table, ignoring the pit in my stomach that no amount of enjoyment can seem to fling off. I can't deny, amid all the inspiration, there's also a little piece of me once again performing for an audience of no one.

I barely notice when my phone rings, but after a few moments I grab it out of my bag and answer the unknown Italian number.

"Signora Park! Excellent news. The baggage company has rung to tell me they dropped off your bag at the hotel. All your worries are now through!"

Chapter Eight

One year ago

I hated being late with Elena. We'd lived together for the past six years, which meant everyone was used to us showing up as a unit. But usually at least one of us was on our game enough to get us to places on time, like the flippers on a pinball machine taking turns every time the ball comes at one side. So things really had to have been going down the drain for both of us to screw up a time.

But that, of course, was where we found ourselves on the rainiest of spring days, dodging puddles and aggressively large umbrellas to dart down the street toward dinner at Rezdôra.

Elena's tiny frame had her sprinting even more than I was, but I couldn't slow down to help her along—we really were that late. At least she was wearing her understated start-up gear of jeans and a short-sleeved black turtleneck. My decision to wear a flouncy red dress meant that my legs were soaked and I was already shivering.

We finally reached the restaurant and melted into the cozy atmosphere, pasta and wine humming through the air. The hostess took pity on our soaked facade and kindly scooted us right along to our table upstairs, where Cat and Subrata were already deep in conversation.

Cat had ordered a bottle—her rigid consistency seemed to have won out, and they were drinking one of her favorite Argentinean reds, despite a wine list mostly populated by Italian vintages. To be fair, considering she traveled four days a week for her consulting company and her family was a mess, having some steadiness with the wine selection was probably necessary.

She waved as we climbed the stairs, and Subrata turned, dewy skin glowing with excitement, wearing an outfit that for anyone else would have seemed conservative, but on Subrata I knew it was her version of going all out—a light-gold silk shirtdress paired with dainty dangling earrings and the item on her hand we'd all been waiting to see.

I took a deep breath and tried to divert myself from all the images of my difficult, blindsiding day flashing through my mind—unnecessarily nitpicky edits littering the draft of my latest article; the overwhelmed pit lurking in my stomach while I was made late to another meeting by one of the senior editors droning on well past the point of necessity; the rude text from the guy I'd been trying to ghost who clearly couldn't take the hint; the churning anxiety over the nights of extra recipe testing I had on my plate that should have been delegated; and running into Charlie. That had been the ultimate kick in the teeth. I think I was still in a bit of shock from it.

My rain-soaked mop of hair and disheveled dress were a perfect exterior encapsulation of my insides. But I had to quickly center myself to get my face to reflect the version of myself I wanted to be for Subrata tonight. *Fake it till you make it. Whistle a happy tune. Don't cry out loud.* I was so adept at getting myself back into gear at this point that it wasn't even a stretch to plaster on a smile and get myself in the mode of believing that I was totally fine. *If I believe it, then I am.*

Thankfully Elena was even better than I was at switching modes—that was the sales professional in her. "Okay, show us the ring, for crying out loud. I've had to wait all damn week to see it!"

She grasped at Subrata's graceful hand, manicured with a perfect rose-pink color that made her look like a hand model for engagement rings. The gold band and square diamond gleamed back at us, and it was all I needed to melt the fake smile and become warm from the inside. My kindest friend, my gorgeous pal who was so elegant she practically floated, my quiet but tough little cookie, was thrilled to be engaged.

I couldn't help but smooch her cheek and barrel her into a hug. Elena wrapped around us while Cat beamed from her seat, sneaking the chance to roll up her blazer sleeves and answer some work emails while she thought we weren't looking.

We all piled into our chairs, and Cat filled up glasses for Elena and me. The tenderness of this moment caught me off guard. All four of us had survived adolescence into our twenties in part because early awkward teenage exchanges in uncertain dorm rooms had solidified into an unshakable foundation that all of us had grown to count on. We were never the most effusive with our feelings, but that almost made it easier—I could count on these women without saying a word.

And now it was a new chapter. We were shepherding the first of us to take this particular leap by giving her our own version of a safety net. We were all gathered at the ready to celebrate and support and delightedly take our marching orders for what would come next. We were not celebrating rings or even the idea of marriage—we were celebrating our friend's happiness on her own terms. It melted away the grime from the previous portions of my day.

"So I have some exciting news," Subrata said, fluttering.

"If you're telling us you're engaged, I'm a little worried that you hit your head in all the excitement," Elena teased, taking a big gulp of her wine.

Subrata shook her head at the obviousness of the joke and barreled on.

"No, Luca and I have decided where and when we're having the wedding."

"No City Hall?" I said, a bit surprised.

Subrata might have made a living from design, but it didn't mean she liked fuss. She'd always said she wanted to get married at City Hall and do a small dinner and call it a day. ("Think of all the other more permanent things you could spend your money on!" I'd heard her say on more than one occasion.)

But looking at her blushing face now, I could see those were all the musings of a woman who hadn't yet gotten caught up in the romance of engagement. I couldn't help the amused smile that took over my face as I saw her sheepish expression.

"Well, no," she said, the blush on her face rising. "The more we talked to our parents, the more excited everyone got about having a big wedding. So we are actually going to do the wedding in Italy, near where a lot of Luca's family is from."

There was no hesitation from any of us—if this group could do anything, it was to be supportive even through a curveball. We all oohed and aahed and asked details about the location, the plans, the venues, and the food. Subrata was lit up from the inside, gushing out all the details she'd clearly been excitedly waiting to share.

But I couldn't manage to bat away the rumbling hiss that was seeping in at the edges of my attention.

Samuel.

If Subrata was having a big wedding, then my yearslong streak of dodging any event where Samuel might show up was probably going to come to a swift end. I'd always been quietly grateful that Subrata and Luca had never been the holiday party or Super Bowl bonanza type of friends.

Their penchant for small gatherings meant I was never forced to have to pretend in front of my friends that Samuel was just some guy I'd hooked up with one summer. I hated that I'd skirted over the details with them, that I'd kept such an intimate secret from the women whose support of me was a given.

I couldn't even explain to myself why I'd avoided ever telling my friends what had happened with Samuel after the summer was over. At the time it happened, it hurt to even think about him, and we were all so far away from one another.

And then, as the years went on, it seemed like I'd be ripping open a wound if I ever had to verbalize the details. Maybe the wound healed improperly, but it was healing. Avoiding talking about love or men or the acute dread that filled me up at even the hint of letting someone in eventually coalesced into the only way to push down the anxiety. It can go away if you don't look at it directly.

The reality of the crummy day I'd walked into the restaurant from now pooled together with every day for years before it. I had left college thinking the same thing I had when I'd entered it—that a new stage of life could render a new version of me. But instead I'd just been running on a hamster wheel in the meantime. Moving up too slowly at a job whose function I liked but where the company itself was thankless. Using the companionship of daily routines with Elena as a replacement for an intimate relationship I was too scared to embark on.

The obvious realization smacked me in the face as suddenly as the fact that I hadn't had any real relationships last more than a couple of months since I'd last seen Samuel. When it was all spun together, it felt like an awfully bleak track record to face.

But I've always been great at rolling my shoulders back and snapping myself into what matters. Everyone has these late-twenties insecurities. This was just a normal reaction to the first of my friends getting married, and nothing more. Maybe enough time had gone by where seeing Samuel would seem like ancient history. Mind over matter.

I listened to Cat's questions about logistics and laughed along with Elena's jokes about family drama.

Three shared pasta courses later (hey, we liked to double down on a good thing, okay?), we paid the bill and wandered outside into the tapering drizzle.

"Should we go get a drink?" Cat asked as I raised my hand in confirmation instantly, happy that Cat was clearly ignoring her usual two-drink maximum policy.

"This week has worn me out," Subrata admitted. "You ladies go and have another drink for me. Love you all so much."

I linked my arm into Elena's, trying to ensure that she couldn't beg off an escape to go along with Subrata. But she gave me a kiss and said she had too much work to do. We all gave the bride-to-be hugs and kisses and parted ways, Elena and Subrata heading home and Cat and I off in search of another drink.

When we snagged a table at Corkbuzz, a wine bar a few blocks away, Cat immediately ordered us another round, and we sat silently for a moment, companionably assessing the magnitude of Subrata's news.

"It's crazy that her tester pancake turned out to be perfect," I finally said.

"Her what?" Cat chuckled.

"You know, the tester pancake," I explained, hoping that the preceding glasses of wine wouldn't make this analogy impossible to follow. "Like, when you're making pancakes, you don't just start off by dumping all the pancake batter onto the griddle and assuming everything will be okay. You have to start with one and then test it out to see—is the griddle hot enough? Is the batter not too thick or not too loose? Does the butter melt at the right sizzle? Does the batter have the right ratio of blueberries—"

"You mean chocolate chips—" she interjected.

"I mean blueberries for my fictional theoretical pancakes, thank you very much. Anyway," I said, clearing my throat, "you need the tester pancake to help you adjust. Not to mention you might spend years refining your pancake recipe to get to the one you want."

"But sometimes the tester just works," Cat argued wholeheartedly.

Such a hidden sap. It made no sense, since she—like me—had essentially been single since college. But I knew she was a softie beneath her badass consulting and math-brain exterior.

"Besides," she said, "they always say when you know, you know."

Her words made me sizzle under the surface. They resurrected memories of tingling touches and sharp inhales of breath. I pictured a pancake recipe whose tester was perfect but that I somehow hadn't been able to ever even come close to re-creating. And now, after years of pushing those memories down, I might have to face them again in a year.

The thought unsettled me, but I couldn't focus on that for long, since my mind broodily recalibrated to Sophie. The prickly nearness of my run-in with Charlie today was still permeating, like a layer of dirt I couldn't manage to scrub off in the shower. How long had she thought she'd found the perfect pancake?

Cat's changed demeanor broke my thoughts.

"Do you think Subrata thought I was being a little morose in there?" she asked.

I wasn't following.

She caught my quizzical look and sighed. "I just . . . I got a little sad at the thought of a big wedding. I thought we'd be doing City Hall."

I instantly took her hand in mine once I realized what she meant.

"I'm sorry, Cat. Watching someone else with their mom at a full-scale wedding is probably going to suck."

"Yup," she said, downing the rest of her drink.

I sat silently, waiting. I was kicking myself for being so distracted earlier.

Cat was always so put together and externally restrained. But ever since we were twenty-one, she'd been dealing with a sick mother and then, a few years later, grieving the loss of her. She was always type A, but the accelerated adulthood pushed her even further. That slight specter of sadness was always humming under her surface, hidden by her excellent facade of control. She could quip about pancakes and down a drink without one of her best friends noticing her strain. Not sure if it was a superpower or a major liability, but sometimes I hated that she'd gotten so good at maintaining composure in the face of hardship.

I tried to go after the lowest-hanging fruit to make her feel better. "First of all, no, I don't think Subrata thought you were anything but perfect, because I stupidly didn't notice anything, either, and Subrata is even more oblivious in her excitement than I am on a normal day."

"Thank you for that." She smiled, still a bit lost in thought. "I wouldn't want to ruin Subrata's happy moment."

"I think a bomb dropping on the restaurant couldn't have ruined Subrata's mood tonight," I replied, and she snorted a little laugh. Good. I wasn't totally useless in a crisis.

"No, I imagine probably not. But still, I was caught off guard thinking about everything that comes with a whole wedding," she said, pausing at the admission. "I guess we're at that age, though. Gonna have to face it eventually."

"Well, but once Subrata's done, you know at the very least I won't subject you to a wedding."

She frowned. "Don't say that, Stella."

"Why?" I hated when she tried to romancify me. "No one would want to go into a lifetime of dealing with me."

Cat narrowed her eyes. "Well, I've put up with you for half my life, so now you're insulting *me*."

"You know what I mean," I said, wanting to placate her a bit.

"I really don't."

I squirmed, uncomfortable with even the thought of having to dredge out all my insecurities as proof, to show Cat I was better off keeping my relationships casual.

"Absolutely no interest, thank you very much," I said, redirecting as flippantly as I could. "Besides, I've seen how that movie turns out."

"I know you have," she said, ignoring how I'd made my own baggage ooze onto hers. "I've watched my dad suffer for years now from his own version of losing the person he loved. But it doesn't mean it's not worth it. He'd do it all over again."

"Soph wouldn't," I countered, thinking of my now almost forty-year-old sister and her gun-shy approach to dating over the last decade.

"Maybe not, but I just don't believe every good guy is secretly hiding a Charlie underneath."

I paused, but at the mention of his name I had to tell her.

"I ran into him today," I said quietly, the thought still almost too absurd to say out loud.

"You *what*?" Cat replied, sitting up and staring at me. "You let me wax on about my mopeyness when you were carrying *that* bombshell around?"

Leave it to Cat to take her perfectly normal grief and try to minimize it.

"Your mopeyness is totally justified," I said firmly.

"No, I know. I'm not avoiding." She looked at me pointedly, and I knew she wasn't going to take no for an answer. "But that must have been awful. What did you say?"

I sat back for a moment, and the sledgehammer of the run-in hit me all over again.

"I was walking outside my office to grab some lunch, and I ran into him with some coworker. And he acted the way you do when you see someone random you're delighted to catch up with after not seeing them for a long time. Do you know what he said?"

My voice caught, and I tried to brush it off.

"He introduced me to this guy and then said, 'Oh, Stella was like a sister to me!' *Was* like a sister—can you imagine? That man taught me how to ride a bike. He bought me my first tampons because I was too embarrassed to tell my mom. He married my sister and ditched her after six months. The audacity to act like it was all just a phase of his life."

But the sentiment I couldn't articulate was that maybe that was actually the scariest part of all. That someone could fall out of love, and for them, that was all it was. A phase, a moment, a blip. Not a great love worth fighting for. I was collateral damage to Charlie's about-face, and I had to watch the agonizing fallout knowing that Sophie had done nothing wrong. The first love I'd watched bloom died in an instant, and Charlie was still out here in the world, unbothered and enjoying himself.

Cat was silent, and I wondered if she was going to wait me out the way I'd just waited her out. She knew there was nothing to say about this, the same way there was nothing I could say to bring her mom back. We both had our worldviews implode in front of us at a young age, and we'd had to see the consequences up close—Sophie's yearslong depression, Cat's father's avoidance. I hated that we had this misery to bond us. I hated that we'd both learned early how to shut down anything that could cause us pain. But I appreciated that we both understood the impulse.

"I hope you slapped him," she said seriously, and I couldn't help but laugh.

"No." I shook my head. "I had to act like I didn't care. I got away from the conversation as quickly as I could. I didn't want to give him one second of satisfaction thinking that anyone in our family ever thought about him."

"Perfect. Much more mature."

Cat gave me a small smile. Oh, how good we both were at papering over the painful things. How utterly expert at finding the silver linings.

"Besides," she said, "who needs men anyway? I mean, great for Subrata and all, but who needs it."

"Exactly!" I replied, much happier to get Cat aboard my silly man-hating train (even if I knew Cat didn't really believe it), rather than a wallowing one. "This fear of needing a man to make us happy is a product of our bullshit Disney princess culture that also taught us a man can fall in love even if a sea witch stole the woman's voice. She was pretty damn awesome as a mermaid first!"

"Hear, hear," Cat said, clinking her empty glass against mine. "And at least we have a year to sort out our emotions before this wedding so we both can keep Subrata under the false impression we are normal functioning adults."

"Totally," I concurred.

I tried to push the percolating thoughts of Samuel out onto the periphery, not wanting to think about how no year of sorting was going to be able to prepare me for that run-in. But maybe if I survived seeing Charlie, I could survive anything.

We'd gotten stronger, after all. We were heading into a new era, and we had to face it. We all wanted to believe that a wedding could just be an event; but really it was the start of our lives branching off in their own directions of our choosing. We'd all gone to school, on to college, and then into the professional world—but Subrata was starting the chain reaction of the next phase. Who gets married and who doesn't? Who will have kids and who won't? Who will stay single by choice, and who will be stifled? Who will move to suburbia, and which of us won't be able to leave our urban enclaves? We all had choices, none right or wrong, that would take us off this moving sidewalk we'd all been on and put us on divided pathways. I hoped we were older and wiser enough to handle it.

But as if Cat could read my mind, she put her head on my shoulder, and I grabbed her hand for a squeeze. We had each other. No matter what changed or who chose what path, the four of us would be cheering each other on from the sidelines. It was the one thing that made my insides feel warm and my exterior secure.

At least on that front I was incredibly lucky.

I downed the rest of my drink and said a silent prayer. One year was going to come at us all pretty fast.

CHAPTER NINE
THURSDAY, PRESENT DAY

I can't help but feel affection for the voice over the phone—my beleaguered baggage man has finally found some joy in my good news. I gush and tell him *grazie* at least a dozen times before I hang up and see all the eyes at the table looking at me expectantly.

"My bag finally arrived!" I cheer, as though it wasn't obvious from my exclamations and effusive thanks moments earlier on the phone.

Anjana starts a round of applause, and I take a dramatic curtsy.

"I should probably get back so I can actually change into some clothes that fit me," I exclaim, almost giddy at the prospect of removing my ill-fitting skirt.

"Well, I'll drive you, if no one else is going back," Cat says, always ready to step up, but I can hear the hesitation in her voice.

Crap. I hadn't really thought about everyone else's desire to have another leisurely stroll through Spoleto on their short trip to a magical destination.

"Samuel was going to go back after lunch anyway to finish up some work, and I was going to catch a ride with someone else either way, so I could stay longer," Hadley quickly replies, leaning around Elena with a smile. "Go with him, and I can always hitch a ride with your crew when everyone else is ready to head out."

She clearly does not care in the slightest about suggesting her boyfriend take me alone in his car. Obviously it is not an issue in any way for him. He has an adorable girlfriend and a whole New York life parallel to my New York life, and this Umbrian jaunt just happens to include me—a person of no consequence to his current existence. I'm a bit embarrassed by how depressed that thought makes me. I try to shake it off.

But when I look over at him to see how he will respond, the way he looks at this suggestion is akin to someone who has accidentally swallowed a bug. He is fidgeting with his shirtsleeves, clearly trying to look comfortable with a situation he has no interest in. Well, that's even worse than being of no consequence.

It isn't like *I* suggested it. Does my face look as horrified as his? I'm trying to plaster a cool and calm expression on my face, but who knows what that looks like in reality. There's an awkward silence while Hadley's comment hangs in the air. Finally he clears his throat.

"Oh, sure, absolutely," he says, all traces of discomfort wiped from his voice. "That was, indeed, my plan, to go back a bit early. If you need a ride, feel free."

It isn't exactly a ringing invitation, but there isn't really a polite way to decline. I had openly stated I wanted to go to the hotel, and only one person is imminently driving back. And somewhere in the pit of my stomach, I can't tell if the lurching inside is from dread or some sort of tingly anticipation at being alone in a car with him. I can *feel* the last time we spoke to one another alone, viscerally, as though I could reach out and touch him before he slammed the door one last time.

How is it so tangible for me but clearly so faded for him? I can't stop the rattling of tension I get every time I look over at him.

But maybe that's exactly why this is a good idea. Maybe it will be good to have some forced small talk to get us past whatever awkwardness is lingering. Maybe the yawning hole of the nine-year gap in our communication can be filled with pleasantries and catch-ups and stories about work. Didn't we once like talking to each other? Wasn't that, at one stage, the main thing we did? We were really good at talking to each other once upon a time. Surely we can find a way back to that—in a platonic pals sort of way—for the sake of this one weekend.

The rest of dessert slowly drips by as I keep glancing over at Samuel to see if he's glancing at me. He is not.

It isn't until the bill is paid and everyone has stood up that he finally, deliberately looks over at me and says, "Shall we?"

I nod my assent, hug everyone goodbye, and wave absentmindedly as they all turn and move in the other direction.

He's standing close to me as they all walk away. Not so close that any part of our bodies are touching but close enough that I can register him taking up space in my general space. I want to lean a little closer and see what he smells like, see if he still wears the same cologne and smells like some sort of herby ocean, or if he smells like clementines and bergamot from the hotel soap, just like me. But the space between us is like an electric fence, fizzing away next to me but with an unknown level of power I can't even fathom trying to break through.

I can feel him breathing and deliberately not looking at me as the moment registers. We are alone, and neither of us moves for a moment. It is as though once the act of saying goodbye to our friends is over, we have to both put on some sort of mask and pretend that everything is normal, and it seems like neither of us is quite ready for that. I need a deep breath before I can bottle back up so many years of wondering and plaster on a smile.

But he must have taken his deep breath first, or not needed one at all.

"The car is this way," he cheerfully announces, pointing back down the steps we came up from.

"Great!" I respond, trying to muster up all the enthusiasm I can for the location of a car that is parked in the same place we both were previously.

We start to walk down the steps. I am looking at my feet, ostensibly to make sure I don't trip over the slick stones, but I'm also giving myself an excuse not to look up.

"How was your drive over?" he starts, nonchalantly keeping to as inoffensive a topic as possible.

"I honestly don't know," I reply, chuckling a bit and looking up, a bit sheepish. "I sat in the back and think I slept through most of it."

"Is that your plan for this drive then? Didn't get your requisite eight hours last night?"

He looks over at me and smiles. It jolts me so much that I have to ball up my hands to stop them from tingling.

It feels tentatively like he's decided to be himself around me. It was a simple comment, but it contains multitudes. It was a joke; it was an *inside* joke for someone who knows me, and knows I don't like staying out late or missing out on sleep. It is as though the previous tactic of ignoring me—or being indifferent—isn't going to work when we have to spend an hour in each other's company. The magnetic pull that once existed between us still exists somewhere for him, too, and that realization allows me to suddenly breathe a bit more easily. It was ribbing. It was an opening to being friends.

We can be friends.

I can do that.

We haven't ever *really* been friends.

But that was a long time ago. Almost a decade has gone by, and I haven't heard from him in years. The past is in the past, and I could enjoy his company again. He probably barely remembers anything that happened anyway. This isn't a big deal. I need to stop my brain from overthinking something that is clearly not important anymore.

I smile back at him. "Well, with the jet lag and the loss of sleep from the first night, I'm really aiming for more like ten hours a day, so I'm a little bit behind. Car sleeping might be the key to this whole weekend."

"And what are you going to do tomorrow, when you have wedding obligations all day?" he says with faux curiosity.

"Oh, I'm definitely planning to sleep on Subrata while she gets her henna done. She can rest her hand on my head while I lie on her lap, and then that'll allow her to keep it elevated. It's really a win-win for both of us. As long as I don't drool on her, it's the perfect solution."

He snorts at the imagery. We prattle on, now taking the stairs a tad quicker and with more lightness in our steps.

The decision to kid around is like a truce, steering us away from whatever awkwardness was lingering, giving buoyancy to our movements. As we approach the edge of the steps, my joke of a sleeping plan has become more elaborate—naps in the corner while everyone else dances on Friday, sleeping under my seat while the long Indian wedding ceremony takes place on Saturday. We are laughing by the time we reach his car.

We can be friends.

That is, if I can unball my hands and get them to stop tingling.

Chapter Ten

July, nine years ago

I held up two dresses in front of the mirror. I picked the tighter of the two and threw it on. I added another layer of mascara.

It had been over two weeks since I'd last seen Samuel. I hadn't been avoiding him exactly, but I had feigned a bit more busyness than might have been accurate. Every time I thought about him, I wanted to stick everything I felt into a box and shove it down.

Our date fizzed on the edges of my brain, loopy banter that oozed its way into my thoughts. I tried to plug the holes and ignore the giddiness that that evening made me feel, because the giddiness crashed into the pit weighing me down in the center of my stomach. He felt more complicated than what I wanted for the moment. He wanted a capital *D* Date, and I wanted to fling around the city and make memories fade.

But the voice mails did not let up, as promised, and the texting became a daily occurrence (which I certainly contributed to), and it didn't seem like another date could hurt, exactly. I gave him a day and time a week out so that, fourteen days after our initial date, my memory of the repartee and the kissing and the chivalry had started to fade enough to make it all seem like a tantalizing prospect.

Maybe I could get him to sleep with me without getting attached if I just *willed* the situation into being.

Maybe I was reading too much into his good guy routine, and he was less interested in a relationship than I was projecting.

Maybe seeing Marc at the office every day, with a few interludes at his apartment, along with a silly and slightly overserved night out with an old fling, had blunted Samuel from feeling like anything particularly special to me.

One more look in the mirror, then I opened the door and hopped in the elevator.

He was waiting downstairs in jeans and a crisp button-down shirt in a picture-perfect light shade of blue. He had cut his hair a bit since the last time I saw him, and he looked so much more put together and sexy than he had in the previous khaki debacles. He had told me to get dressed up but wouldn't tell me where we were going.

Suddenly seeing him looking all swoonworthy, I instinctively touched my own hair. Knowing I'd put more effort into myself than I wanted to admit, I immediately felt nervous. I'd relegated him to those edges, and I hadn't been prepared for how much his smile would make me spark.

I went up to say hello, and he pulled me right into a kiss on the lips. He wasn't going to let me fidget my way out of letting this be a real date. I wasn't convincing him to casually meet at a diner in the Village anymore—he was taking me out, and I had agreed to it, and now he was doing it up properly.

"So where are we going then?" I said, trying to sound as breezy as I could make myself.

"Well," he said, clearly excited about his plan, "you made me wait two weeks with some pretty nonsense excuses"—*Okay, so maybe I haven't been playing that angle as cool as I thought I was*—"and since I know your birthday is this week"—*How? How does he know that? What kind of stalker radar does this dude have?*—"AND since I know you love theater"—*fair, that has been discussed*—"there was really only one option that I could think of for your one birthday date in New York with me."

He stood there beaming at himself, waiting for me to ask him again. I wasn't sure I wanted to give him the satisfaction.

"How did you know it was my birthday this week?"

"Do you think a birthday is *that* hard to suss out?"

He wasn't going to let me steal any of his joy right now. But I was not ready to let it go.

"But why would you need to suss it out?" I replied.

He shook his head and gave me that exasperated-but-charmed look he seemed to have perfected.

"Because I like you and I heard it was your birthday, and I wanted a really excellent excuse to take you on an over-the-top date despite your total commitment to getting me into bed without any care for my sensitive soul and its deep desire to woo you properly."

I stared at him. His tone had a jesting quality to it, but it was clear he was dead serious. He really flummoxed me with this brutal honesty. There was nothing to do but throw it right back.

"You can't just keep saying you like me when we've only been out once."

"Sure I can. I said it before you even agreed to go on a date with me," he said with a self-satisfied smile.

How could he be so assured at every moment? It was hard not to let suspicion linger over someone so damn sure of his feelings.

"You didn't say that to me," I corrected him.

I wanted to poke holes in his theory. I was trying to find some excuse to make this into less of a thing than he was making it.

"Nah, I said it to my buddies after I asked you out, even though you turned me down multiple times over the course of one evening. The first date was just proving the point. So now we're well past that, and I was right the first time. I'm an excellent judge of character."

I rolled my eyes at him and couldn't come up with a quip. He'd totally disarmed me. I was starting to wonder whether giving him another shot was really such a bright idea. I had to change the subject.

"So, where is this magical outing, then?"

"You'll see."

We took the subway to Times Square, which didn't exactly inspire confidence in his plan. He grabbed onto my hand, and I tried to casually let it go, but he gave me a look that said *Relax, this is Times Square*, so I let him pull me along. We turned down 49th Street and walked until it became clear where we were going.

"You got us tickets to *Book of Mormon*?" I said, shocked at the extravagance of him procuring one of the most popular tickets in the whole city.

"No, I got *you* tickets to *Book of Mormon* for your birthday, and I decided I'd make an excellent plus-one for you."

I looked over at him. Those shades of nervousness were back, just a little bit, behind his confident smile. He was interning for the summer, and he had gone out on a limb to buy a girl he liked hard-to-get theater tickets on the off chance it might impress her. It *did* impress me.

I had told him about some of the off-off-Broadway shows I had gone to since I'd been in New York. He knew I liked theater. He knew there was no mistaking this for anything other than a grand gesture. He had *somehow* known it was my birthday so that I wouldn't have an excuse to tell him it was too much. How could I not be impressed after all that?

More worryingly, I really, really did not want to see any of that nervousness on his face turn into disappointment. The thought made my stomach knot.

I leaned against him and kissed him, right in the middle of the street. I hadn't intended it to be more than a simple kiss, but once he started kissing me, I was drawn into him. He tasted like a cinnamon mint of some kind, and he smelled like men's soap; probably he'd just showered before meeting me. I pulled back before I could get carried away and looked him right in the eyes.

"Thank you," I whispered quietly. "That was really thoughtful."

My sincerity made him glow. He took my hand and led me inside.

As we took our seats, I found my eyes gazing toward the elaborate golden ceiling of the 1920s theater, with elegant carvings and chandeliers rising high to the rafters. It was beautiful even before the show started.

"So you like to go big?" I said to Samuel as we waited for the rest of the crowd to get into their seats. "Trying to set expectations high?"

He shrugged. "No, I just believe in high-impact moments."

"What does that even mean?"

"You have to know when the timing of something is significant. You can do every small thing right, but if you nail the high-impact moments, you'll always be memorable. If you go really far out of your way when someone's going through something difficult, or if you show up and cheer in their triumphs, they'll remember it forever. Like, my brother was sick a few weeks ago, and my mom was out of town. Instead of ordering in, I made a big pot of chicken soup. I could have cooked him dinner every night for a month, and it wouldn't have had the same effect as the soup when he was sick. You need the high-impact moment."

I rolled my eyes. What a show-off of a theory.

"So you think if you dazzle me on a second date that happens to be adjacent to my birthday, that makes you more memorable?"

He winked at me. "Well, I *did* get you to openly admit that this is a date for the first time. So that's something."

The lights dimmed before I could respond.

Two and a half hours later, we streamed out of the theater laughing and dissecting the granular details of the play. It had been thrilling to see something so transportive and hilarious, seemingly on a whim. I've always had a particular blessing (or curse) that when I watch great theater or read a compelling book, I get fully sucked in—everything else around me falls away, and I'm really *in it*. Other than during the intermission, where I staunchly refused to leave my seat ("Only fools try to go to the women's bathroom at an intermission, Samuel"), I'd been taken out of my long, hot New York City days and into the rabbit hole of hilarity.

"So duly noted that going to a play with you is like watching a child walk into a candy store," Samuel said with a pleased grin as we walked back toward the bright lights of Times Square.

"I'm sorry, I get a little cheesy when it comes to musical theater," I replied with a shrug.

"No, I loved it," he gushed. "I was watching you almost as much as the play."

I blushed a bit but attributed it to the heat that had started to really hit us outside the confines of the air-conditioned theater. He was rolling up his shirtsleeves, and I was distracted by the muscles in his arms. The heat was getting to me in more ways than one. I jerked my head up to look at his face. I could see the wheels turning in his head.

"Do you want to get a hot dog? Did you eat anything tonight besides my plethora of theater snacks?"

I had indeed eaten a lot of theater snacks. But I was hungry, as usual.

"Sure," I said. "Here?"

"No way, we're in Times Square."

"So?"

We had stopped next to the big red steps in the center of the neon island, and tourists swirled around us, moving and talking and taking in all the bright lights and noise that emanated up. But he and I were just looking at each other, and all the exterior sounds seemed to fade into background noise.

"You can't really ask a New Yorker to stand in Times Square for anything other than a Broadway show," he said, his eyes twinkling a bit with the ribbing.

"But little old me isn't from around these parts, and I just find all this big-city stuff so exciting," I replied in my most dramatic southern voice.

He laughed heartily and shook his head.

"You are enough excitement for any city, and I think you're probably going to end up more of a New Yorker than me someday," he said with affection. "But for now . . . why not."

He grabbed my hand again and pulled me toward a hot dog cart. He seemed to be finding ways to make me hold his hand, even though I found ways to get my hand back every time the moment had passed.

I wasn't against it in principle—but I didn't even like holding hands when someone was my boyfriend. It made me feel unable to move as freely, like my body had to contend with someone else's movements and choices.

I was too wiggly to be a hand holder. I was too used to doing things on my own. And with Samuel it felt like it was a subtle way of making us a unit—us taking on the world together, hands intertwined to get somewhere without going out of lockstep. The thought made me anxious. I quietly unknotted my hand from his the moment we'd stopped.

"What would you like?" he asked.

"No," I said firmly, "I'm getting this. You bought the Broadway tickets, for Chrissake."

I turned to the vendor. "I would like two hot dogs with ketchup and mustard for myself, and for my friend—"

I saw him wince ever so slightly at the word "friend," but he didn't let it stop him from responding quickly.

"I'll have the same, but add onions too. And spicy mustard for me."

"Basic yellow mustard of the plebeians for me!" I chirped next to him.

I handed over cash while Samuel mumbled next to me about the extortionate prices of the same hot dogs just because the cart was in Times Square, and in that moment I could see him as an old, wizened

New Yorker sixty years from now still complaining about every change under his breath while he vocally fought to the death against anyone who insulted the city that coursed through his body. It was all so endearing.

When he grabbed for my hand again while the vendor got our hot dogs together, I didn't pull away. We stood silently, sweaty hands clasped loosely while we watched ketchup, two kinds of mustard, and onions piled high on top of our hot dogs.

We detached when we each needed two hands to grab onto our hot dogs, and we moseyed up to the very top of the red staircase to sit among the tourists who were resting or taking selfies.

We sat close together and ate in silence as the sea of people hustled about below and yellow taxis crowded in the streets. Straight ahead everything was lit up by all the signs and the giant video ads, and you could see the New Year's Eve ball, waiting patiently in the summer while it bided its time until it could be the center of the show again once the year dragged on.

I felt Samuel turn to look at me, and I enjoyed staring out at the insanity of Times Square with the knowledge that his eyes were solely on me. The whole world could be imploding around us, shouting, teeming, never ending, and yet his focus was only on watching my face. I turned toward him.

"You have a bit of mustard on your lip," he said, gently pulling my face toward him and kissing the mustard away.

"Now I've conned you into eating my cheap yellow mustard instead of your fancier spicy variety," I whispered in his ear.

"I'll take that trade anytime," he said.

And the bright lights and cacophony of sounds around us were drowned out by going in for seconds on a mustardy kiss.

Chapter Eleven
Thursday, present day

Once we leave Spoleto, the conversation flows easily as Samuel and I drive speedily along the small winding roads that lead us back to Norcia. Green, rocky hills give way to small towns every few minutes, dotted by ancient stone walls, sprawling fields, and trees that have been growing for centuries.

We spend the first twenty minutes catching up on the small talk basics, as though we're simply old acquaintances who have a passing familiarity with each other's lives. That same ease we always had in each other's company is right where we left it, and all we have to do is fill in the time gaps from when we last caught up. Neither of us mentions anything about the last time we saw each other, but we both have clearly decided not to pretend we don't remember anything personal about the other.

It's easy, and I like it. I hear all about the nonprofit his brother is working for and whether he would ever move out from the ease of living with their parents. I share stories from the chaotic pace of working at a magazine in a digital era, punctuated by lots of descriptions of recipes I've been working on. I deflect his questions about what I want to do next by doubling down on how much I love what I'm currently doing.

He laughs his way through a story about a client who can never seem to locate her glasses, which are always on top of her head.

I look out the window most of the time. He has to stare ahead, since he's driving, and it feels a bit too perilous to look right at him. Every few minutes I point out something along the road—a herd of goats; a small pizzeria that still has a crowd drinking away the late afternoon; a bus stop with a little old lady sleeping on her groceries; a sign for a pasta festival we both agree would be sad to miss.

Somehow that easy connection between us, that ingrained inevitability to our conversations, is still there. Yesterday's awkward debacle has completely faded. I'm grateful to have had this excuse to spend some time alone together. Maybe being friends with Samuel isn't such an impossible idea. I am relaxed for the first time in days.

"So what else did you eat in Spoleto?" he asks, a small grin forming as he glances toward me.

"Same as you," I deflect.

I can feel his eyes continuing to flicker back toward me every few seconds, a soft spot of disbelief written all over his face. Clearly he hasn't lost his ability to read me like a book.

"Okay, fine," I say, his smirk tugging words out of me. "I got a pistachio gelato when we arrived. But I *needed* to get it, and it wasn't on Subrata's plan."

The dubious expression on his face just makes me want to double down.

"Okay, see," I continue. "This particular shop uses three types of Sicilian pistachios and slow roasts them for twenty-four hours. Forty-seven judges from a gelato university crossed the world trying to find the absolute best, and they picked this one. So how could I not do that?"

"'Gelato university'?" he chuckles.

"I know, right? I definitely missed my calling," I reply, and I love how his laugh gets a little deeper.

"But at least you didn't miss the gelato."

"Exactly!" I smile, relishing the lightness between us once again.

"What else is on your list?" he asks.

"Definitely more lentils, and this region is known for truffles, so I have to do that. But they're also really known for their meats here, which is interesting. Obviously the cured meats we're used to when we think of Italian charcuteries is here, but also a lot of roasted pork as well, and boar. And sausage! I read a recipe for amatriciana with sausage instead of guanciale. Umbria's actually one of the few regions of Italy without any coastline—"

"So you did no research at all before coming?" he says, sarcasm peppered in with a smile.

"Please, I'm just getting warmed up. I haven't even gotten into the olive oil varietals. And pesto! That pesto we had at the dinner last night on the lamb chops—that pesto that has marjoram and walnuts instead of the one we're used to from Liguria, with basil and pine nuts."

He glances back over at me, a humored glint in his eyes.

"I'm glad to see you're still the best person to eat a meal with," he says.

I'm trying not to feed off the spark that exists between us, but I can't help it. Chatting with Samuel feels like playing a friendly tennis match with a former teammate and getting back into the rhythm of muscle memory. I know he has a girlfriend, and I'm sure this awareness is just residual enjoyment of that easy banter we'd always had. There's no harm in two old acquaintances having a laugh once again.

I am deliberately ignoring the way my whole body reacts every time his eyes merely flick over toward me.

But the thought is pushed aside when I spot something and can't help myself from shouting out. "Oh my God, Samuel, stop the car!"

He pulls over so abruptly and quickly it stuns me.

"What's wrong?" he replies, short of breath.

It feels strange for his eyes to be straight on me again after so much time seeing his face looking at the road. He looks concerned. I didn't mean to make him so worried so fast.

"No, no, nothing is wrong," I say quickly, trying to deescalate a confusion clearly of my own making. "I just saw so many poppies, and I thought you should get to see them too."

I point weakly out the window as though a vast bright field of flowers is enough of an excuse for scaring the shit out of him.

"Oh," he breathes out, his expression calming immediately, and I can see the wheels turning in his head as he has to adjust his expectations of what's going on. "Well, let's get out and look then."

He parks the car off to the side and opens the door without giving it another thought.

I get out of the car feeling slightly guilty at the unplanned stop on such a short drive. But stepping into the field shifts my feelings immediately. I have really never seen anything like it.

It is a field as big as a football stadium carpeted every inch with bright-red poppies. The red is like the kind of color that you see only in oversaturated photos, the kind that doesn't seem to truly exist in real life. Thousands and thousands of poppies stretch out in front of us, one right after the other, as though if you squinted, it would look like a giant red blanket had been laid on top of thousands of gangly green weeds. Dense olive trees line the edges of the field, and behind them, sloping green hills take over the skyline against a cloudless blue sky.

I bend down and pick up a poppy, its inky-black center surrounded by delicate red petals clustered and fanning out. It is all so dreamy.

I can't contain my excitement as I wander deeper out into the poppy field, aimless but going farther and farther into the sea of red. I turn back to glance at Samuel. He is looking at me, tentatively, clearly unsure about what I'm doing.

"Are you coming?" I ask, more expectantly than I would have liked.

"Sure," he replies, nodding his head as though he's trying to convince himself, even as he starts tentatively following me out into a field with ankle-high flowers and no path.

He steps gingerly, as though aware that every step he's taking is crushing a few poor flowers beneath his feet. But they seem to pop back up with every move forward, as if they're meant to be briefly trod on and then cover the tracks of whomever has wandered into the center.

Once I reach far enough in, I lay down and look up at the sky. After a minute my view is blocked by Samuel, standing, looking over me.

"What are you doing?" he says quizzically, his shadow removing the sunny heat from my face.

"Come on!" I murmur sleepily, as I swat him out of the way in order to get my sunshine back. "How can you possibly not want to lie down in this giant field of flowers?"

"Bugs?" he replies with a smirk.

I sit up and look at him, tilting my head like a teacher who's lost her patience for a favorite student.

"You're a buzzkill," I respond, chuckling and lying down again to stare at the sky.

Who cares what Samuel Gordon thinks anyway? How often do I get to be in Italy, away from work, away from promotions and expectations and my sister making dramatic life U-turns that I'll have to deal with soon enough? If this isn't a moment to stop and smell the poppies, then I don't know what is. I don't care what he thinks of me anymore, and I am not going to let him stop my few moments of soaking it in.

Even if he did happen to be the person driving me home.

Oops.

I sit up. "Sorry, I know you have work. Do you want to go?"

He stands silently for a moment, clearly contemplating what to do. But to my surprise, he finally plops himself down.

He does not lie back in the way I did. But he leans back on his arms and looks up at the sky and takes in a deep breath. His upward gaze gives me a moment to really look at him, peacefully breathing in the smells of a field in the middle of nowhere. Up close it is clear that he's even more handsome now as he's gotten older, like a man who's finally grown into himself. Aging looks deeply sexy on him, and I wish I didn't notice it so readily.

"I guess you're right," he finally says, still staring up at the cloudless sky. "When you see something that feels necessary, you have to grab it and hold on. When are we going to be in a field like this when everything is blooming again?"

We.

"Exactly," I reply, not really knowing how to respond.

I lift myself up onto my elbows too. He looks over at me.

"Do you feel like you're doing that right now? At work I mean, grabbing onto it?"

He'd always been ten steps ahead of me. Always. I guess my work deflections hadn't really worked as well as I thought.

"Not really," I reply honestly, after a beat. "I do love it. The work I'm doing, at least—I can stand in a kitchen all day tinkering and somehow feel rejuvenated and excited when I stumble out of work after dark. But I missed out on a promotion right before I came here, so it's sort of making it all feel unsettled."

"Why didn't they give it to you?"

He has the uncanny ability to ask questions in the right way. Not *Why didn't you get it?* or some other phrase implying the fault was my doing. He automatically assumed they didn't give it to me for some reason out of my control.

"It wasn't anything I did so much as this other guy in my office just constantly tooting his own horn," I say, slowly. "He shouts from the rooftops every time he does something that should just be a normal thing in his job description. I sort of merrily roll along, putting out excellent content and coming up with ideas that everyone loves and that do really well. But it's the expectation that that is what I will be doing. No one is impressed that I once again delivered."

He nods, thoughtfully, not rushing to respond or make a judgment.

"That must be frustrating," he finally replies.

"It is," I sigh.

I'm surprised that I'm admitting as much so openly. I lay back down and look up at the sky, nothing to see but a giant patch of blue.

"I think I'm just a little too comfortable there," I finally say. "I know I have a job that so many people would kill for. I know I'll move up eventually. But it feels like I'm spinning my wheels a bit at a time, when I do have a lot of energy to create and I don't always feel like it's being utilized. I know I don't express that enough to the people around me—I want to be able to accomplish things on my own, not bother people, be easy to work with. I hate the idea of rocking the boat, even though logically I know I should."

I haven't really been able to articulate that before, but something about this field and the ability to say whatever I want out loud to the sky, with no one else around, makes it feel feasible. I stop talking and turn to look at Samuel. He's still calculating, still considering, not quick to come to a conclusion after such a dense admission.

I close my eyes and try to enjoy the smell of being surrounded by flowers. But after a few moments, Samuel finally speaks up again.

"Do you think maybe having parents that let you go on your own path sort of alone, without pushing, made it so you don't quite see when you *do* need a little push?"

I jolt up and look at him. My heart tightens in my chest. That was more than a throwaway inside joke, like his one before about my sleeping habits—he has held on to my family dynamic somewhere in the recesses of his brain for all these years. Some little piece of my young mind has stayed etched in his. He had always seen that my parents' trust and expectations were a blessing and also a load. His ability to see me clearly hasn't been frayed by time.

It makes me ache for what we've lost. Or what I lost when he left. The memory makes me prickle toward him.

"Probably," I finally say, not sure of how else to respond. I need to change the subject fast before he confuses me anymore. "I bet that's not a problem for you at work," I mention casually, trying to lighten the mood.

"No, not really," he replies gingerly, as though the previous commentary on my life and inner soul has been as simple as the weather.

He can sense a change of topic and roll with it when needed.

"Law firms are pretty prescribed. You do the work well, you move up. The people around you can also move up. I've been lucky and have had a lot of good cases, but I feel happy with my trajectory."

I doubt it's as simple as that. He always pushed for what he wanted—he pushed until he got it exactly his way, regardless of whether people caught up to him or not. He's probably being modest, but at least he's shifted the conversation easily. He explains his day-to-day at the firm, and I listen intently, thrilled to be getting this little peek into his current life, even if I'm not a part of it.

"How's your sister doing now?" he asks, although it's immediately clear that he's clocked the change in my expression at the mention of Sophie. "That great, huh?"

I soften a little.

"Sorry, it's just . . . a funny time to ask about Sophie, that's all. We sort of had a little disagreement right when I landed yesterday. I was tired and I didn't handle it well."

Understatement of the century.

"What happened?"

He's so earnest, so clearly ready to allow me to waste his time with my nonsense problems. To anyone else I would give a stock answer and wave the thought away, but I find, in this moment, that I want to tell him about Sophie.

"So, she got divorced around ten years ago," I say, nervous that maybe I'm skating a little too close to territory of our own. But he just nods, indicating that he remembers without any additional commentary needed. "And she hasn't really dated since then. She never really talked about it, so that's been sort of the status quo. And a few months ago she started dating this guy—I mean really, she can't have met him more than three months ago—and they got engaged yesterday."

"And you're concerned for her."

"Yes. I'm concerned for her," I repeat back softly, realizing I haven't even said that basic fact out loud until now. "I'd lost my baggage, and then I couldn't handle it when she dumped even more baggage on top of me."

I give him a weak smile.

"Well, maybe it's a good sign they found it then."

He pats my hand, and it singes me, as though all the touches we had years ago left marks that are now recognizing his return. I'm sure he didn't even give it a passing thought, but I can feel it lingering long after he's moved his hand away. My heart is beating faster, and I desperately will myself to make it stop and pretend it didn't notice. This entire conversation about Sophie feels way too close to acknowledging what happened between *us*.

We sit in silence for a moment, me avoiding his gaze for fear it might actually burn through me. I worry that I've gone ahead and ruined our chance at friendship before it's even begun. *Typical Stella.*

"But you haven't discussed your concerns with your friends yet?" he finally asks, clearly oblivious of the tension aching through me while I chastise myself for being so pathetic.

"Well, there hasn't really been time," I counter weakly, embarrassed that he can see right through me once again.

"You should, you know," he says quietly. "You don't have to hold everything so tightly. You can be like that gelato and rely on three types of pistachios instead of going it alone."

I try not to smile at the terrible analogy, but it's impossible to hold it in. Being seen by Samuel again makes me want to *not* hide my cracks from everyone else. Maybe I *could* make different choices. He always excelled at chipping away at all my hardened angles, seeing the spots in need of buffing that I'm so good at hiding from everyone else.

I am consumed with an urge to reach out to him and touch him in some way. It feels like this empty field has somehow collapsed time to a moment when we were comfortable saying anything to each other and even not saying things and happily sitting in silence together. So much time has passed, and yet we have the same cadence, the same shorthand with each other.

I've always assumed that my impression of him as a person who *understood me* was rooted in some sort of teenage infatuation. Like my frontal lobe hadn't evolved enough to know what was lust and what was actual connection. But I can feel it in my bones now that that was just an excuse I've been telling myself for years. That attraction I had in his orbit still feels primal and unmovable in this moment. It is somehow both surprising and also completely not.

Samuel always was my favorite person to talk to. I'm just now realizing how much I missed that ease.

I need to remind myself that this weekend is merely a blip, and we'll go back to not knowing each other once again when we leave Italy. The thought sits in the pit of my stomach, and I hate how much it pulls me down.

And because of that, I can't help but scratch the obvious itch that's in front of me. The way my body is now dizzy around him makes it seem *necessary* to bring up Hadley. Maybe if I can steer us to the topic of his girlfriend, I'll be able to shake off this feeling.

"Hadley seems really nice," I suggest, looking up again as though the cloudless sky suddenly holds something of keen interest.

"Oh yeah, she's great. We met in law school, and I've never been able to get rid of her," he says with a chuckle.

I look over at him. What a weird thing to say about your girlfriend.

And since I have no tact, and especially never have around Samuel, I have to say it out loud.

"What a weird thing to say about your girlfriend. No wonder she let you drive away from her into the sunset this afternoon."

He isn't looking at me anymore. The mood has perceptibly shifted. "Hadley isn't my girlfriend."

"Oh?" I squeak.

My heart is beating so fast that I think the sound of it thumping might be picked up on by cars on the road. I try to breathe in more air with every breath but quietly, so he won't notice that I've suddenly gone completely stiff and weird with information that my mind can't quite process.

"No, Hadley is just my friend," he finally replies. "She's like the sister every man dreams will take over his small apartment's couch when she and her girlfriend break up three months after starting law school together."

He snickers at a memory that is well trodden for him but is currently melting a hole in my brain after having to completely erase an entirely different narrative that was taking up space and paying rent.

I can't quite think of what to say next. I want to ask more questions, but none of them seem like appropriate follow-ups. *So she is gay? So when she links her arm through yours, that's like a friendly best friend move and not a sign that you get naked together when you're alone? Why did you need a best friend plus-one at a wedding with a bunch of your friends anyway? Does this mean you, in fact, do not have a girlfriend? Am I, in fact, panicking for no explainable reason right now?*

"We've lived together ever since then, and it's worked out really well," he continues, oblivious to my internal freak-out over nothing. "Although my mom is always waiting for her to realize she's straight, and I've had to explain to her that she's really not allowed to say that out loud or, preferably, even think it."

I laugh when he laughs, because I don't know what else to do. I've been mentally putting him in a box ever since I saw him standing with her the day before, and suddenly I need to not have all my feelings startlingly uncaged and rattling around my body. He has smashed through the box and is in jarringly too-close physical proximity to me.

"That's great, it's so nice to have a best friend you can live with," I say like a robot parroting back some stock response to whatever sentence has just been thrown its way. "Should we go back to the car? I didn't mean to keep you away from getting back to the hotel for so long."

I stand up. He looks surprised for a second but rolls with it and stands up next to me, wiping at the nonexistent dirt and theoretical bugs that he was so wary of keeping off his pants.

"Yes, definitely," he says quietly.

But then the moment has truly ended, because his mask is back up. He smiles a perfunctory smile at me.

"And you have a suitcase to reunite with!" he exclaims with more enthusiasm than I would have expected.

We walk back to the car and get in. He turns on the radio, and we sing along to the classic-rock songs that are mercifully on as we pull away from the cocoon of our poppy field.

Chapter Twelve
August, nine years ago

Braveheart is such a stupid dude movie, but I'd insisted we watch it since I couldn't believe he had never seen it. Whenever I said I went to college in Scotland, most men replied, "Oh, like *Braveheart*," which, in itself, is dumb because obviously people aren't running around like Middle Ages warriors today (well, no sober people are anyway).

But now here I was, lying in the bottom of my bunk bed wearing nothing but an oversize T-shirt and shorts with Samuel's arms wrapped around me while we sort of half watched a movie that I didn't really like that much.

Well, he was watching it. With interest. I guess all boys love war movies, so that should have been a given. But I was not able to focus on the movie. One of his hands was placed oh-so casually on my stomach and the other just barely perched on my leg. It felt intimate and possessive and way too hot for someone who still seemed unmoved by my attempts to get him actually naked in my presence.

I had sort of given in to Samuel after our Broadway date. I guess he was right about high-impact moments—that one softened me. He was so sincere, and I *liked* him. He had a Jedi-like ability to convince me of doing what he wanted, even when I wasn't quite sure I'd reached the place where he was. I figured I could add him to my rotation, even if that wasn't all he was looking for.

But frankly, it didn't matter what he was looking for, because all his sincerity couldn't counterbalance the evenings on the phone with my sister. For all of Sophie's attempts to make me think she was fine, covering her melancholy and resignation was like hiding a bullet hole with a Band-Aid. Her decimation was my hardening. Her blindsiding was my wake-up. At every stage of my life, Sophie had been my ten-year advance team, and for the first time, I didn't want to have what she was having.

I wasn't getting attached to Samuel; I was merely proving my point that I could keep things light. This was what I had to give, and he didn't question it. It was like the summer was a bubble, and we were simply going to live in it as long as it didn't pop. I let him take me to the beach, to an outdoor movie, for long walks around the reservoir in Central Park. I let him kiss me and feel me up, and I tried to get him to come home with me. That was the only area where I'd been failing—and at this point I really couldn't figure out why.

When he'd mentioned the movie, it seemed like the easiest way to get him to come over. An afternoon in bed watching a movie while my roommates spent the weekend out of town was not going to end in frustration.

So now we *were* watching the movie, but I was mostly anticipating its end. Every so often I would plant a little kiss on some other part of his body, as though I had to keep his Spidey senses alert and aware that I was here and I was not wearing a bra and I had some plans beyond watching a movie.

When the credits rolled I turned to him and started kissing him, slowly, trying to be as subtle as I could while also climbing on top of him (so . . . not very subtle then). A three-hour movie with his hands on me had made my body vibrate with anticipation. It was the first time we'd been in private together, after so many outings and kisses in public.

I was about to just take my shirt off already when he rolled me over and we were lying alongside each other, face to face, but not kissing anymore. He simply looked at me, searching my face, and I couldn't have told you what was inside his head if my life depended on it.

He wasn't rejecting me, and I could certainly *feel* that he was interested. But he had stopped, deliberately. And was just looking at me.

"Why?" I finally said, intuiting that it was pretty clear what *I* was hoping for.

"How many guys are you sleeping with right now, Stella?" he said softly.

I sat up, startled by the blunt force of his words. It was such a strange feeling hanging between us. He wasn't accusing and he didn't seem mad. He was merely asking a question that he clearly wanted a simple, direct answer to. I was obviously not mature enough to respond in kind, so I had to muster a bit of indignation first.

"Why is that your business?" I replied haughtily.

"My business?" he said with a smirk, but still as calm and cool as if we were talking about flavors of ice cream. "You're trying to have sex with me right now, and it is unusual to you that I might be interested in ascertaining how many other men are currently enjoying the same privilege?"

I didn't really know how to reply. My first instinct was to pretend like I *hadn't* been trying to have sex with him, but I quickly discarded that since it was about as obvious as daylight and that wasn't going to get me anywhere. Defensiveness became the next logical step, now that indignation had been summarily disregarded.

"We have never had a conversation about being exclusive," I finally said.

"I'm well aware."

"So why does it matter?"

"I'm not saying you can't do whatever you want. On the contrary, your body, your choice, et cetera. We are in total agreement."

He stopped, as though he expected me to say something else, but I didn't really know how to argue with that.

So he continued: "But it's also *my* body and *my* choice, and I choose not to sleep with you when you clearly don't want to be my girlfriend."

The word "girlfriend" landed with a thud right between us. I could feel the simplicity of our summer bubble suddenly starting to take on water, and I was about to drown.

"Why?" I finally said, again.

"I like you too much for that."

He said it so simply, as though it was such a logical explanation to him, but that to me felt like a foreign language.

"If you like me, then why isn't that enough? I like you too," I murmured, as though maybe if he heard it from me, that would be sufficient.

It was difficult to admit that out loud, but I wasn't going to get anywhere without giving him at least that. And, frankly, as much as it scared me, it was the truth.

"You have made it very clear from the moment we met that you don't want a boyfriend. You have not indulged me with the particulars on why that is. I'm not going to speculate. I want to spend time with you; I think I've made *that* pretty clear. Obviously I'm extremely attracted to you."

I couldn't get over how he said things with such ease—*Obviously I'm extremely attracted to you; I like you too much for that.* The things everyone else tried to obfuscate were basic facts to Samuel, no use trying to hide them.

"But," he continued, "I'm not going to do that to myself. You don't realize how hard it is at night, when you're too busy to be with me, not to visualize you with some other guy. I don't need the full picture."

Well, that was blunt. Totally surprising, and certainly not the normal way most men dealt with things, but it was pretty clear that Samuel did not operate the way most guys did.

"So I'm very content to wait until whenever you decide you want to date seriously."

It was another startling revelation. I couldn't control my face from looking so quizzical that he started laughing.

"What?" he finally said.

I sputtered out, "That's your move?"

"What do you mean?" he replied, looking more pleased with himself than he should have.

"We literally live on different continents most of the year. You're telling me that your goal all this time has been to get me to date you 'seriously' . . . how?"

"Why does it matter?"

"Why does it matter that in a couple of weeks we are going to be living thousands of miles apart when I go back to school in the UK and you go back to school here?"

"Correct."

He was starting to piss me off now.

"Why are you being like this?"

"Like what?"

I couldn't tell if he was genuinely that obtuse or if now he was just trying to goad me. Either way I didn't like it.

"Like someone who literally does not see logic," I responded, feeling my irritation pour out of me along with a few blunt choice words. "We have known each other for less than three months, most of which I've spent kind of avoiding going out with you, and now that we're having fun, you're telling me that your expectation is a long-distance, cross-continent relationship where you wouldn't see your girlfriend probably until Christmas? That's your endgame?"

He nodded along like this was the most normal scenario that had ever been suggested.

"If you want to be with someone, you make it work. I don't want to date anyone else. I've felt that way since I first met you."

The sentiment hung in the air between us, heavy, and with everything I *wasn't* saying lingering in and filling the space.

I obviously did not have that level of clarity on my wants. Yes, I liked him. Yes, I liked him more than I thought I would. Yes, I liked him more than anyone else I was seeing, but I wasn't going to date those guys either. I was young and in college and was not going down a messy path that only led to heartache.

But I couldn't admit all of that.

"It's not you—"

I stopped myself. I could not give him the whole "It's me, not you" shit when he was so good at being honest.

"I really wasn't being coy when I said I wasn't dating. I have a lot of family stuff on my plate, and I am processing that and trying to simply have fun this summer. I don't need emotional complications at this point in my life."

"I know, and I get it."

"Well, clearly you don't get it," I said a little testily.

"I do. And I'm happy to wait for you to figure it out."

"I'm not figuring anything out," I spat back, finally letting myself show a bit of anger at the absurdity of what he was saying. "I'm saying, no, I don't want to date you."

"Right, yes, you've made that *abundantly* clear," he said with a chuckle.

I knew he could read the bewilderment on my face, because he changed tactics.

"Look, I don't want to be your friend. I think you know that. But I am not here to pressure you or make you less cynical in an instant after obviously going through some crap with men who are clearly idiots—"

At that I shot him a look, because his impression of my hesitation was obviously something as trivial as having been dumped by a high school sweetheart. He was *lucky* to have no idea what could happen when you opened yourself up to someone. He was *lucky* to not know how much young love could eventually rip your heart out. He was *lucky* to not know what it felt like to realize you weren't good enough for someone.

But I'd seen it firsthand.

"It's really not about you, Samuel," I finally said again, trying to get my original point across while still deflecting from the parts of my reasoning that hurt too much to articulate. "I don't want to deal with *any* relationship. Everyone at this age—and at any age, really—acts selfishly. We hurt people, we break our promises, even with the best of intentions. And that's *normal*, but I just don't want to deal with someone else's shit right now. I don't think that's so hard to understand."

Maybe it was unfair to not give him deeper insight into my reasoning, but he wouldn't understand anyway. He would simply argue with me, even though I'd already seen the truth and he hadn't.

"Besides," I continued, trying to find some way to lighten the mood, "you just like going big. This is all a high-impact moment for you."

"I can't help that," he said, giving me his lopsided smile that's always made it hard to say no to him. "That comes with the territory of being a first-generation overachieving big brother. I like taking care of people. I like going all in. I'm not going to pretend like I don't. But that doesn't mean I don't know when something is *worth* going all in on."

"Well . . . ," I said, stalling and biting my lower lip, trying not to let his well-aimed words slip past my defenses. "You and I are just going to have to agree to disagree on that one for the moment."

"Sure. For the moment," he countered, clearly completely ignoring my skepticism.

He reached for my arm and started drawing slow circles on my wrist. "I do, however, also think that when something is meant to be, it'll eventually be. So let's have fun this summer, and we can keep in touch and maybe someday you'll feel differently. And if not, that's fine too. I like you, and this"—he pulled me toward him, so our faces were so close they were almost touching—"is very, very fun for the time being."

He moved his whole body on top of mine and started kissing me so deeply I thought I might have a stroke from how much I wanted him.

I had just spent three hours anticipating him touching me, and now he was here, pressing into me, but without any ability to actually get what I wanted. What a particular brand of torture this was.

I put my hand around his back and felt his muscles tightening from the pressure of holding himself over me. I kissed him to forget everything he had just said.

When something is meant to be, it'll eventually be.

I kissed him to forget every time I'd foolishly swooned when Charlie whispered to Sophie how much he loved her. The sting of their implosion muddled and intertwined with everything Samuel had said to me moments ago.

If you want to be with someone, you make it work.

The only way to end the muddle was to keep kissing, and keep hoping that maybe just for once I could stop letting words ricochet across my brain. I moved my hands to the top of his jeans and tried to unbutton them before he gave me an exasperated look.

"You're really not going to have sex with me," I sighed, trying to remember why we had started this entire baffling conversation in the first place.

He shook his head and collapsed on top of me, then rolled to the side and pulled me into him, holding me tightly but gently up against him and stroking my hair.

"Not yet anyway," he said with a smirk.

CHAPTER THIRTEEN
THURSDAY, PRESENT DAY

My suitcase is in my room when I arrive back, but I can't open it just yet. I flop onto my bed and stare up at the ornate ceiling fan, moving slowly in languid circles. If I stare long enough, maybe I can focus only on how many times the fan is going around and be able to avoid facing how fast my heart is racing.

I should be better at it. I am the queen of avoiding. A master at ducking out of any new relationship that even starts to seem close to the *word* "relationship." Just merrily roll along as long as I don't have to shift or alter anything. Keep life easy and drama-free by never even starting something that could turn *into* drama.

But I can't seem to shove this one down far enough to make it go away.

The rest of the car trip after the poppy field was filled with music and small talk, and we had a perfectly friendly goodbye when we went in opposite directions toward our rooms once we got back to the hotel. But something has shifted.

Maybe it's all simply an insane rattle in my brain, and he hasn't noticed a damn thing—didn't *feel* a damn thing for the last two days while my insides have been doing the tango—but for me, the afternoon was suddenly like a floodgate had been opened after being stuck tightly shut for almost a decade.

I haven't let myself think about Samuel for more than a fleeting moment for so many years. Even though I knew logically he would probably be at this wedding, I didn't allow myself to think about it beyond that basic fact. And I didn't actually articulate that fear out loud to anyone before I got on the plane. I was so caught up with work that I was able to bat away the niggling sense of some kind of excited dread that had burned around my periphery for months. If I didn't have to see it, then it wasn't real. And once it was real, at least there was a person in between us who made it simpler.

Having a girlfriend who is *here* and who is *nice* packaged him up into a glass box with a tidy bow tied on top and a stamp on the side that said DO NOT TOUCH. Even when things seemed so easy and normal between us once we started talking in the car, even when his nearness made me shiver, the distant presence of Hadley was like a nice stop sign that kept my brain from spiraling out of control.

But the glass has shattered, and I am now alone in a room and all my memories are flooding in. Every ounce of love Samuel poured onto me when we first met is churning with his eventual withdrawal from my life. The memories are crowding me like an elephant sitting on my chest, and my lungs are full of shards of glass, prodding and poking me, without any way to escape.

This anxiety is consuming me. It is impossible to ignore the glaring reality that this is why I have been, essentially, single my entire adult life. I have worked so damn hard to be in control, and in one fucking week, it is like the universe is trying to remind me that no matter how carefully I plan and plot and protect, I can't avoid that all-consuming anxious frenzy from taking over again.

I've kept on such a straight and narrow at work so that I wouldn't be blindsided and unable to breathe.

I've kept relationships casual and ended them before they can begin so I wouldn't spin out.

I decided long ago that the best path forward for me always is to get in front of problems. To not allow anything lurking to *become* a problem. So maybe that's hindered my ability to have a boyfriend—but deciding against vulnerability because it causes mild panic attacks seemed like a worthy trade.

I am lucky to have met people I trusted well before adulthood, and those people have been enough for me. Subrata, Elena, and Cat have been able to see most of the messy side of me. That is plenty open. Anyone else seeing it is too overwhelming. I started my career and created an orderly pattern and a bubble that have kept me safe and happy for years.

I *am* safe. I *am* happy.

So why does it feel like the first drops of a thunderstorm falling swiftly onto my head? What long-covered scar tissue has Samuel's reemergence somehow cut through?

I cannot delve into this shit right now.

I put a pillow over my face and breathe in and out, willing myself to think about anything else. I start ruminating on an article I should be writing and allow myself to escape down that pathway until I've tricked my brain so thoroughly that I can't feel my heart racing anymore.

"You were that tired?" I can feel the voice dulled through the pillow that's still on my face.

"Hmm?" I say groggily, not wanting to move yet.

I fell asleep and have no idea what time it is now.

"You didn't even open your suitcase."

I take the pillow off my face and sit up. Elena is standing over me, with a quizzical look in her eyes.

"Oh, yeah," I respond airily. "I still have so much jet lag."

"Are you zonked from all the work stuff?" she tries.

"Yeah," I say, giving her partial honesty. "It's just very overwhelming to think about what I should do next."

"Well, maybe see it as an opportunity to move forward, you know? You've had the exact same routine for like six years straight. Maybe it's okay to leave the safest option behind for a little bit. You're strong enough to take some leaps, Stel."

I blink back at her, wondering if all we're talking about is work. Elena is nothing if not incisive. She can be the silliest friend when you need to blow off steam, yet she also is always somehow the thoughtful person who sees when you're flailing below the surface. But it's hard to be sure what she means because she's already moved on and opened the closet, where all her clothes are neatly lined up.

I look at the clock—it's already five thirty. Shit. Time to get into gear. I stand up and start unceremoniously unpacking my suitcase.

"We missed you in the car, but Hadley is so much fun," she says as she wanders into the bathroom and starts washing her face. "Did you know she does family law? Like divorce and custody and everything. She basically is a defender of women from their asshole ex-husbands, and she's the kind of lawyer people hire when they do *not* want to set-tle. It gets nasty, apparently. I'm not sure I could do that kind of work, especially with so many kids involved."

"Oh, interesting," I say, mostly distracted.

Elena is bi, so with women I can never tell when she's telling me about a friend or if this is just some unconscious way to babble on about a girl she likes. And I've had to recalibrate my entire view of Hadley in the last few hours, but maybe it's all been obvious to Elena all along.

Ugh, I can't think about Elena and Hadley suddenly being friends or an item or in some other scenario that would mean I'd now have to see Samuel once this trip is over. Nope, shoving that thought right back down.

I am hanging up the contents of my suitcase and mentally kicking myself for every single thing I have brought. Subrata helped me pick out outfits for the various ceremonies, but everything else seems to pale in comparison to the gorgeous Italian surroundings.

I pick up a *taralli* from the bowl on the counter. The little circular Italian snack is like a tiny cross between a breadstick and a pretzel, and gnawing on them is easily the best thing for my nerves. I need the distraction while I stare at my clothes with disappointment.

"Wear that one," Elena says from the bathroom, pointing to a butter-yellow jumpsuit with a pink-and-red floral bloom print on it with a knotted sweetheart neckline. It does look like a burst of Italian spring sunshine.

I look at my face wash and makeup nestled into my suitcase and feel a glow of satisfaction that at least *that* is there for me. I throw the jumpsuit over my shoulder, grab onto my toiletries, and join Elena in the bathroom, secure that at the very least my mask has arrived.

Cat pulls her car in front of the ornate stone arch and wooden door of the Palazzo Seneca, and she, Elena, and I all ooh and aah. The small hotel is this evening's locale for another meal that's sure to be incredible. Because Subrata wanted to have a traditional Indian wedding, tomorrow will be the sangeet, so Luca's family wanted to throw their own Italian soiree tonight. I certainly wasn't complaining about the plethora of excellent events on the calendar.

Palazzo Seneca is in the center of Norcia's old town but down a quiet side street. Walking into the boutique hotel, you certainly feel all the five hundred years of history the building holds. Simple antique furniture, a massive painted globe, and a surely priceless, elegant old piano sit near the entrance.

I want to gawk at everything around us, but we are led down the hallway toward Vespasia, the Michelin-starred restaurant that resides within the hotel. This is definitely fancier than last night's event—I can only imagine what could top this the following two nights. We are taken out to a courtyard garden where the dinner will be held.

"What do you think Subrata would have done if it had rained?" Cat says quietly in my ear. She is always the one thinking through logistics, and I'm not surprised that's where her mind went.

"Probably a ten-step backup plan," I whisper back, and we both try to contain our giggles, imagining our friend planning everything meticulously from afar.

All four courtyard walls are lined with dramatic arches. Some are doors back into the restaurant or hotel, and others are floor-to-ceiling glass windows. Small hedges line the center of the garden, which is blooming to the hilt with a variety of herbs, packed together. Their aromatic smell wafts through the space, which is open to the sky but completely stilled by the surroundings.

Wrought iron candle lanterns sit on the ground and are perched as sconces on the walls so that the whole scene is bathed in candlelight. They match the intricate iron chairs nestled into tables topped with white tablecloths.

I wander around each table until I find our name tags. My stomach sinks a bit when I see that Elena, Cat, and I are all separated by Luca's various male relatives, a neat trick to even out the genders at the tables despite living in the twenty-first century of *Who Still Gives a Shit*. Italians, I guess.

I take a seat, waiting like a captive to see who I will have to make small talk with for the next three hours, minimum, with a view mostly of the windows instead of the array of people Cat and Elena get by sitting on the other side of the table.

But when our table mates arrive, I am pleasantly surprised. Luca's cousins are actually kind of cute and exceptionally entertaining in that way that Italian men who think they are charming can be when they want to amp up the evening. They immediately latch onto stories about

Cat's crazy travel/work schedule and seem to be engrossed in the idea that *Such a young, beautiful woman has to be out of town so frequently* (ugh, their words, not mine). Cat is lit up with the flattery.

Other than Subrata, none of us have been particularly successful at relationships. Cat had a college boyfriend, but I always suspected she was hung up on a childhood friend she'd always talked about when she visited her dad's family in Argentina, so the boyfriend didn't last. And then her mom got sick, and she generally just worked too much, so since college she's always had easy excuses for avoiding relationships.

Elena had an on-again, off-again high school boyfriend whom we all despised and a very intense girlfriend for a few years around college, but generally she is like me and aims to keep things pretty light. In short, we are all pretty pathetic when it comes to dating.

So a bit of an ego boost never hurts any of us relationship-challenged dolts.

Everyone coos when little appetizers arrive—a puff of bread with a thin slice of prosciutto draped over the top (we all practice copying the waiter when he says, "*Gnocco fritto*," rolling his *r* delightfully); a pork rind with some other cured meat adorning it; and a savory little pastry that looks like a cannoli stuffed with goat cheese and nuts.

I start to tune out the conversation. I know all of Cat's best stories, and she is certainly getting a cackle out of the three men sitting with us, helpfully aided by Elena as a wing-woman with much experience. But I am not really in the mood to flirt and banter, so I find my mind wandering to all the small details of the courtyard.

Every table has a little wrought iron birdcage with a candle inside, like a smaller and more intricate version of all the other candleholders spread throughout. The napkins are a shimmering white.

Our waiter brings the next course, the creamiest bowl of lentils I have ever tasted. He seems both obligated and excited to share the whole history of lentils in Umbria, with their three-thousand-year tradition and protected designation of origin. History aside, every bite is rich and nutty, and I am *definitely* going to have to find myself some of these small Castelluccio lentils to pack in my suitcase.

Within five minutes I've got a handwritten note from the waiter describing the best shop in town for purchasing them, the secret to softening them in only twenty minutes, and the best sausages to pair them with. I can see Cat rolling her eyes at me, but I can't help it if I find the food conversation more interesting than the subtle *Can I get in her pants?* innuendo conversation happening across from me.

I turn around to see how the other tables look amid the excessive candlelight. My eyes immediately catch Samuel's, looking right at me from across the courtyard. I feel the entirety of my insides jostle. It's amazing how little he has changed, really. Most men caught staring would look away, pretending like they haven't been looking at all. They dart their eyes away, leaving you wondering if *you* were in fact the person staring and if *you* should be embarrassed.

But Samuel isn't a coward, even in the smallest of instances. I turned to see him watching me, and now he just keeps on watching. I can't stop myself from watching right back.

His face has almost no expression; I can't read what is in that brain of his. My heart is beating faster, like I've been startled, and I'm glad he's too far away to see the physical effect his eyes are having on me. I squirm in my seat.

Finally, after what could be ten seconds or ten minutes (probably the former, but it feels like the latter), his lips curl up ever so slightly to one side, and he raises his glass. Like a mirror, my mouth does the same, and my hands hold up my drink. Among all the talking and laughter and music and flickering candles surrounding our tables, we have a small "cheers" from across the room just for us, eyes locked, expressions at ease, at least one of us with a tingle down her spine.

"More wine, signora?"

The waiter has broken the reverie.

"Oh, sure," I reply quickly, looking up at him encouragingly as he pours more of the local bottle of grechetto into my almost-empty glass.

I drink probably a little too fast in the hopes of numbing the pulsating edge that is lingering across my skin.

Another set of waiters swoop in and place a risotto in front of us, regaling us with the provenance of these particular truffles, hunted by a local forager and his dogs just this morning in their nearby family-owned plot that they've been cultivating for over a century. The whole elegance of the explanation of each dish is like dinner theater with a side of pasta.

By the time I'm able to peek back over at Samuel, he isn't looking at me anymore. I can't quite fathom how I can have the largest quantity of truffles I've ever seen in front of me and feel such disappointment.

After dinner ends, the party moves inside to the hotel's library, and somehow everyone is sampling various Umbrian amaro that are not doing anything to make anyone less drunk and fizzy. All the older family members have gone home, and most of the friends are standing in corners next to heavy wooden bookshelves or sitting around tables in high, deep-red leather wingback chairs. Two of Subrata's friends from work are enamored with a bookshelf that is actually a hidden door that leads into what looks like—boringly—a conference room of some kind.

I enjoy watching and sipping. I probably *shouldn't* be sipping any more, after my liberal consumption of all the glasses of wine that were placed in front of me. But this wood-paneled room with old books behind glass, brass picture lights, and a rotary phone is so much more interesting to observe with a warming beverage in hand. It feels like I've stepped back in time. Or maybe my brain is so hazy that it makes it feel that way.

"Whatcha drinking?"

I turn to see Samuel standing next to me. My drunkenness impairs my ability to conceal my insides from showing on my face, and I glow at his arrival. His nearness lights up my whole body. And also, frankly, is doing a lot of other things unsolicited to my body.

A sober voice in the back of my head is shouting at me to not say anything stupid, but the amaro and the wine are in cahoots to make sure I ignore whatever rational thoughts try to peek their way through.

"Amaro al Tartufo," I trill in my most dramatic Italian accent, stringing out every possible vowel and probably sounding way more idiotic than it seems to my sloshed little brain.

"Which is what exactly?"

"I dunno, herbs and truffles and whatever else Norcia is known for turned into liquor."

I realize that despite being a writer who is supposed to be focused on culinary exploits, I have really dropped the ball on this one. But I can't truly be blamed for being overserved. Blame the waiters.

Samuel looks amused and then beckons as though he wants me to hand over my glass. I don't know how to react, so I slowly hold it up for him, and he gingerly takes it out of my grip, never touching, although the proximity of his hand is doing something to me. He smells the drink and takes a sip. It gives me an excuse to stare at his mouth. Maybe for a little longer than is appropriate.

"It's good," he says. "Not necessarily the thing I would pick out of a lineup, but, you know, when in Rome."

"It's Norcia, actually. Rome is that way."

I point in a random direction (maybe in the direction of Rome, who knows) and smirk, exceptionally pleased at my *excellent* joke (maybe not as excellent as it feels in this particular tipsy moment, but who's to say).

"Well," he replies dramatically, "when in Norcia then."

He lifts the glass again into a sort of cheers. My whole body is now sparking, like I could simply reach out and grab him, and we might fuse together. With the alcohol quietly removing all my carefully erected defense walls, it's suddenly like I'm standing with a lost limb that I can't quite reattach. How can we be standing so close but as such utter strangers?

We are looking at each other again and not saying anything, and the weight of everything not said is hanging in the air between us, the heaviest humidity imaginable. Any strangeness I've been feeling about the afternoon clearly has not affected Samuel. He seems emboldened, actually.

Here I am, freaking out and wondering if I'm making a total fool of myself, and Samuel has taken the events of the afternoon and turned them into a whole new comfort level. How does he always do that? How can he have it so easy while I'm standing here so tortured, with every little spot across my body heightened?

We spent an afternoon driving and chatting and standing in poppy fields, completely and utterly ignoring the fact that the previous time we'd spoken to each other had resulted in slamming doors and so many things that could not and *had not* been unsaid.

The memories are all gurgling up for me, and I have no idea what he is thinking. But for the life of me, my slightly alcohol-infused brain cannot think of a single reason why I shouldn't be kissing him right now instead of standing here making stupid jokes about Italian cities. It has *not* been nine years, and I am *not* an idiot, and there *has* been a time in my life when the way he looked at me contained more love and affection than any person I have ever known before or since.

But that is wrong.

Because I can't read what his eyes are saying to me. Because I do not really know him anymore. Because I am not a child with a crush. Because there was a real and valid reason why he walked away from me at the time and neither of us ever looked back.

I try to open my mouth to say something, anything, to get myself out of this spiral and go back to some normal semblance of normal acquaintance when, thank God, Cat strides over. She is exceptionally sober (as one's designated driver should be, and, frankly, how Cat almost always is, with her much more judicious mind that keeps her out of embarrassing scenarios).

"Hey, drunko, wheels up in five minutes," Cat trills. "I need to get some sleep before tomorrow's shenanigans, and you for sure need to drink some water."

She holds up a glass of water she's already procured for me and hands it over. "I'm going to go get Elena from wherever she's disappeared to—I think that secret room might just be a conference room?"

She bounces off in a flash, and I am left with water in one hand, amaro in the other, and an amused Samuel, who has *definitely* noticed the "drunko" label. Great.

"She runs a tight ship," he says with a smile.

"Thank goodness someone does. Captain, my captain!" I respond playfully back.

Why. Why am I like this?

"She would rather not drink the whole evening than take a cab?"

"Oh no. She hates being stranded without a way home, and she barely drinks anyway because nothing ever gets her out of control," I say with all the affection in the world. "I would not say that our darling Catalina is a taker of chances."

"Well, sometimes you need people like that around you," he replies without any hint of anything.

I nod and take a big sip of my water, suddenly very aware of how little I have hydrated and how I will be feeling it tomorrow. Samuel watches and tilts his head buoyantly toward me.

"Well, since I don't think we've figured out how to be frogs yet, I bet a glass of water is probably the best we can do."

I lift my eyebrows. "What?"

He suddenly looks a bit panicked. All the hairs on the back of my neck stand up, and I have the strangest feeling of déjà vu, but I can't quite place it.

"Oh, just, you know, one time you said something to me about osmosis and frogs and water," Samuel stammers. "That just . . . her handing you the water reminded me of that. It was funny. At the time. I thought it was funny anyway. It's a visual that sticks in your mind."

He is blabbering. Why is he blabbering? The panicked expression has been wiped off his face and replaced with something more neutral, but he is still yammering on about nothing, and I don't quite know what to make of him right now. Maybe he is drunk too. But it's weird to see his calm demeanor suddenly so thoroughly twisted.

To stop the awkwardness, I try to come up with any kind of reply.

"Maybe I'll be luckier with the osmosis now that we're in Italy."

I make absolutely no sense, and now I'm wondering if the babbling is rubbing off on me. Maybe the building will collapse and crush us so we won't have to dig our way out of this conversation. That would be preferable.

Thankfully Cat comes back with Elena in tow and grabs my hand, saying a halfhearted goodbye to Samuel as she drags me off. I lift up my free hand in a soft wave to say goodbye, locking eyes with him and looking back even as I am being hauled out.

He lifts his hand up and watches me; it seems like he has something to say but can't quite bring himself to. I want to ask, but I'm being forced out the door.

We get in the car, and Elena turns on some loud music. I think she's probably just as tipsy as I am. Cat starts the car, and we lurch forward.

She looks at me in the rearview mirror.

"Oh man, I almost forgot that you hooked up with Samuel that summer we were all living together in college. No wonder he's trying to chat to you again now."

A part of me wants to confide everything that happened after the summer to Cat and Elena now, wants to allow the bottled mess of nine years ago to come pouring quickly out. But that stopper has kept me safe all these years from panic and self-examination—even with Cat's comment as a sliver of an opening, it feels too extreme to let the oxygen in now.

"Something like that," I say with a sigh.

CHAPTER FOURTEEN
SEPTEMBER 4, NINE YEARS AGO

Letter from Samuel to Stella:

Stella—

I'm really not that good of a writer (which can be a problem at times for a student whose primary function is writing essays), so please forgive me for anything clichéd or awkward.

First and most importantly—thank you for letting me throw you a little going away party and for eating bagels and lox for dinner since I needed to send you off in proper New York style and that seemed the most fitting. I know you'll secretly wear that Yankees hat and will definitely not light it on fire as stated.

I asked you not to read this letter until you got on the plane because it's not meant to pressure you in any way. I know how you feel (as we have established) and I do just want us to keep in touch. I hope you know you can always call me or reach out—or mutually send each other essays to edit, as you so brilliantly suggested to get us each out of our writing ruts.

But, I realized I had not really told you how I feel. I know I've sort of danced around it and I know you've kind of avoided having to actually talk about it. But it doesn't feel right for you to not know and it also didn't feel right to make you talk about something you clearly would get VERY uncomfortable having to watch me say out loud to your face (even though you are extremely adorable when you are uncomfortable. And oddly sexy—not sure what that's about). But as such, it seemed like a letter was the best way.

So, here goes.

I love you.

And I am saying it because I have to. You make me happy from the top of my head all the way down to my toes. Talking to you for even one minute makes being with you seem like an undeniable inevitability. I love you and always will.

I don't want you to change and that is not symbolic or a line. I know this might be hurtful for you to hear, either for what it is in itself or for the memories it brings back, and for that I'm sorry. I just could not imagine having you leave without telling you how I feel. I could not imagine you not knowing.

To be honest, my brain knows what you are going to say (or not say. I do love a brush-off from you and I can't wait to get an email tomorrow asking how classes are going and whether I ate some slog in the cafeteria, or something equally breezy). I knew where you stood and where you stand, you've told me before. But my heart told me that if somehow, someway, I could bear telling you how I actually feel, I might be able to reach past your disbelief of me (and, as I'm mostly hopeful this is not a me-specific issue, men generally), even if only for a second.

I'm going to take the chance that maybe you'll let a small part of yourself believe that I am sincere, that it's not ridiculous that I love you, and that it's not ridiculous for me to say that that feeling is never going to change. Not for the rest of my life. I know it.

Did you know that I hate ice cream? I don't want my desserts to be cold and slippery—I truly find it gross and it baffles me that anyone likes it. Yuck. But on our first date (yes, it was a date) you really wanted to buy me gelato and I ate the whole damn thing. Because I would rather eat a slimy, disgusting ice cream (shudder) than see any sadness on your face for one second. I knew I loved you from that very minute.

Maybe this is selfish, because if I don't want you to be sad or feel pain I am sure this letter is certainly causing some of that. But if it is, then I promise it's the last selfish thing I'll do and we never have to talk about it again.

You said to me once, sort of offhandedly, that everyone acts in selfish ways, breaks promises, hurts the people they are close to. And that's mostly true. Some make that choice purposefully, some make it in self-preservation. Most of them are not bad people. But the problem is you've managed to stumble across that one who is different.

—And right here is the point where your cynical side (and it is only one side of you) is waving red flags. Big bells and whistles (and possibly firecrackers) are going off warning you that this guy telling you that he is "that" guy, that he isn't part of "it," that it is an impossibility for him to hurt you, is either lying or doesn't know himself well enough. But please do me the favor of ignoring those noises for a few more minutes and letting me finish.—

I don't mean to be immodest, but this is just how I am and I can explain to you why if you want. But I know it's true. You don't have to believe me. I just needed to put it onto paper, so for the next months and years you can know I said it and I meant it.

So why am I writing this letter? I know that, given your experiences, it is impossible for you to believe me outright. I accept that. But I also know that I can't give up on the chance that you will one day be able to believe me. I know that circumstances are circumstances and that right now you are sitting on a plane home and then in a few days you'll be on another one headed to another continent. I know you can't abandon all your cynicism in one fell swoop. But I am willing to wait until you think you can.

Until then I hope we can be friends. You know, just the kind of friends where I'll be over here madly in love with you but never breathing a word about it again until you want me to. And that's a promise I intend to keep, so this letter is truly the last you'll hear about it unless you bring it up.

Have a safe flight and don't watch any movies that make you laugh too hard or your seatmates will think you're a weirdo.

All my love,

Samuel

September 8

> Email
> From Stella
> To Samuel
> Samuel . . .
>
> How are your classes going? Did you eat any slog
> in your cafeteria? . . .
>
> I watched Weekend at Bernie's on the plane and I
> definitely was that weirdo cracking up in the middle
> seat. Oh well.
> Don't be a stranger.
>
> Stella xoxo

I'd intended to write something better back. I hadn't gotten as far as what to actually say or what I'd even *want* to say if I could get a coherent thought together.

But in the end, I just couldn't.

I'd arrived in Raleigh for the long weekend before school started back up again, ready to revert into the version of myself I became whenever I got to breathe in the humid air of home.

When I was born, my parents were older, Sophie was halfway to being grown up, and they never really were able to go fully back to baby mode. For as long as I could remember, they treated me like another member of that mature circle—self-sufficient, able to tackle any challenge. And I relished that confidence.

With Sophie, though, I got to be the baby. She always snuck me a little extra candy or cuddled me a little tighter under the blanket. She was the only person in my life who saw me for who I was but still believed a lion cub needed coddling too.

But the past summer I'd been the one coddling and cuddling. And I was ready to put that disordered mayhem behind us. She'd had a year to grieve, and I was convinced this summer would be different.

Except, the steeled Sophie I'd chatted to on the phone the last few months wasn't standing ramrod straight like I'd expected, still willowy but now with stronger roots. It was the opposite. She was somehow coated in an armor so thick I could barely see through it and yet was as delicate as a glass vase that a slight breeze could knock right over.

The first night I got home, I was surprised to see how *settled* she was in her old room. What had been a temporary fix until she found a new place to live suddenly seemed like a stasis.

"How's the apartment hunt going?" I asked as we set the table for dinner, out of earshot from our parents.

"Oh," she replied, distant, like the thought hadn't even occurred to her. "I'm saving up. I'm not in a rush."

"Is it weird, though?" I continued, undeterred. The answer to that seemed fairly obvious, even though I didn't know how to tiptoe around this version of my sister. "Like, what if you want to have people over?"

I didn't dare ask if she had dates over.

"I don't really. I mean, I go out with my friends sometimes, but mostly I'm enjoying being alone. I never really got to be alone before."

Before. It hung in the air. It made me want to set the cutlery down as gently as possible, lest I make a slight noise and upset this indelicate awkward balance.

"Well, you deserve a little time to yourself."

"I do. I definitely do," she said. "I think it's good. Keep things small. I'm happier like this."

She wasn't looking at me. The napkins were being folded with a level of precision you'd expect from a soldier. No one had ever seemed *less* happy, and yet we were just going to stand here and nod at each other without really meeting eyes, pretending like this bony, sallow person was the same woman as the boundless, optimistic light of a sister I'd always known. It was too painful to say it out loud. So we just said words like "I'm happier" and left it at that.

We ate dinner that night with a conversation I couldn't really bring myself to focus on, a bunch of chirping birds making incoherent noises around me. Warbling sounds went in, but they went right past us all, unable to do anything for Sophie but mercifully pretend that she was happy. I guess maybe we thought that if we kept playing at it, eventually, someday, down the road, it could be true.

The twilight zone version of my family stayed put the whole weekend, pretending in ways we'd never had to before: lying to my sister by omission and hoping that that could eventually bring her back to us. Four days later, I'd never been so relieved to board a plane.

The lead balloon of the state of my sister had sat on the buoyancy and confidence of Samuel's letter. Every time I even tried to think about what he'd said—let alone try to craft a coherent response—I couldn't help but let the life experience in front of me paint right over his facade. It was a nice idea. It was even a tempting idea. But no love is worth that chance at devastation.

I'm too young for this, I couldn't help but think.

But, but, but.

I wanted to talk to him. So it couldn't hurt to respond a little bit, right? I'd been living for days in a world of plausible deniability. It wasn't perfect, but it was working.

So I responded the only way I could. And for now that would have to be enough.

CHAPTER FIFTEEN
FRIDAY, PRESENT DAY

A mehndi party the day before a wedding is a brilliant concept that really all cultures should adopt. It's basically like getting a spa day during which all the women at a wedding gossip and eat before having to deal with everyone else.

On Friday morning, Subrata's bridal suite at Villa Amati is just down the hall from our rooms, but it is like a different world (one that's suddenly made our *extremely cool and beautiful* room seem like a hovel).

Subrata, the interior designer in her bursting at the seams to show us everything, has already pointed out the intricate detailing of the original seventeenth-century frescoes with whirling florals in green and red against a golden background. The fireplace mantel is in the same floral pattern but instead is carved in marble (just like I have in my New York City apartment, of course. HA).

Squishy velvet couches in whites and beiges are offset by colorful pillows strewn about. Bottles of prosecco sit in ice buckets, and giant snack boards piled high with fruits, meats, and cheeses are on every table.

But the Italian is not to be outdone by the Indian flair. Subrata's mother arranged to get more flowers than I could have thought possible in one room—the arrangements are more elaborate than most weddings have, and she also had garlands made of the most colorful blooms. She draped delicate Indian-inspired fabrics over every table as tablecloths. She has also somehow found six skilled mehndi artists to create traditional henna patterns on our hands. The combination of the Renaissance room and the Indian additions is like falling into some dreamworld that only Subrata could have conjured up. It is perfect.

I, of course, am trying to master the art of having someone paint my hands while also stuffing my face with as much cheese as possible. It's a delicate skill, but someone has to do it.

"You could stop ramming cheese into your mouth for like thirty seconds, and you probably wouldn't die," Elena says with a chuckle.

"Probably isn't definite, though," I reply.

I pop another hunk of cheese into my mouth while keeping my other hand as still as possible so that the paisley design that's almost complete on my hand won't get ruined.

"Do you think if I itch my nose I'll get henna on it and then walk around looking like Rudolph for the next few days?" Hadley whispers over to us.

The younger women are all grouped together, while Subrata's aunts and older family friends are still milling around with their free hands to eat and drink as much as they want. Lucky. I try to stifle a laugh while Cat reaches over with her one unpainted hand and scratches it for her.

"I knew I loved you guys," Hadley says with a laugh, her tall frame looking uncomfortable sitting cross legged on the floor.

I want to be annoyed at how easily she's slotted in with my friends, like we've all known each other our whole lives. But she is impossible to dislike. She is somehow both blunt and easygoing. Direct, but warm. Sure of herself, but not cocky. I can see why she and Samuel get along.

We pepper Subrata with questions as our artists finish with us and move to start on Subrata's aunts. We've been given smaller designs, but Subrata's artist insisted that, for the bride, she needs *at least* three hours to do it right. So Subrata is stuck in the same spot with both hands unusable.

I keep trying to feed her cheese, and Elena keeps shaking her head at me. But Subrata seems grateful for the sustenance, even if she is avoiding liquids since she isn't allowed to get up.

And with every question about the wedding, she gushes. She glows. She looks so happy I think stars might shoot out of her and set off fireworks. She's spent many, many months planning this—the perfect combination of Italy and India melded together by someone for whom design is deeply enmeshed in her blood. I've never heard someone talk about flowers for so long and with so much enthusiasm.

But the best part truly is the way she speaks about Luca. For all the pomp and glamour around the wedding, the central thing for her is still this person she is tying her life to. She is so giddy to be his partner. It's hard to imagine trusting someone enough to let your heart open that wide to them, knowing they could crush it. I've spent a decade deliberately avoiding it.

"It's so nice that you'll already be over jet lag and ready to simply enjoy your Italian honeymoon," her cousin Anjana gushes. "We'll all go home to our boring lives, and you will stay in Italian paradise."

"Yeah, I'm really glad we planned it this way," Subrata says with a nod. "I didn't realize how tiring and overwhelming this all would be, and the thought of getting on a long flight after having to be on for all these events seems impossible."

"I don't know what you're talking about," I joke, shoving more cheese in my mouth now that I've gotten both hands back. "I just can't wait to go back home and slave away in a job where no one appreciates anything I do despite being the best at it. Way better than a honeymoon."

I chew on my cheese as everyone stares at me.

"What?"

"If you're so unhappy, then do something about it," Elena says bluntly.

"I'm not unhappy . . ."

I'm realizing maybe I've said too much, and I'm really bringing down the vibe of what is *supposed to be* a light, effervescent day of lounging around before our best friend gets married.

"I think your job sounds so cool," Hadley pipes in.

Have I even told her about my job? Why is she inserting herself?

But I get the feeling that anything I say to Hadley could make it back to Samuel, so snapping at her is probably not what I'm going for right now.

"It *is* cool," I say, tentatively agreeing with her. "Well, the actual things I do are the parts that I love. Tinkering with recipe combinations and nerding out about ingredients with the rest of my test kitchen colleagues never feels like actual work," I finally reply. "It's all the internal politics and personalities and hierarchies and nonsense that gets exhausting. I wish I could just write and edit and test recipes all day without also having to suck up to terrible people and sit in meetings where half the point is just to let some narcissist drone on and hear their own voice."

Cat snickers, "Don't hold back or anything," and we all laugh.

I do feel a bit lighter for getting it off my chest. But Hadley doesn't seem to want to let it go.

"Is there a world where you could do all the parts you like but get out of the parts you don't? Could you ever go freelance and just say yes to the things you want to say yes to?"

I hate that she's had this insight. Elena's words from earlier ring in my head: *You're strong enough to take some leaps, Stel.*

I can't deny that I've played it safe in pretty much every area of my life. Maybe that's made me stagnant. It's not like I *haven't* thought about quitting. I have enough contacts at this point, and it would be a hustle, but I could do recipe work for corporate clients to make the bulk of my paycheck and then get to write the things I want to with the rest of my time. But I've never quite been able to muster up the courage to do it.

I hate the part of myself that likes *saying* where I work—it's so much easier when you say the name of a magazine that everyone knows, and suddenly that makes your creative and sort of abnormal job make sense. The external validation counts for too much when it isn't what actually makes my day-to-day shine. And frankly, I'm scared of putting myself out there in such a defenseless position.

But clearly I can't say *that*.

"Yes, I've definitely thought about it, but I'm still working my way up in my industry." I finally settle on the one area no one can argue with.

"I hear that." Hadley nods. "I like my firm, but I definitely want to start my own whenever I feel established enough. But it's for sure too early. Still a lot to learn!"

I sort of hate that she has an analogous situation to relate to mine. I also hate that my insides are so petty. She is trying to be nice. She *is* nice.

Knowing she isn't dating Samuel somehow has actually almost made it harder with her. She gets to be his best friend *and* be the person he tells everything to. It's hard not to remember that for one small period of time I got to be that person for him. The reality of it smacks me in the face every time she talks.

The conversation glides along as everyone talks about work and what's coming up for them and their busy summers visible in the distance. I'm mostly just trying to see how much I can eat without anyone noticing.

"If someone could run Italy out of cheese, I imagine you'd be the person to take the cake," Subrata says laughing, and I notice we're alone in the sea of people, everyone else flitting in and around while she has no choice but to sit still.

I scoot closer to her and shove another piece of cheese in her mouth for good measure.

"I'll also take some cake, too, if you're offering," I say.

She rolls her eyes.

"You're impossible, Stella," she mutters sloppily through a mouth still full of cheese, and I can't help but grin.

"But you love me anyway."

"I really do," she responds sincerely, and my heart warms. "Are you doing okay?"

I don't know where the gear switch has come from, but I'm determined not to make any of my problems Subrata's problems on today of all days.

"Oh yeah," I say, as breezily as I can muster. "All this work talk isn't really important today. We're just making conversation. I'm fine, really."

Subrata shakes her head, exasperated at my attempt at nonchalance.

"I'm getting married, I'm not having a lobotomy. I can be excited for the wedding and also focus on your life too."

I appreciate her so much in this moment, held down by henna artists and surrounded by a million tiny details but still laser focused on everyone around her.

"I know you can," I say. "I'm not trying to avoid. But my problems at home aren't a huge deal, and they'll still be there when I get back. I just want you to have the perfect day to go with your perfect hubby-to-be and live happily ever after for me, okay?"

She snorts. "No pressure at all then."

I shake my head. Ugh. I guess I'm ruining this too.

"No, there's no pressure," I say, determined to say it better this time. "I just mean, you deserve to have this wonderful weekend. You guys have been so solid for so long and you know what you're doing, and that's a beautiful thing and we should all focus on it."

"No one knows what they're doing, Stella," she says, although the sentiment is a little overshadowed by her attempts to crinkle her nose so she can get rid of an itch she clearly has, but that she can't scratch because of the henna.

I put her out of her misery and scratch it for her.

"Thank you. But seriously. Marriage is only a leap of faith. I'm still scared things could go wrong. I'm still scared we won't always be able to work our way out of every fight—"

"You do not fight!" I exclaim.

"Of course we do!" She rolls her eyes again, and I'm wondering if I'm going to exasperate her so much I'll ruin her eye makeup too. "Nothing is guaranteed. It's all one day at a time. But it's worth it to have some optimism."

I'm starting to suspect this conversation isn't just about her; she's being about as subtle as a rhinoceros.

"Well, I'm glad you have it," I finally say.

"You can have it too," she says with a nudge. "For yourself, and maybe for Sophie too."

I groan. Of course Elena didn't *actually* let it go after hearing my conversation with Sophie in the car. She was just waiting for the right time to pounce on me and make me be a better person, damn it. Smart to go through Subrata, I suppose.

"You and Luca are a *world* different from Sophie having a fling."

"It's been a long time, Stel. Wounds can heal. It's okay to let people in."

"Sophie hasn't let someone in in a long time. So it's natural I'd be a bit protective of her."

"I meant you."

I breathe in deep, not sure how to respond. I gently put a wayward strand of hair back behind her ear, ignoring the earnest stare she's hitting me with.

"I'm fine, Subrata."

"I know you're fine. You're the strongest woman I know."

That pumps a little warmth back into my cold veins.

"I'm just saying you could also trust the people you love to take care of themselves sometimes. And hell, maybe even let them take care of you occasionally."

"A little rich, coming from someone who needs her friends to feed her while she gets elaborate designs appended to her body."

"See, and I *let you!*" she says smugly.

"And I let you guys in too," I retort.

"I'm simply saying, if you leaned on us a little harder, we wouldn't break, you know?"

I feel a prickle behind my eyes and try to shake it off. Maybe she's right, that my status quo isn't really working for me anymore. I do probably need a change. I just don't know how to get the fog off the glass and make it stay clear. If Sophie really has moved on, then why can't *I* move on?

But before I can go down that exceptionally scary mental road, a small shriek punctures our chatter. We look over toward the aunts getting their henna applied, and see that Subrata's mother is having a bit of a panic. Subrata cranes her head but can't quite see, and the artist working on her arm gives no indication she would allow a break.

"Will you check on my mom and try to resolve whatever is happening? You and your GSD nonsense can handle this," Subrata says to me.

I look over at Elena, who's standing by the window sipping a coffee and also seemingly wondering what's going on. I am not enjoying the "get shit done" motto slander, but she is laughing. I shrug it off and immediately hop up and dart over. Subrata's mother is looking at her hands and sighing.

"What happened?"

I look over to see what is wrong. She turns to me.

"Oh, I don't know why I'm being so dramatic, really. It's my fault. She was doing my mehndi and I heard my phone ring, so I moved my hand without thinking, and she got some henna on my nail polish. I didn't bring the color with me, so now I have one orange finger!"

I nod, trying to think of how to resolve this for Subrata.

"I'll just run out to the store and get more nail polish then—there has to be something that comes close enough that will look better than this?"

Subrata's mom is already nodding her head, but the henna artist turns to look up to me with indignation.

"Absolutely not," she replies. "You shouldn't be folding your hands at all on a steering wheel for at least a few hours—this is not the moment to go dashing off to a car."

"Maybe someone else can drive me," I say, scooting away and trying to get out of her clutches before she stops me.

I don't want Subrata's mom even a little bit upset today, and the sangeet is only a few hours away. If I'm going to solve this, I need to solve it now.

"Okay," I say to Subrata and the rest of our group, now congregated back around her. "So the good news is it's not a huge deal. Your mom accidentally got some henna on her fingernail, and her nail polish was light, so now you can see it. But it can easily be covered up by matching some new nail polish and slapping a few coats on. Bad news is the artist who did my henna does not want me to drive and potentially ruin it, even though I think we can all agree that my henna is like the least important henna that anyone would be looking at."

Subrata's artist has nodded along with everything I said, so I guess she agrees both that I should not drive and that I am inconsequential.

"So you need someone else to drive you," Cat states, logically moving me forward.

"Yes. But we'll need a dude who has not had artistry applied to his hands, seeing as all the women are either done or in the middle of getting theirs done."

"What are all the men doing today?" Elena asks.

"No idea," I say honestly. "But somebody in Luca's family has got to want a high-impact moment to impress Subrata's family."

I don't know why I've phrased it like that. There is only one person I know who uses that phrase.

"Oh my God," Hadley says, laughing, "Samuel is *always* talking about high-impact moments. I didn't know anyone else said that stupid phrase."

I am cringing. I've opened a can of worms. No one else *does* say that. It's a Samuel thing through and through. But Hadley is already dialing on her phone, and before I can figure out what's going on, she has the phone up to her ear.

"Samuel?" she says.

Ugh.

"I have a high-impact moment opportunity for you."

She is already laughing at his reply.

"I know," she continues. "You get to save the mother of the bride, so this is like the thing most in your wheelhouse."

I am slowly filling with dread and anticipation.

"Yeah, Stella needs to get new nail polish for Subrata's mom because she accidentally got henna on one of her nails. But they said Stella can't drive because of her own hands. So we need a getaway car."

She is smiling encouragingly and giving me a thumbs-up as Samuel responds, and I cannot hear what he is saying on the other end of the phone.

"Yeah, exactly. She already knows what the color looks like and so she can point out whatever is needed, and you can use your unadulterated man hands to grab it and pay and drive. Very manly."

Hadley keeps nodding and looks up at me.

"Okay, he says meet him outside—he's just in his room doing work like the boring sod that he is, so he's available for our whims immediately."

She laughs and starts speaking into the phone again. "Yes, I did call you a 'boring sod' because you are. Stella is coming out now. Bye!"

She hangs up her phone and looks pleased with herself for solving the crisis. I stand there for a moment, briefly dumbfounded by somehow getting myself into another situation in the course of two days where I am going to be alone in a car with Samuel.

But I can't stand there for long or I'll look insane. So I take a deep breath, give Subrata a kiss on the head, run over to her mom, and share the plan. She is so delighted and thanks me profusely, and I take a photo of her nails so I can be sure I have the right color.

Then I dash off for my high-impact moment.

Chapter Sixteen
October 2, nine years ago

I woke up groggily (and slightly hungover) next to Callum and immediately turned over to look at my phone, shielding it from him. It wasn't that Callum would care—we'd been sleeping together pretty casually for a few weeks since the school year started back up, and I'd only slept over because it was so late last night. He was clearly not interested in whatever messages I was getting on my phone first thing in the morning.

I was mostly trying to avoid how much *I* wanted to look at my phone.

Since "The Letter That We Did Not Speak Of" (which, true to his word, Samuel Did Not Speak Of), we'd somehow gotten into the habit of evening (him) and morning (me) emails as a result of our time difference. He wrote to me about his day and evening while I was asleep, and I responded in the morning when I got it. We both woke up with some missive from the other. His were always longer and better. He mostly told me stories about his ridiculous roommates and the shenanigans they all got into, along with whatever small complaints he had about the mountains of homework he had on his docket.

The emails had originally begun, as promised, with essay edits—it actually was really nice having someone not in my classes to look over whatever I was working on. And I secretly sort of loved getting to nit-pick at his essays and see how his focus on a topic might be different from the way I'd approach it. He was always so serious and took each essay as an opportunity to argue vehemently for some inconsequential academic topic that no one would really ever care about.

And somehow it had just sort of evolved. I'd let it evolve. I kept wondering how I'd allowed myself to get into a weird daily secret routine with this guy I knew was not in this as a friendly pen pal, but . . . I didn't want to stop. So I didn't.

It didn't mean anything, though. It was just some essay edits and bits of friendly banter. Nothing more. We lived too far away from each other for it to mean anything more.

Callum was snoring, so there was no chance my movements had woken him up. I opened my phone and turned the brightness down on the screen.

From Samuel
To Stella

I'm currently in the library. I went up and got Matias a Fresca just now and decided to write you an email, so those are my big exciting breaks for the evening (ha). I hope your talk with your mom went well. Today was very productive for me otherwise, I finished that first response paper. Maybe if I'm done tomorrow, will you look it over for me?

In any case, I'm so happy I've gotten into a good working groove. Even though I've done a lot of work, none of this has seemed hard to me. Please remember me saying that when I'm on page 3 of

a 30 page paper next week, and you can laugh at
me then.
Hope you slept well,

Samuel

I read it three or four times before getting up. I quietly slipped my
clothes back on and tiptoed out the door. I really didn't need to have
any morning conversations with Callum—he wasn't particularly good
at conversations at any time of day. Especially when I was in such a
buoyant mood and it had nothing to do with him.

The mornings were so peaceful in our quiet university town. All
the pubs and bars and restaurants that were alive with music and
voices last night were now dark and sleeping. The stone buildings
looked the same as they clearly had for hundreds of years but just
shifting ever so barely with the passage of time. Open and shut, morning and night, over and over again. The history of the place made
everyday drama seem so small.

I arrived at my little red-doored house and jammed the key in
the lock to open it up. My roommates were also still asleep, so I
slipped into my room quietly. I closed the door and lay back down
in my bed, pulling the covers up over me and breathing in my own
space. The walls could not be more of a college room cliché—a red
sarong hung across the wall like a tapestry; a poster of Barcelona's
Parc Güell was tacked up from a visit last year. A corkboard with
photos of nights out with friends, intermingled with family photos,
concert tickets, and sticky notes giving off reminders that were probably overdue.

I stared up at the ceiling for a few minutes until finally I pulled
my phone back out and reread the email. It would be rude not to
respond.

From Stella
To Samuel

Call with my mom was good—thanks for asking. I avoided writing that paper for Anthropology because I needed instead to test a theory about tahini in my chocolate chip cookies and the good news is that THE COOKIES ARE AMAZING, but the bad news is that my paper is still looming. So I'm off to write it now. Wish me luck! (But yes, obviously I'd love an excuse to procrastinate so please send me yours whenever you have a draft).

—Stella

Short, sweet, and to the point. He had said to keep in touch, so that was all we were doing. What was the harm of having a little conversation to look forward to each morning?

No harm that I could see.

CHAPTER SEVENTEEN

FRIDAY, PRESENT DAY

I get outside and Samuel is already there, car keys in hand, looking at me with anticipation. His eyes light up when he sees me, and the corners of his mouth turn up into a grin. I can't help but return the sentiment.

"Thanks for being my getaway car," I say. "Again."

"You know I can't resist a high-impact moment," he says knowingly.

He is wearing some kind of Italian-looking beige linen shirt, and he has a bit of stubble on his face—like he's allowing his face to go on vacation along with him and relax into itself. It is frustratingly hot.

We get into the car, and I'm careful not to move my hands too much, imagining the ire I will attract if I return with any henna even slightly altered. He turns on the radio and we are off.

"I love that you remembered that," he says, chuckling.

"Remember what?"

I'm not avoiding looking at his face this time. The view is too good.

"Oh." He turns to look at me as much as he can without taking his eyes off the road. "I just meant the high-impact moment thing."

"Oh, well, it was Hadley's idea really. To call you."

"Ah," he says.

Something has deflated in him, and it is my fault. *Shit.* I want the grin back. I want the grin directed at me again.

"No, I mean, it was a great idea. As soon as I said that, we all knew you were the man for the job."

Everything I'm saying sounds so hollow. I'm a moron.

"Here I was thinking you remembered my penchant for those kinds of things."

His voice is quieter. Not accusing, simply the way he always was able to say exactly what he was thinking without bias or judgment. But the tone is softer, and it makes my stomach tighten into a knot.

"I *do* remember that," I say slowly, as though I am delicately holding a ticking bomb. "Of course I remember that."

I am not sure why I've admitted this, but I couldn't stop myself. I couldn't stand the idea of disappointing him by lying about remembering something about him. If he only knew—it was absurd to think I could have forgotten that.

His eyes are on me again, and I'm wondering how much he can look at me and the road at the same time, but I don't say anything. I feel already like maybe I've said too much and crossed over some invisible line we've both been avoiding.

He finally murmurs, "I'm glad," and we pull into the parking lot of a drugstore.

Damn tiny Italian towns with their close proximity to things.

I look into his eyes, not quite ready to get out of the car, not quite ready to let the moment pass. That heaviness is in the air again, with all the unsaid things lingering and hovering between us. Somehow now I feel an intense urge to say something else, to give him something else, so that he'll know I haven't forgotten him. That I could never forget him.

"Why don't you have social media?" I finally blurt out, and I'm so embarrassed I almost clamp my hand over my mouth.

He sees the shock on my face over the admission that I must have *looked* for him on social media to know he doesn't have social media. But his face just reads as almost relieved.

"I don't really understand the point of it," he finally answers.

"To share your life?"

"I do share my life, just not with strangers."

It feels like a jab, even though I know it wasn't intended that way.

"I just mean . . . ," I say to fill the silence, not really knowing exactly *what* I mean. "It's not for strangers. Acquaintances. Or like aunts and uncles or people you went to high school with."

I deliberately do not say *and women whom you used to know who have never been able to stop dreaming about where you are and if you are happy.*

"It's nice for people to see what you're up to," I finish blandly.

"You don't share anything personal on social media, only recipes," he counters tauntingly.

Damn him, seriously. Here I am swallowing myself whole and wanting to curl up and die because I've openly admitted to him that I've stalked him casually for *years*, wondering when he would just open a goddamn Instagram account already, and here he is easily and freely admitting that he has kept tabs on me without a care in the world. Nothing fazes him. Nothing.

And he isn't going to let me out of responding. He knows how much I hate awkward silences, and he knows I'm trapped because I showed my hand nervously and he brazenly showed his, and now it's my move.

I have to admit, though, that it feels like a breath of fresh air to not be playing it safe, the way I do every day back in New York. Maybe I *should* directly say what I'm thinking more, the way Samuel always has.

I finally retort, "No, well, social media is sort of required now if you write anything. I have to post about work."

"Right, well, I don't. So I don't."

He is smug. He is going to wait for me to say something else and not let me wriggle out of this torture.

I grumble, "How nice for you," and he laughs.

I love his laugh. I love that right now we are like a living approximation of the walls all around Norcia—still there but crumbling a bit and with vines and sunlight peeking through. I want to bask in it and hold on to it and forget about the fact that an anxious mother is waiting for us to bring her some nail polish in a heavily decorated room before a wedding.

I want to tell him he's an idiot but that maybe in this moment I could forgive him for being such an idiot. Maybe I could even find a way to forgive myself too. But instead I open the car door because Subrata's mother is waiting for me, and I am nothing if not a dependable person who can ignore her own anxiety to get shit done. For other people.

It's incredible how many colors of nail polish there are, even in a random drugstore. It is also impossible to match them to a photo taken in different lighting.

"I feel like maybe this one is the best?" I venture, pointing toward one of about fifteen various pale pinks that could all potentially be options.

But Samuel is shaking his head.

"Screw it, let's just buy them all, and I can bring back whichever ones we don't use. This place is only like five minutes from the hotel, and I'm not doing anything before the sangeet anyway."

He bundles them all up in his hands and walks them over to the counter. He starts chatting to the sales clerk, but it is clear he doesn't speak English. Samuel turns to another woman browsing and asks her if she speaks English.

Within moments she is translating the situation to the clerk, and they are all laughing and nodding and clearly everyone is on his side. A high-impact moment indeed. And I'm merely standing here like a statue without any ideas whatsoever.

The clerk rings up the nail polish, and Samuel throws everything into a bag as he hands over cash, looking very pleased with himself. He beckons me to leave with him and I comply, jumping out of my trance to follow him out the door and back into the car.

"So we'll go and see which one works the best, and then I'll bring the rest back. The guy is totally on board."

I'm irrationally irritated by how much satisfaction I'm feeling from knowing I'm helping someone I love in a meaningful moment— acquiescing to the joy of high-impact moments is *not* the ego boost I need to give to Samuel right now.

So instead I nod and say nothing, and we both get back into the car.

We ride in silence for a minute, and I don't know how to get back to the honesty of a few moments earlier. It's gnawing at me, like I need it back to fill a gaping hole that has now opened up inside me, but I'm paralyzed by the fear of saying the wrong thing.

I shouldn't have worried, though—Samuel is never content to simply sit with something lingering.

"I do like your recipes and articles, though. I obviously don't make anything, since I'm an abysmal cook, but I like seeing what you come up with."

It's an opening and he knows it.

"Oh, so you *do* have social media," I tease back.

"Definitely not. But I subscribe to your magazine, so I always see whenever it's your byline."

Casual, so casual. My heart is stopping and I'm practically fainting from truth bombs, and he is just casually sharing whatever damn thing comes to his mind.

"You subscribe to a food magazine?" I say incredulously.

"I subscribe to *your* food magazine."

"It's hardly *my* magazine."

"You know what I mean."

Do I? What exactly is he saying?

It doesn't matter, because he shifts the subject in his own special, completely unsubtle, unfazed, and unselfconscious way. "You should have a portfolio website with all your work. It would help you if you wanted to do freelance work."

"How do you know I don't?" I ask, teetering on the edge of what I really mean.

How much do you know Samuel? How much are we admitting to here?

"Ah, so you have a secret portfolio page that no one can find? That must be extremely effective at garnering new work and potential clients." He is enjoying teasing me now, and I can't help but enjoy it too. "Maybe that's where you've been hiding that tahini chocolate chip cookie recipe of yours I've always wanted to try."

My eyes widen.

"You remember that?"

We pull into the driveway of the hotel, and he gets out of the car and hands the valet the key, never really taking his eyes off me. He comes so close to me that I can feel the heat coming off him, and it makes my insides swirl.

"Stella, I remember everything about you."

Chapter Eighteen

Nine years ago

October 22
From Samuel
To Stella

Attached see my edits on your paper—this was a really good one!

So what an evening this was—first I had the most pointless newspaper meeting of all time. One would think that a pointless meeting would only last 15-20 minutes or so (you know, just enough time for the kids who like to hear themselves speak get their fill). But no, this one was a whole hour. Then I went to the library to say Hi to all my studious friends. But they were all working and no one wanted to make conversation. Losers. (Please note here that, yes, I went to the library with no studying to do and I am calling other people losers).

Matias is now consuming an entire box of fruit roll ups and I have to get away from the sugar high. Those salmon burgers you mentioned sound 8,000 times better than anything in my current diet. Which, speaking of, I'm actually going to visit my brother over Thanksgiving because he is at LSE in London (did I mention?) and they don't get the holiday off (because obviously the Brits could care less about a holiday of a former colony). If I'm going to be in the UK, maybe I could pop up and say hello.

Hope you had a wonderful night's sleep that did not include a sugar high from excessive unhealthy pretend-fruit snacks.

Samuel

October 23
From Stella
To Samuel

I feel like your newspaper meetings all seem useless. Why do you do editing again? Aren't newspapers dying and you also have no desire to be a journalist? Write, like me—then you can just submit recipes and notes to the paper without having to actually do the rest of the work. That's a pro tip right there, for free, from me to you. You're welcome. Although maybe I shouldn't knock your editing right before I say . . . thanks so much for the edits to my papers! Let me know when you have another paper and I'll gladly read it over.

I have attached the salmon burger recipe so you don't combust on fruit roll ups as your only option. I promise even a cooking luddite like you can make them.

And sure, let me know the days you'll be here, that could be fun (you do know that London to Scotland is not really so much a "pop up" though? Wouldn't want to waste your time with a lot of travel).

—Stella

Chapter Nineteen
Friday, present day

I know I'm supposed to be listening to happy speeches about the happy couple and watching dances that cousins and relatives have spent a lot of time working on, but I can't stop my mind from racing.

I remember everything about you.

I'd cajoled him into telling me something, hinted at similar things myself, but I was stunned by his ability to easily cross over every line of normal conversation. I didn't know how to respond. I just sort of gurgled something incomprehensible, thanked him for the ride and the nail polishes, and dashed off back toward the room.

He followed me with the ever-important nail polishes, since I was an imbecile, and he handed them over proudly to Subrata's mother while all the aunts and older ladies oohed and aahed at him and pinched his cheeks and told him how incredible he was. He winked at me, and I thought I might keel over from how much it flustered me.

But as soon as Subrata's mother chose her color, he bowed dramatically to cheers from the appreciative crowd and took the rest of the nail polishes back, on his way to dutifully returning them to the store.

I didn't really pay attention to much for the rest of the afternoon. Thankfully my outfit was preplanned—Subrata took us shopping in

New York to her favorite store, where we all picked out Indian outfits to wear to the sangeet tonight. Mine is a dark mint-green lehengha—a long skirt embellished with golden beads and designs—along with a short blouse in the same color and beading, leaving my midriff bare. I love the way lehenghas move much easier than saris, and Subrata smiled quietly with clear delight when I picked it out.

Putting it back on, I was relieved to at least feel like I had the appropriate thing to wear, the memory of my lost suitcase not yet faded. I got ready quietly and quickly and was sitting in the room working on an article on my laptop—gingerly making sure not to mess up my mehndi (a success) and trying to not let the fireworks going off in my stomach distract me (a total failure).

I was relieved when Elena finally declared it was time to go.

Luckily the sangeet is at our hotel, so it's easy to mosey over. The ballroom of the hotel has been transformed. Lights are strung up across the ceiling from every angle. If I thought the flowers at the mehndi were extravagant, I clearly could not have imagined this evening's floral arrangements—lush bouquets in vibrant colors shooting up from every table, with equally bright tablecloths beneath them.

A buffet with a mix of Indian and Italian food beckons. It's like a fever dream from the bonkers corners of my recipe-obsessed mind—samosas stuffed with zucchini blossoms and creamy ricotta; chapatis with tomato and mint chutneys made with local produce; artichoke pakoras topped with cilantro and ginger; local truffle panipuris, and even more truffles on the creamy turmeric lentils. There's a chef slicing a porchetta that's been rolled up with cardamom, cumin, black pepper, amchur, and coriander. The air is spiced and herbaceous, and I dive in the moment I see others partaking.

But what gives the evening its true color is the involvement of every guest who has arrived. The evening is full of dances and toasts and entertainment, because that is the essence of a sangeet. It's the party before the serious event. It is the warm-up act that tries its damnedest to do better than the main act, even if we could never *really* be distracted from the main event. It's the revelry and music and party before we get down to business.

Some of Subrata's relatives are doing gorgeous traditional dances, and some of Luca's relatives are truly embarrassing themselves while having the best-possible time.

I should be getting nervous about the dance that Anjana has *insisted* that Elena and Cat and I have to participate in, one that I have most definitely not practiced enough of. She obviously had no faith in our abilities to learn Indian dance moves because the video she sent us to learn from is painfully elaborate, detailing each step as though we are toddlers in need of assistance (which . . . is fair).

Elena has pulled the video up on her phone and is trying to watch it surreptitiously without being noticed. I'm planning to stand in the back and hope the muscle memory kicks in. I have bigger things on my mind.

I remember everything about you.

Everything he said prior to that was light and jokey, but that last sentiment was almost a challenge. It isn't in Samuel's nature to dance around anything. To his own detriment, and those around him, he just barrels his way through to getting or saying what he wants. He's never cared what other people think or how his words might affect them.

I always found it charming and disarming when we were younger, but now it terrifies me. Maybe that's what makes him such a successful lawyer—who wouldn't want a brash, unafraid champion in their corner?

The chasm of time that sits like a giant question mark between us seems only like a knowable series of events that we haven't covered; even from our brief interactions over the last few days, I know there has not been a significant shift in who we fundamentally are as people. He has checked boxes—graduate from college, go to law school, get a job—but his inherent Samuelness hasn't changed. We are the same people, older for sure, *maybe* wiser, but still able to burrow deep into each other's roots and find the kernels of what makes the other tick. It doesn't feel like time has inhibited that between us.

Once we both realized it, it was probably inevitable that we would poke and prod until we'd each asked all the questions we wanted answers to. Samuel has not grown out of that quality, clearly.

I am on edge, eyes darting, feelings jumbled and instincts fractured. *Everything?*

I have spent so many years forcibly pushing down so many memories and not unboxing them, but that doesn't mean they haven't been there all along, preserved for the moment when I finally allow them to come rapidly tumbling out. And they are currently, fully, entirely, tumbling out.

I play conversations from nine years ago over and over in my head, holding them up to the moonlight and examining them from every angle. What went wrong? Did I make the best choices for myself at the time? What on earth am I doing right now?

His words are, once again, years later, stunning me from their directness and simplicity. He didn't remember me only once he saw me—he's always remembered me. All the nights I lay awake over the years wondering; every time I went on a date and just knew I'd had more with someone else; every time I found myself searching his name on social media, just in case he'd finally popped up somewhere. I always assumed he wasn't mirroring my behaviors.

But there's an unease swimming alongside the electricity roiling inside me. I was never casual for Samuel, and the thought is driving me in circles. I can't make assumptions based on so many years ago—he might have felt one way at that time, but today is not then. The strength of those feelings was youthful lust, a first crush. Maybe even a first love. *Maybe.*

But no one holds on to those feelings for that long. He has had an entire adulthood. He has dated and whispered into other women's ears. He has fallen into bed with women he cared about and maybe some he didn't. He has celebrated losses and triumphs. He has grown as a man and with his family and friends.

A declaration of love at twenty is not a serious undertaking.

And staring me in the face is the undeniable fact that *he* was the one who ultimately left. He'd promised patience and understanding, and instead I ended up exactly where I'd always suspected I would with him. I'd based almost a decade of identity on the fact that the first love I truly believed in had shattered right in front of me, and *then* the first man who told me he loved me was able to move on as quickly as if it had never happened. If my heart had been locked by Sophie and Charlie's demise, then Samuel threw away the key. I know Samuel *thought* he loved me. But he gave up anyway. And because of that, he was the one I have never truly been able to forgive. He broke me—and us—in a single gesture, and it altered me. He might remember everything about me, but I remember everything he said the last time I saw him.

That one memory has been a perverse safety net—proof that I wasn't wrong to be so cynical. Proof that protecting my heart wasn't some misguided choice based on only my sister's life. I was skeptical of being loved, and in the end I wasn't enough. I never could have been enough—he truly didn't understand what he was promising. No one does at that age.

And ever since then, I've taken solace in staying in control. I've reveled in my ability to stay away from getting emotional because my entire well-being has centered on my ability to get shit done and be there for everyone who needs me.

My feelings for Samuel were a mistake in another lifetime, because romantic relationships aren't worth it anyway. He is my own cautionary tale that's waved its red flag every time I've gotten close to starting down a road with some other man. That's kept me sane and focused on what really matters—like work, and my friendships—for all the years since. And it's allowed me to keep work and friendships in their own safe box. I was safe from experiencing that kind of pain again. He was the past.

Until he wasn't.

What does Samuel want from me now? A trip down memory lane for a weekend? Maybe. I don't truly know him anymore. He might have memories and a lingering attraction, but the way things ended has to hang over him the same way it's hanging over me. Instead of listening to speeches, I am currently playing his words over and over in my head, like a skipping stone that continually resurfaces but feels farther and farther away.

And for all this mental ping-pong I'm doing instead of paying attention to the events happening in front of me, the most nerve-racking thing is that I haven't actually *seen* Samuel yet tonight. It's not unusual—the venue is dark, with spotlights on whomever is dancing or telling stories or giving speeches or fire breathing (this was a hired act and thankfully not a family member). I'm seated with Subrata's side, so we're far from any of the Luca crowd. But there is something extremely unsettling about knowing Samuel is in the room and that I can't quite wrap my mind around where he's standing.

The MC (Subrata's twelve-year-old cousin, who is actually doing kind of an amazing job, and whom I might want to hire as my personal hype man to just live in my apartment and make me function more like a confident adult) calls our group, and I walk up like someone on her way to the guillotine. A dance about a love story set to a particular high-octane bhangra pop song is really not what I need right now. But Subrata is grinning in a seat next to Luca, casually clutching his hand, and I know this is not the time to make anything about me.

I stand as far in the back as I can in a group of eleven people. Anjana is front and center in a perfect pleated bright-pink sari, so really, all eyes will be on her. The music starts and I'm moving, the moves coming more easily than I would have expected. My eyes start to adjust to the lights, and I can see more of the crowd. I don't have much to be nervous about, considering now I can *see* that every single person is looking at Anjana. She is like a beacon of grace, a focal point in the heart of an indiscriminate group of fairly clumsy women who fade into the background as their leader sets the pace and the tone and keeps all eyes locked.

All eyes except one pair.

I see Samuel watching me from the back corner near the door, and I immediately feel myself faltering. I can't pull my eyes away from his, which naturally makes me unable to watch and copy Anjana, which makes me probably look like a wounded giraffe, legs going in the opposite direction from wherever they should be. I know I need to look back and focus on what I'm supposed to be doing, but I just can't. He is looking at me the way he used to; he is staring at me with the abandon he always did, without a care in the world other than soaking me in.

All the intrusive thoughts that were barging their way in and pushing memories back to the forefront of my mind aren't any match for how Samuel's gaze makes me feel, like a warm knife dipping into butter. I want to ignore the warning bells and just give in to the magic of this place and this moment in a world so far from our normal, everyday lives. I want to know if that explosive chemistry I'm remembering is a figment of my imagination or if my body is reacting so excessively to his presence because everything I've tried to forget is real. And with his eyes on me, today it's tangible.

He remembers everything about me.

The dance mercifully ends, and even if I hadn't just made up my mind to walk straight to the back corner of the room, it probably would be wise to do so anyway. No one is going to feel anything but uncomfortable having to attempt to congratulate me on my brilliant and completely believable performance.

Samuel is watching me as I silently glide my way through the crowd, smiling at various friends and family but not stopping, and not losing his eyes along the way.

I finally reach him, and he grabs one of my hands. My hand feels his like a memory, as though all of a sudden I can hear the bustle of Times Square and I can smell a hot dog and we are about to climb a set of red stairs in the midst of a sticky summertime evening.

But instead he wordlessly pulls me out the door and into an alcove behind an archway of wisteria, and the memory morphs into the here and now.

Chapter Twenty

Nine years ago

November 9
From Samuel
To Stella

So you know how I'm supposed to have Fridays off normally (kind of like your Wednesdays)? Well apparently somebody didn't get the memo on that one, because, inexplicably, tomorrow is busier than any other day of this week. My calendar is like a ticking time bomb from 8am until 2am (newspaper editing never sleeps). But I love being busy, so I'll stop pretending to complain.

Also tomorrow I have to decide who gets to introduce the Senator at our newspaper fundraiser. I bet this won't get political (yeah right. Also, ha, political). I've already had three kids tell me they are "owed" this introduction—great! I'm also going to have 18 student groups jumping down my throat for "special access" to the event and that will be a shitshow in and of itself. The good news is the day after I am on my plane to the UK and not looking back. They can all maul each other for the chance for a selfie. I'll be outta there.

Okay . . . I'm gonna stop procrastinating so I can get a few hours of sleep if I'm lucky.

See you soon,

Samuel

He was coming in eleven days. Just like that, he was going to be at my door in less than two weeks. My not-so-subtle attempts to let him off the hook were not taken up. The distance from London to me wasn't a problem. The time away from his brother wasn't a problem. He'd been fishing, and unless I'd outright said no, I got the sense there was no way I was going to stop him from coming here. And despite having drafted several emails to that effect, I could never find myself actually able to send an email with a logical excuse to tell him no.

I had stopped responding to Callum a few weeks ago, and he had taken the hint. There was no other man to distract me from my digital emotional dependency.

I was living in this state of limbo where I woke up smiling from the promise of an email and then went about my day like nothing was abnormal in my life. It had been easy to write it off as just a nice way to start my morning that didn't really mean anything. I was *determined* to keep interpreting it that way.

But the visit popped that bubble. I didn't say no. I didn't dissuade. I found myself daydreaming about what I would say when I opened the door to see him standing in this other version of my reality—so far from

New York and the heat of the summer and everything we had said and not said all those months ago. I was restless with both fear and anticipation.

We were both living on some sort of high-wire act—afraid if we discussed the trip more than in passing that we would have to *actually discuss what was happening*. We hadn't discussed anything. I had no idea where he was planning to sleep. I hadn't even really asked if he was planning to stay at my place. I had no idea what he was intending to happen.

It almost seemed ludicrous—a game of chicken that was going to end with him ringing a doorbell and both people hoping we'd gotten the other person's impressions of a situation correct.

There was nothing to do now but wait. And respond to his email like everything was normal.

> November 10
> From Stella
> To Samuel
>
> I hope when you are reading this as you mentally prepare yourself for your crazy day that you remember that college students are completely rational beings who always take things gracefully. The event will be a cinch. No one is ever going to hold anything against you when you are just doing your job.
>
> HA. Just kidding. What a fucking nightmare. I'm cheering you on from this side of the pond, even if everyone is about to hate your guts.
>
> See you on this side soon.
>
> Stella.

Chapter Twenty-One

Friday, present day

There is no more staring or innuendos or pointed queries. Everything we both admitted in the car has put a stop to that, and we've both made up our minds. He pulls me outside, and our mouths immediately lock on each other, and we are kissing like everything that's been pent up this whole week (or maybe these whole years) is bursting through every crevice and we're unable to have any more space between us.

His hands are in my hair and mine are around his neck and we are trying to walk backward away from the party without tripping over ourselves. We are pawing at each other with an urgency that can't possibly be sustained. His hands are on the bare part of my stomach, and I am wrenching at his bow tie to undo it and unbutton the top of his shirt and kiss his neck. He tastes like sweat and the same cologne I remember from so long ago.

We back up into a wall of wisteria vines, and I feel petals falling into my hair from the force of knocking against them.

I laugh and start trying to pick the flowers out of my hair, their scent now exploding around us like a flirtatious fragrant reminder to keep pushing forward.

His whole face is flushed.

"I'm sorry."

I can't help but chuckle softly as I try to catch my breath.

"No, you're not."

"No. I'm not," he whispers back, more to himself than to me.

We stand and let our eyes adjust to the moonlight, seeing each other's faces more clearly as the seconds pass.

"I just meant more for mauling you and getting flowers all over your hair," he says with a small grin. "Not sorry for pulling you out of the room, because I don't think I really had control over that."

I nod my agreement, still not entirely in control of my own actions anymore or, for that matter, breathing.

The grin widens to a smile like a kid with a confession, but slightly more wicked.

"I saw you in your bathrobe, you know."

"What?" I can barely get out a sentence, let alone try to figure out what he is saying.

"Hiding from me."

It clicks. Oh God, that first day when I didn't have my suitcase. I can feel the blood draining from my face. Well, that is mortifying.

"I wasn't *hiding* from you." I am trying desperately to save some dignity. "I was just surprised to see you when I was *wearing a bathrobe* and didn't really know how to react."

"I kind of loved it."

"The bathrobe?"

"No, the hiding."

I wait for him to say something else, but he doesn't. I am, per usual, unable to think of what I could possibly say and just stay mute. But he doesn't let the moment linger. "I was nervous to see you after so long, and I wasn't sure if I could handle it if you were all nonchalant."

His smile fades a bit at the thought, and it stings right in my center. I know exactly what he means. I know it because it was how I saw him that day—standing so easily with someone whom I had assumed was his girlfriend. The panic of his apparition stabbed me, and I was glad he felt that way, too, somewhat, but I wasn't sure I could be brave enough to verbalize it right now.

I go for airy instead. "Well, obviously I am nothing if not nonchalant when running away in a bathrobe," I say with a flick of my wrist, and I get the laugh out of him I was hoping for.

"At least you didn't have to bring a security blanket with you."

My quizzical look apparently speaks volumes.

"Hadley," he responds. "I figured that was obvious. Well, obvious once you stopped thinking she was my girlfriend, which is mildly hilarious for anyone who knows Hadley."

"What was obvious?" I ask.

He kisses my cheek and softly pushes a bit of my hair behind my ears. He is soaking me in, enjoying the moment.

"I needed a buffer. In case you brought someone," he finally says. "Hadley sort of wrenched the whole story out of me after I invited her, and then she agreed to come because she didn't think I'd be able to hack it alone, which is most definitely true."

I suddenly realize that he'd come here as nervous as I was to be face to face with each other again. It melts me. I want all my affection for him to envelop him and express what I cannot possibly bring myself to say.

I feel a pang of jealousy for their friendship—not because of her, but because it is clearly so easy for him to share all this with his best friend. I am surrounded by my best friends, and yet I am weathering my own internal storm inside my mind on a boat with no other passengers. I am a lonely ship's captain battling wave after wave of anxiety and regret and longing, and my crew is standing at the shore without even knowing I've taken off.

I could have told them more. I *should* have told them. Years ago. Or at the very least last year, when it was clear I was going to have to see him again here. Cat and I sat at that bar, unloading her fears about her mom and my distaste for my run-in with Charlie, and I couldn't bring myself to open up just a little bit more. Subrata nudged at me this morning to let her in, and I didn't really tell her I was feeling confused. I avoided it.

My complicated feelings for Samuel were always the hardest thing to share, because admitting to *any* feelings opens up a possibility of caring that I haven't been able to address. The only way I can fend off anxiety and panic attacks is to push the things I can't control down as far as they can go.

But I have never understood until this moment that leaving things unsaid doesn't make them go away.

I kiss him to keep myself from dwelling too much on all of it and to make my mind stop. It's slower this time, and I'm addicted all over again, all thoughts and doubts once more disappearing. My tongue slowly searches in his mouth, and his responds to mine as though we have all the time in the world. He wraps his arms around me, and we kiss for so long I can feel my lips tingling, bruised from pressure and pleasure.

He moves his lips to my neck, and I lean my head back, more petals falling on my hair, but I couldn't possibly care less if I tried. I'm in an Italian dream with a hazy glow of moonlight and the heady wallop of the smell of wisteria. He is caressing my arm and kissing my neck, and I loop my fingers into his waistband. I am tranquilized in feeling him all over me again after so long.

His kisses are the same. That's the part I can't quite wrap my head around. He tastes the same and moves the same, and while his frame is broader and he's gotten stronger, I could close my eyes and know those were his hands from a mile away.

A thought crosses my mind, and I can't help but smile. And because I am me, I can't stop myself from asking the question, even if losing his lips on me makes me suddenly feel like I'm missing an essential part of my basic framework.

"Wait, so does that mean that Hadley has been actively trying to find excuses to get you alone with me?"

He grins, and I can see all his love for Hadley contained in that one beaming smile.

"Yeah, clearly I'm a stubborn idiot, and I was determined to be very cool and aloof—"

"As you are known to be, always—" He laughs and shakes his head.

"Yes, that was obviously a plan with failure written all over it. I think I managed it for maybe the length of one lunch."

I think about him in Spoleto, quietly avoiding me, and it squeezes at my heart to think of him noticing my every move the way I was tracking his.

"I think," he says, considering, "Hadley was relishing the opportunity to finally get to be my wing-woman and somehow took it to extremes by offering me as a chauffeur on a consistent basis."

"You do make an excellent chauffeur."

"I don't think a chauffeur is supposed to be ogling his passenger."

His eyes are fixed on mine so intently that I wonder if he's going to burn a hole into me. I put my hands into his hair and push the pieces back away from his eyes. He is soft and flushed, and his stubble prickles against my wrist.

I nuzzle into his neck, and he curses under his breath from the sudden shock of pleasure.

He pulls me in closer and holds me as I wrap my arms around him. My body is in a suspended animation—desirous but unsure of what to do next and whether I even dare to do whatever comes next.

Logic has let cravings push it aside, and instead of the typical anxious buzzing, my insides are as serene as a glassy lake. We stand there holding each other as the sounds of the party waft toward us from inside.

"I'm supposed to go back to Subrata's room when the sangeet is over and stay there tonight," I finally mumble, unsure of what I'm trying to imply.

I can feel him nodding against me, and he kisses the side of my neck again, tenderly, as though I am suddenly so much more fragile than the woman he was previously holding on to tightly like a life raft. I wonder if he'll be a good guy to the end, like always.

I can sense a tension rising in him, and I'm curious if this need to modulate himself is unnatural, like life's experience has taken away his brash ability to just plow forward and say whatever he believes is the right answer. Maybe to him I'm like a wild animal that, if he moves too fast, will jump and run away. I don't like that time has taken away some little piece of his tenacity. Or maybe I took it away.

But he brushes away any tension in his body as quickly as it arose.

"Is that what you want to do?"

He takes my chin in his hands and looks into my eyes. His voice is laden with innuendo, and he isn't hiding it, but I can tell he doesn't want to pressure me.

"No," I admit softly, unable to say anything other than the truth. I feel a twinge of guilt that I have already been so distracted and, now, absent. But Subrata is busy, and this nostalgic magnet drawing me toward Samuel is scrambling my brain.

The anticipation reverberates across my body, and I can tell his mind is going a mile a minute, back and forth between decisions, as though they are ping-ponging across his brain and making it impossible to decide.

I chew on my lip for a moment, wishing his mouth were back on mine so I wouldn't have to think so much. Or maybe so I could let the lust I'm feeling make my answer for me and push out any of my remaining thoughts.

"Can we . . . go to your room?" I finally say, shocking myself a little with my brazenness.

He looks at me so intently I can barely breathe. His eyes are smoldering, desirous and filled with questions. I should win an award for stopping myself from dragging him away right here; I'm vibrating with so much energy that I don't know how he is still standing still in front of me. I'm surprised I'm not in my own head, already anxious about the consequences of my question, but I guess horniness is winning against rationality.

I can see those wheels turning again in his head, and I am desperate to crack him open and get a clearer glimpse of what's going on inside. Is he wondering whether he wants to go with me? Does everything from the past bubble its way up for him too—making it so difficult to not blurt out every secret and thought that he has to breathe from the pit of his stomach just to stop?

But no, that's just me. He is being typical Samuel and thinking ahead.

"Yes, but maybe you should tell Elena you're going to bed early so she doesn't waste her night trying to find you, when you're *supposed* to be heading back with Subrata."

"That's a very thoughtful and, frankly, also diabolical point," I laugh, kissing him again because I'm so damn relieved his mind is exactly in the gutter where mine is.

"Should we . . . reconvene after?" I wave my hands between us, probably a little too close to his pants, and he snickers.

"'Reconvene'?"

"I'm not sure which dirty thought wouldn't offend your delicate ears, so I felt 'reconvene' was the most genteel word I could come up with."

He wryly shakes his head as his hand strokes the side of my face, and I want to melt right into him. His delight at my complete idiocy has always made me radiate.

"Sure, we can reconvene." He looks as giddy as I feel. "Why don't you go back in first so it's not completely obvious we were outside together. Although . . ."

He grins as he picks out the rest of the flowers from my hair. I look at his bow tie and give him an apologetic look—he certainly looks disheveled. It's hot, but probably more obvious than either of us would like. I smooth his hair back into place and then cup his face in my hands.

"I'm in room seventeen," he finally says.

I kiss him again, pressing my body against his, and a few minutes later, when I'm back inside the party to say good night to Elena, I am still finding little flower petals every time I look.

Chapter Twenty-Two
November 20, nine years ago

I was nervous. My foot was tapping against the couch as I sat there waiting, *willing* the doorbell to ring.

Our game of chicken was finally about to collide head on. He was taking a train up from London and then somehow finding his way from the train station to my door.

We had emailed about the plan, and it made sense at the time, but now it seemed woefully casual. *I'll just hop in a cab when the train arrives and come to your place—I'm easy, don't plan anything around me.* Oh sure. Just a casual visit across an ocean, then up north, to visit a woman whom you declared your undying love to and then hadn't discussed it with since, but instead we regale each other with minute details of our day every single day for months.

Very, very casual.

I had pretended for so long that if I didn't stare directly into the sun, it wouldn't burn me, but maybe I should have applied sunscreen or put on a better top or used some other metaphor that would explain why my insides were doing somersaults and I was freaking out for having left so many conversations for this exact moment.

But the doorbell rang and I jumped up and there was no turning back now. I skipped down the stairs and opened the giant red door at the landing.

Samuel stood there clean shaven but with his cheeks red from the excessive wind that always came in fast off the sea in the mornings. His hair was tousled, and he had a duffel bag in one hand and . . . pancake mix in the other?

"I figured I couldn't bring you bagels or pierogi if I was stopping in London for a few days, but American-style pancake mix would last the journey and give you your home fix."

His grin was so sincere. His joy at standing on my doorstep after crossing an ocean and sitting for hours on a train and dragging along pancake mix and seeing my face was palpable. It was all I could do not to kiss him.

But why not kiss him?

I pulled him inside the door and pressed my lips to his. He tasted like a mint, clearly recently consumed in the hopes of this exact kind of greeting. He dropped his bag and the pancake mix on the floor of my entryway with a clang, but I didn't care because he felt so good and I couldn't pretend like I was anything other than goddamn happy to see him.

He wrapped his arms around me and held me tightly while he kissed me, like I was a mirage he had been dreaming of but didn't yet believe was real.

After so many months of speaking every day without speaking, it was a sensory overload to have him here. He knew almost everything about my life—every class, everything I ate, every mundane roommate conversation—without having actually inhabited my life here. Our summer delineation had been chipped away at, one email at a time, and he existed in my present every single day. But he hadn't existed physically in it.

And I was surprised by the relief I felt to have him standing in my house, kissing me, and making the affection he had sent every evening across the ocean feel effortless in person.

"Can I give you the grand tour?"

I pulled my face away from his, ever so slightly, to see his eyes. I was a little breathless from the greeting.

"You don't live in this entryway? That's why I put my bag down here."

"I'm sorry to disappoint you."

His eyes glinted at mine, and I couldn't stop smiling.

"Thank you for the pancake mix."

He picked up his bag and handed over the tin. I stared at it, a jewel that had been unearthed just for me. I took his hand because the lack of physical contact was starting to ache, and I led him upstairs to my room.

He put his bag down in the corner and looked around. My college room aesthetic did not scare him away, but instead he looked at every photo on my wall like it was a treasure waiting to be examined. He turned back toward me after a few moments of poking around.

"So this is where you write your extremely long and expressive emails to me every morning."

The smirk was back, and I hadn't realized how much I'd missed it.

"I'm a minimalist, can't you tell?"

"I'd say the Sticky Tack behind your haphazard poster kind of gives it away."

I laughed. "I like to stay true to the cause in both my words and decor."

He snickered, and I put my hands in my pockets, unsure of what to do with them when all they wanted to do was grab him.

"I like it," he said quietly. "I like being able to picture where you are now. I can see your face scrunching up, sitting in bed trying to think of how to write me back and be witty without being too obvious, or editing my essay, shaking your head at how terrible it is."

"You know you're a way better writer than you claim—stop fishing for compliments."

He reached out for me and pulled me back toward him. I moved my hands from my pockets into his back pockets. I liked this proximity better. I tilted my head up toward him but didn't move to kiss him. I just wanted to watch his face. He lightly touched my hair and pushed a piece behind my ears.

"Hi," he said finally, his lips upturning but nothing else moving.

"Hi," I whispered back.

There were so many things to say and ask and share and confess. But nothing felt better than a simple hello and the very existence of him in my room.

"It's really nice to be here," he eventually said, eyes still locked with nowhere to go.

"I'm a little stunned you're here, to be honest," I admitted. "But I like it."

He smiled at me, both of us unsure what to do next. But he broke the tension.

"I'm starving and I do need the grand tour. So want to go for a walk?"

I nodded and grabbed my purse. His duffel bag stayed right on my floor. I guess that and all the kissing answered the question of where he was intending to stay. I felt a heady mix of excitement and nervousness. As we walked out, he tried to casually hold my hand again, but I grabbed onto the banister instead and hopped down the stairs. When we got outside, he didn't try again.

We spent the morning and afternoon walking and eating and walking some more. We walked along the town streets while I pointed out old buildings with interesting historical backgrounds or potentially less accurate ghost stories attached to them.

We stopped at the fish-and-chips shop that tourists came from out of town for, and I pointed out all the local awards and newspaper clippings that they displayed so proudly in their windows. I insisted he get the mushy peas and put vinegar all over everything to get the real, local experience, and he spent the next twenty minutes extolling the virtues of malt vinegar.

We walked along the beach and bundled ourselves against the wind, shouting to hear each other, until it finally was too ridiculous and we walked back to get to some semblance of normalcy. We stopped into my favorite café for tea and a scone, and he claimed he was too caffeinated already for the day, so he got hot chocolate with the most absurdly large marshmallows I had ever seen. I picked one out of his cup and shoved it into his mouth and then kissed him. He took a bit of whipped cream, dotted it onto my nose, and then kissed it off. We both tasted like sugar.

We walked along the pier and pointed out all the boat names that we loved. Some were primary-colored little dinghies, and others were fishing boats that were too proud to add a name. But others told tales of lost loves, high winds, and family ties just through the names painted on the back: *Scottish Hurricane, I Sea You, Parcel of Rogues, Wee Lass, The Codfather, Iona Gal.* We made up backstories for every single one.

We dipped into my favorite pub for a pint of cider and a bag of salt-and-vinegar crisps while I tried to explain the rules for rugby before having to admit that I decisively did not know a single rule of rugby.

I had to stop myself from pointing out my favorite ice cream shop. As I started mentioning it, the words in his letter smacked me right back in the face. *I would rather eat a slimy, disgusting ice cream than see any sadness on your face for one second.* I couldn't break our perfect day by summoning the things we didn't speak of. Thinking about his letter made my pulse race, and all that nervous uncomfortable energy started flooding in from the sides of my brain. Every part of me that had deliberately kept all my vulnerabilities tucked away suddenly felt extraordinarily exposed.

I took a sharp left down an alleyway with beautiful old houses to distract myself. The colorful shutters against the gray stone gave me something else to talk about, something to focus on, instead of the thoughts that were nipping at my heels.

I dragged him to my favorite kebab shop, even though he kept insisting that he wanted to take me out for a proper dinner. I waved him off, telling him there was no better meal to have in Britain than a döner kebab out of a Styrofoam container. It's quintessential student food because of its magical abilities to cure a hangover, but for me it had become more the greasy, spicy, gamey combo I craved whenever I needed comfort food.

I made Samuel pour as much white sauce on top as possible—convincing him that the yogurt-garlic-mayo-za'atar combo of this particular establishment was unmissable.

But maybe I also wanted to have an outdoor casual meal because I was pushing down the niggling fear that if I removed us from this forward momentum of ambling and talking, the magic of the day would be broken, and I would be forced to contend with the consequences. I was outrunning my conscience by putting one foot in front of the other and shoving more and more food down my throat.

I didn't have to consider what Samuel wanted from me.

I didn't have to admit that I was more enamored with him than I was allowing myself to believe.

I didn't have to wonder what was going to happen when we got back to my apartment.

I just soaked in every minute of our perfect day. I sat down on a building stoop with him and balanced a Styrofoam container on my lap. I took a sauce-slathered piece of kebab meat on my fork and put it gingerly into his mouth, narrowly avoiding dripping it on myself.

He sighed happily and I beamed. "Isn't this just like a piece of heaven?"

It was dark outside by the time we got back to my house, but I was grateful that no one seemed to be home when we returned. I'd shared vague half truths with my roommates about a man potentially coming to visit, but I wasn't sure I was ready to be put so gloriously on the spot as I would from introducing him to someone I lived with.

I took him back into my bedroom and closed the door. He sat down on my bed and watched me as I fumbled around busying myself. I took my watch off and set it on the dresser. I tidied up some notes off my desk. I pushed the chair back into place. His eyes were like an explorer's, taking me in and tracking me as I jolted around with fidgety energy.

"You're nervous," he said.

It was a statement without discrimination. A fact of life about this woman he was inhabiting this room with. It was radiating off me. My gaze stopped avoiding and finally caught his.

"I am nervous."

"Why?"

"Aren't you?"

"Should I be?"

He looked around dramatically, jokingly, like someone was going to jump out from behind the curtains. I shook my head and softly laughed.

"I just mean . . . I don't really know what we're doing here, Samuel."

"Don't you?"

I sighed. I wanted to say so many things. I had to say some piece of the truth.

"Somehow you've gotten under my skin."

It was an admission. It was the thing I'd been afraid to articulate. Every email we'd sent was like a slow bread-crumb trail leading up toward this moment. He stared at me, his lips slightly upturned, looking amused and bewildered at the same time. I wanted him to say something, but I could tell he was trying to formulate the right answer.

"You already know you've always been under mine," he said softly.

I nodded, unable to keep looking at him. I did know that. He had made sure I had always known that. He had been an open book, ready for me, and I had wriggled and squirmed and tried to fight him off.

"I just don't know what we're doing here."

I was repeating myself, but it was the only truth I could muster. I *didn't* know in any rational way. I knew I wanted him here, and I knew I loved his emails, and I knew he made me feel alive.

But how had we gotten here? And was I ready to have this piece of me opened up and exposed? Those were questions I really didn't have answers to. I wasn't sure, the way he was. I was scared. I'd watched young love get messy. I'd seen the scars it could leave.

And I really didn't know what he was doing here, in my room, when he lived so far away and there were so many obstacles between us. The thought made me start to feel panicky. I'd previously assumed this would always be a case of him *thinking* he loved me but eventually realizing I was not as lovable as he'd thought. But now I was wondering if maybe *I* had failed at keeping my feelings as casual as I wanted.

"I'm here because I wanted to see you," he said calmly, clearly trying to walk me back from the anxious thoughts he could read all over my face. "That's all. It isn't a big deal. I was just nearby and I wanted to see your face."

He was trying to reduce my skittishness. He wanted me to not think too hard. He knew if I did I would be unnerved. That this glow we had placed around ourselves like a brand-new protective bubble could be popped and go out at any moment.

He didn't delve into the distance between London and Scotland or whether he would normally have visited his brother this time of year at all. He didn't make any romantic declarations. He was here to give me only what I could handle and to treat me as gently as I needed to be. It was swoony.

"I know," I said softly. "I know you aren't trying to pressure me. I just can't help but be a bit overwhelmed that I wake up every day excited to read an email. And now you're . . . here."

I was prattling. I made no sense. But I could see he was following the trajectory.

We both stayed still—him sitting on my bed and me standing a few feet away, watching each other, deciding, drinking each other in. He was so cute with his longer hair and fleece sweater that he'd zipped all the way up against the cold. I walked toward him until I was standing between his knees. He had to tilt his head up to look at me, and his eyes were like saucers, wide and wondering.

"You know," I said slowly, "the last time we were together, you asked me a question, and I gave you an honest answer, but it wasn't what you wanted to hear. But some things have changed. It's only you now."

I could see the flash in his eyes and the whirring in his brain. It wasn't a declaration and it wasn't a promise, but it was a technicality. I had known what I was doing when I stopped responding to Callum. I didn't want Samuel to visit me and not be able to convince him to come into my bed. I couldn't tell him everything he wanted me to say. I wasn't able to, even if maybe a part of me wanted to be brave enough to. I still felt in my heart that his feelings toward me would eventually change.

But I could say that.

I held my breath. If he asked me to elaborate, I knew I would balk. Even after a perfect day, I wasn't evolved enough to pinpoint my feelings and give myself to him in any way beyond my body. But it was maybe enough.

I leaned in to kiss him, to make my case with my mouth, to convince him that even though I might be broken and scared and impossible, he could give himself to me for this moment.

"Stella—"

He caressed my cheek, and I kissed him so he wouldn't say anything else. I needed him, and I needed to make him believe me. I needed to stop every part of my brain that was setting off alarm bells, that knew I wasn't capable of giving him what he wanted, that knew he'd hurt me one day anyway. I was greedy and horny and desirous, and I couldn't stop.

I lowered myself onto the bed on his lap and wrapped my legs around him. I softly bit his lower lip, and he let out a rumble of a groan. I could feel the effect it was having below his waist.

I tenderly lifted his shirt off and kissed him all over his chest, like I was hungry and couldn't stop myself. He followed suit and peeled my shirt off my body, his hands grasping at my bra and his lips mirroring what mine had just done to him. I felt every part of my body shiver. And I knew, despite his own better judgment, his was acquiescing too.

"Okay, Stella," he said with a chuckle. "You win."

Chapter Twenty-Three

Friday, present day

I've feigned exhaustion to (a probably dubious) Elena and snuck out of the sangeet and made my way along the garden path to room 17. I knock softly on the door, and it immediately opens. We gaze at each other from the doorframe.

We are alone. There's nothing stopping us, but for just a moment it is like time has frozen and I'm not able to move. I can't help but remember the last time we were alone together in a bedroom, and I feel such a tender ache for him, even though he's right in front of me.

But I push the feeling down. My body has overridden my mind, and in a flash we're on each other, desperate, kissing like the world is on fire. He removes his jacket, and I pull off his bow tie and start frantically unbuttoning shirt buttons. He is fumbling with the bow knotted at the top of my blouse.

"This bow has been taunting me all night," he says, almost as much to himself as to me.

His fingers finally unknot it, breathing out like he has been holding his breath for too long and he is now the victor in a conquest. I'm a raw live wire sparking and waiting for touch. He unzips the side of the blouse and pulls it over my head.

I can see he is stunned by the lack of bra underneath, and I blush intensely at the way he is looking at me now, eyes dark, licking his lips as though he is going to devour me. But then we're back on each other—I recklessly undo his pants, and he unzips my skirt. I pull his shirt over his head and my skirt falls in a pool on the floor, and we're both in our underwear kissing furiously, hands on every inch without the mental capacity to decide where we want to end up.

He pushes me up against the closest wall and grabs my hands and puts them above my head. His mouth is on my neck, and I can barely breathe. I am going to turn into a puddle and just evaporate. I am in heaven. I am alive and present and faltering.

I lead him away from the wall and to his bed, and he is watching me intently as I pull him on top of my body and kiss every part of him I can find. His fingers, his elbows, his chin. I'm in a daze, and I have to taste every part of him.

And now I'm seeing everything in focus from late-night dreams that have been zipping through my brain for so many years. His hand on the curve of my hip is a physical memory that makes me shiver. His lips on my cheek open up a portal to a time in my life that somehow has never faded. Nine years has compressed into one day, and in that moment it's hard to believe we haven't been doing this continuously for every second we have been alive.

The only thing that has changed is that now I *know* no one else has ever made me feel this way. I couldn't have known, the last time his body was on mine, that my future wouldn't hold that feeling again for so long. Feeling him touch me again, making me shiver and moan so loudly that I feel embarrassed—and he shushes me in my ear, telling me quietly that it is okay, that he understands and that he feels the same way too—it is all tingling on my skin so much more vibrantly because I now know how much I have craved him for years.

I hadn't realized.

I hadn't *let* myself realize that every intimate encounter had been chasing after this one, after this heat, after this adulation. We are moving so fast because we can't possibly stop ourselves now that we've started.

He reaches for a condom from the drawer, and I watch him, hungrily, as he slides it on. I am waiting, wondering, knowing that if I give myself to him like this, there might be a world where I can't forget how good it is and how good we are together. But I had never been truly able to forget, so I might as well let him jog my memory.

I climb on top of him, and he lifts himself up to me so we are face to face. I stretch until we are entwined, and we move steadily with each other, both gripping on for dear life as we feel the intensity heating up. I am on fire and can feel every inch of my body.

I try to burrow my head into his neck, but he lifts up my chin and looks me straight in the eyes as he moves inside me, and I start to come apart. Intensity is like a crashing wave all over my body. I'm shaking and aftershocks and quicksand, and he keeps moving until I feel him tensing, until the moment has ended, and we are both breathing against each other, catching our breath and stilled.

Neither of us moves for a minute, basking in the ferocity of the actions that have muddled both of our brains and caused my whole body to throb. I press my lips to his, slowly.

We haven't moved off each other even one inch, like we are hanging on to the feeling of having him inside me, and the kissing is somehow both desperate and tender. I touch my lips to his collarbone and rest my forehead on his shoulder, taking deep breaths to try and compose myself.

I finally lift myself off him and go to the bathroom to clean up a bit. When I come back out, he's sitting up on the bed, watching me intently, taking me all in more slowly now that we have a moment to drink everything in.

"Hi," I finally say, practically wordless and suddenly shy after the breakneck speed of everything that has just passed between us.

"Hi." He smiles and reaches for my arm. I tentatively give him my hand, and he slowly pulls me down toward the bed until I practically topple both of us over. "I'd say it's been long enough that we deserve a repeat, don't you?"

I laugh as he tosses me back on the bed, and in a flash he's back on top of me, kissing away every doubt.

Chapter Twenty-Four

A few hours later my limbs burn like a gelatinous pool of satisfaction, and I can't do anything other than lie on his chest and listen to him breathe.

"Tell me how you know when a recipe is worth sharing," he says finally, jarring me back to normal adult conversation from the sex-filled banter we've been spewing at each other for the better part of the evening.

I run a finger along his arm, thinking about how to explain such an ephemeral undertaking.

"I guess . . . think of a sunset."

Just from having my ear against him, I can *feel* the smile even without seeing him.

"Please explain to me the twisted metaphor that is going to get a recipe from a sunset."

It wasn't my best-thought-out answer, but now that he's prodding at me—in that way he was always able to, pushing me to examine more thoroughly and articulate with more thought-through purpose—I have to sit up to center myself for an explanation.

"Okay, so any recipe, just like any sunset, gets you to the same place when it's done, right?"

"Right. It's either set or eaten, no matter what it looked like before."

"Exactly," I say, grinning from the knowledge that he's with me on this roundabout mental exercise. "But the journey of each is exceptionally different. The sun is always going to set; the food is always going to be eaten; but before it does, some have an inexplicable magical quality that burns brightly for only a moment in time. Some are simply better than others, and you can't always explain why."

"Okay, but then how do you pick a favorite?"

I throw a question back at him. "What defines a favorite for you?"

"Well, that's the real quandary, right?" he says, now sitting himself up and getting wound up to analyze. It's so adorable, and the déjà vu almost knocks me out. "Is the best one the one you come back to over and over again? Or is it that burst of a single instance that's memorable for being in a certain time or place? Like, if you have a perfect sunset on vacation, is that better than the one you adore from your own rooftop most nights? And similarly with food—is it the best when you have that special something you've never tried? Or your mom's chicken soup the exact way she always makes it?"

I love the look on his face right now. His whirring mind, his ability to attack any question like a puzzle, was always his most indescribable quality. Imagine the curiosity and wonder of a child combined with the analytical mind of a seasoned lawyer; that's the beauty of having a conversation with Samuel. He has the power to take you anywhere and make you believe your opinions matter.

I feel a bit giddy, although I shake it off, rationalizing it's probably more to do with the sex haze than the conversation.

But since I haven't answered him, his mind keeps churning and he continues on.

"I mean, both scenarios are so intangible, right? If you try and photograph either, it'll never compare to the original—you can't capture your senses in a five-by-seven. But some things you can smell years later. And others burn bright in the moment but fade with time and the newness of seeing something else." He pauses, as though he's finally reached the answer. "But when it's good, you just know. You know it when you see it."

"Exactly," I reply, not sure if we're talking about sunsets or recipes entirely anymore.

"So that's the answer?"

"That's the answer."

I am unable to hide my shy smile, a little piece of me glowing that he was able to follow along on my ridiculous logic.

"I share a recipe when I know it's good," I elaborate. "That's why the explanation has to come in a metaphor; it's impossible to explain any other way."

I laugh, knowing how ridiculously vague that answer is.

The warm pads of his fingers intertwine with mine, and the combined heat our friction creates sends shivers all the way to my toes. I roll to my side and bring him with me. How does he do this to me? How can he take a discussion about recipe testing and set my whole body on fire? But I don't dare say that to him.

"Why did you choose Chicago for law school?" I finally ask, swerving the topic into safer curiosities.

"I wanted to see if it was New York or just cities in general," he says casually, his eyes roaming my body instead of focusing fully on the conversation.

"If what was New York?"

"I grew up there, and I always felt as though I embodied that John Updike quote of like, true New Yorkers believe people living anywhere else have to be kidding. But then in college someone told me Updike moved to Massachusetts, so that gave me a pause."

I laugh at the absurdity of the young Samuel I knew, so set in his ways and so sure of his convictions. I feel a little pang of sadness for all the bubbles that were probably popped in those years. It pangs doubly to know one of those was me.

He continues. "And I really liked the law school at UChicago and the professors there, so I went. And I *do* like cities in general, but it became very clear very quickly that New York wasn't going to lose its grip on me."

"Once a New Yorker, always a New Yorker?" I tease.

"I just shouldn't have ever doubted that I know my own mind."

He's still not looking at me, and I can't help but wonder if he's now deliberately not able to meet my eye. That familiar swirl of anxiety creeps into my center, like a clingy friend you were hoping wouldn't show up to the party. I don't think I can open some of these doors to the past, even if Samuel is knocking softly.

I push forward, needing to get the subject back on sturdier ground. "So have you worked for the same firm since you got back?"

"Yup, I interned with them when I was in law school, so it was an easy decision to join and just work my way up. I'd buried myself in law school to keep up my grades for my scholarships, and I really loved intellectual property law. This firm is one of the best at that, so it was easy to say yes."

"And are you burying yourself there too?"

"Yes," he replies. There's no tinge of regret but similarly no spark of joy in the statement. "It's been my main focus, for sure."

"Right, well, what else would be?"

I really hate myself for picking at this thread, but I'm not able to stop, apparently. Maybe I can blame the sex haze for that too. But if he notices that I'm picking, he doesn't acknowledge it.

"Exactly. This is the time to focus and work my way up, so that's what I've been doing. And I guess Hadley tries to make me have a life sometimes, although her brother also lives in the city, so at least she now has another person to badger instead of just me."

He seems content. It's not hard to imagine that he's created a life for himself that mostly involves solving legal puzzles and hanging out with friends in the city he feels enmeshed in.

I feel a twinge of envy for the steadiness he seems to have fostered. Sure, on the surface we're the same: both consumed by our jobs and apparently no semblance of complexity in our personal lives. But his path seems like a rowboat on a glassy lake, needing effort to move forward but with no impediments in the way of getting toward the other shore. Why does my life instead feel like a hollowed-out canoe trying to navigate white water rapids? And how did it take me until this trip to realize that I'd allowed myself to live my life on defense rather than offense?

As though he can follow my train of thoughts, he kisses my collarbone to shake me out of my own head.

"Don't let work stuff trip you up right now."

"I wasn't," I reply, but I can see he's not buying what I'm selling.

"You don't have to do that with me," he says delicately.

"Hm?" It's so tempting to act like I don't know what he means.

"You can obfuscate with your friends and maintain your street cred as the strong person." I roll my eyes, but I know it's only egging him on. "I respect that you want to do that. But I see you, Stella," he says, his eyes on mine. "Don't pretend with me, okay? Be whatever you need to be right now."

His words still me, a verbal bull's-eye.

"All right, Samuel," I concede after a moment, for once not letting myself overanalyze. "Honestly? Right now I just want to ignore everything outside, okay?"

He nods.

I let my fingers roam across his chest, light touches taking in texture and warmth, trying to get my head solidly back in the immediacy of the moment. The bright crowded cubicles of my office disappointments don't need to invade on this hiatus inside a dimmed, dreamy room. I can't let my overactive mind drag me out of this thrilling contentment.

Going with my gut for once feels *good*. Escaping momentarily from the should-I's and ramification-spirals and judgment-fears has been glorious. It's not who I am, but at least I can enjoy being this way here.

He mirrors my movements, slowly caressing me like I'm a rare bird, ready to be carefully studied. When I press him for more stories from work, he gladly shares them, little rays of sunshine poking through the years that have accumulated around us. I like listening to his voice, hearing his timbre, his tales of tenacity and good nature infusing every story he has about the pursuits he's spent the last few years on.

I can feel night start to shift into morning, but with darkness still outside I don't want to pierce through the insulation of the evening. So we keep talking until we both slow enough to catch a bit of sleep for a few hours.

Until I look at the clock and realize that in order to shower and make it to Subrata's in time, I need to go back into reality. Samuel is still sleeping, so I silently extricate myself from our knotted limbs and slip my clothes back on.

I watch him breathing in, his expression blissfully blank, and I think back to the conversation about sunsets and recipes. Until today, I'd never really thought about how much both of those experiences could change when you're experiencing them with someone else.

CHAPTER TWENTY-FIVE

The air is buzzing with excitement as we sit in Subrata's room the next morning with the giant velvet curtains open as the late-morning sun streams in. We try to tackle all the room service we ordered for breakfast, mostly zoning in on the squat cheesy bread, *torta di pasqua*. The mixture of pecorino, rich butter, and bright-yellow eggs arrived with perfect timing, the yeasty hangover cure everyone was craving.

I tried to sneak in as early as possible in the morning so it would appear like I'd gone to bed in my own room and come in once I woke up. But it is hard not to feel a bit bleary eyed, considering how little I've slept, no matter how much fluffy savory bread I stuff down my throat.

The crystals in the chandelier of Subrata's room keep taunting me by twinkling brightly into my eyes, when truly I just want to lie down. But I'm keyed up enough from the excitement of today—and the strong Italian espresso—to barge forward.

Most of Subrata's family are at the baraat, a procession where the groom arrives on a horse surrounded by music and drums. The wedding guests dance around him, and then the bride's family ceremonially welcomes the husband to their family. Subrata's parents have *insisted* on following tradition, which also includes Subrata not being allowed to attend.

But unlike how I would have reacted—seriously, I could never be asked to miss a giant portion of my own party where everyone I loved got to dance around—Subrata is actually calm and collected. There are still nitpicking mothers and chattering aunties surrounding her, but there are also friends, a truly elaborate selection of breakfast cakes, and a chance to take time getting ready before even more insanity sets in.

I am sitting on an elaborate emerald-green chaise lounge chair, curled up like a cat in the sun while I eat a third piece of my "dessert," a hazelnut coffee cake that I am trying to control myself from hoarding. I am surprised by how at ease I feel. Apparently being surrounded by happy friends, even with so many things I'm not saying to them, is like my very own cheat code to unlocking tranquility.

I can see Elena's eyes on me as the morning goes on. Something is on the tip of her tongue but remains unsaid. There is no way my early "night in" didn't surprise her. But there is also no way either of us would make the morning more dramatic by discussing anything other than Subrata today.

So I eat more cake, and pretend not to notice. Cat is oblivious, since the idea of getting into any hijinks is so foreign to her that I could stamp a message on her forehead saying *I HAD AMAZING BUT PROBABLY EMOTIONALLY DAMAGING SEX LAST NIGHT, BUT AT LEAST I SOMEHOW MAINTAINED A SEMBLANCE OF PROPRIETY BY SHOWING UP THIS MORNING DESPITE BEING THE FLIGHTIEST AND WORST FRIEND ALL WEEK*, and she would just look at it in the mirror and say it was backward, so there was no use trying to figure out what the message was anyway.

Subrata is simply glowing, swanning around the room in her hotel robe (decidedly *not* running away from her feelings toward any men— well done, Subrata, for having more poise in your pinkie than I do in my whole body), somehow able to eat more than I probably would if I was about to stand in front of everyone I know. She isn't nervous at all, just ready to get the show on the road.

But soon enough hair and makeup people show up and kick us into high gear. We are all poked and prodded until we stop looking like sleepy hungover monsters and instead appear to be cogent and potentially put-together members of a bridal party. There are no bridesmaids or matching dresses in an Indian wedding, but Subrata did ask for each of us to wear something blue and gold, and I am a little bit in love with my lehengha for the day. I hate that all I can think about is how I want Samuel to strip it off me later.

Is that what's going to happen? I think back to our conversation last night, and it feels hard to imagine that that was it. Tonight seems inevitable.

I can't help the inkling of speculation that creeps into my mind. *If he remembers everything . . . what if he wants more after tonight?*

The thought stops me dead in my tracks and makes nervousness pool into every corner of my gut. We've destroyed each other once already. This Italian jaunt might feel like a dreamscape far away from the real world, but my reality at home is much more complicated. I'm barely hanging on by a thread at work emotionally, and I definitely do not need to complicate my life with a man whose history with me is like a roaring freight train who slams into me and then speeds out of dodge.

But I shake it off.

Who am I kidding? A decade later, I'm not some great prize a person has pined over.

He's gotten more successful and more handsome, and I'm a messy nonpromoted anxious workaholic. We just slept together *one night*. At *a wedding*. Where we're both single and maybe drank too much and are feeling a touch of nostalgia. That's not exactly cause for assumptions.

Come on, Stella, get a grip.

This doesn't mean anything to him.

There's no reason to go overboard here. I can handle a weekend wedding fling. That's all this is: two people who already knew each other and wanted to have fun at a blissful Umbrian wedding.

And it's Subrata's day today—no way I'm going to let anything distract me from celebrating and focusing on this impeccable bride.

I turn toward her and feel bolstered by seeing how gorgeous the whole scene is. We are a tribe surrounding our red-festooned queen as she gets ready, and I can't help but watch proudly as my elegant, simple friend has layers and layers added to her dainty frame—first a red skirt and blouse with intricate beading, followed by jewelry in her hair, and a veil placed on top. Her earrings seem large until piles of bangles keep getting added on top of one another on her arms, and suddenly that appears to be the largest undertaking. When her mother returns and it is time to go out, she adds one last touch of a necklace.

The weight of her entire outfit can't be easy to handle. But as with everything else in her life, Subrata seems to carry it off with so much grace that it's hard to believe it wasn't all spun from the clouds. Meanwhile, I have to continuously look down to ensure I don't trip and fall over my long beaded skirt as we make our way outside.

I can focus today. I have to focus today.

CHAPTER
TWENTY-SIX

The weather is paradisiac as I take my seat for the wedding. Subrata, Luca, and their parents are sitting beneath an elaborate mandap, a temporary structure with a canopy that in this instance looks like every flower in Italy has been attached to it. It is spring come to life as a form of architecture—pink and purple and pale-ivory flowers snake around every possible inch.

A light-green silk fabric with intricate needlework interspersed is like the crown on top, covering them in shade. On the ground sits a white carpet and white plush benches that they all sit on as the ceremony takes place.

I take my seat on the edge of the bride's side, and out of the corner of my eyes I see Samuel. He is wearing a tux again, and he has kept his shade of stubble. A pale-pink flower is attached to his lapel, and even though I can see him staring ahead, I know from the glint of a smile that he's seen me.

Focusing on the ceremony is impossible with him so close. I hear the words; I see Luca and Subrata join hands and circle around a small fire. I see them take seven symbolic steps. I watch as Luca tenderly applies a red powder to Subrata's forehead. My blood is pumping and my mind is racing and all I'm trying to do is just stare straight ahead and look like a model of calm and decorum on the exterior.

As we walk toward the reception, I'm blunted by the fact that there is really no way to get Samuel in private without being obvious. So it's all going to have to wait. But he is torturing me, taking every chance to come over and chat breezily with everyone around me but without ever looking me in the eye. I know he isn't avoiding me, though—on the contrary. He is staying in my vicinity, keeping his body close, letting the heat radiate onto me without ever giving me the satisfaction of seeing what's hidden behind the placid smile on his face.

It's like an entire day of foreplay with no touching and no one else being allowed to sense what is going on.

We are thankfully seated on opposite sides of the tent when dinner is plated. Strings and strings of fairy lights cast a shadowy radiance, and the toasts are funny and heartfelt enough to pull my attention away.

What must it be like to have everyone you love surround you like this and truly believe it will turn out well? There is not a single other person at this wedding who feels cynical about Luca and Subrata's prospects today. The speeches are a sea of "meant to be" and "total partnership" and "ready to take on anything together." No lingering doubts remain. No queries exist over whether these two people are capable of loving each other with all their hearts.

It gives me a dull panicked feeling listening to everyone. The thought of *needing* someone that much gives me anxiety just in the theoretical. I've spent my whole life bursting with self-reliance, convinced that I am better off taking care of myself. That has always seemed like the braver course of action. But snaking through my gut is the sneaking suspicion that refusing to let anyone cross that susceptible barrier has been more protective than brave.

And I have to ignore the glaring fact that I've only truly let one person behind that barrier, and he didn't protect it.

Luca and Subrata get up for their first dance, and I shake the thought from my mind—Luca wore a traditional Indian kurta during the ceremony, but he's since changed into a slick tuxedo that fits perfectly on his lanky frame.

He takes Subrata out onto the dance floor, and they look at each other, incandescent with the glow of the surroundings and all the people cheering them on. When the next song comes on, they beckon everyone out to the dance floor, and I waste no time joining them, pushing every fearful thought out of my mind.

Every song turns into innuendo. Samuel stays close without a word. We dance separately but in the same big groups, and we dance practically back to back, facing our friends without looking behind us. Song lyrics cause our eyes to flicker toward each other and then dart back again. The band plays hits we know and Italian classics we don't. But the high energy never ceases.

Until the band starts playing "La Vie en Rose," and everyone slows down. Friends saunter off the dance floor in search of water and a break. Couples of every age take each other in their arms and start swaying.

And I feel a hand gingerly place itself on the small of my back. I turn around as Samuel pulls me in. With his other hand he takes mine in his, and we move slowly to the music, not saying a word. He puts his cheek against mine, and I breathe him in. The lead vocalist sings softly of heaven sighing, and the horns trill alongside her.

All my thoughts from earlier that morning start rushing back in. I want to believe in a world where we can just have a fling and I don't have to face what happened between us so many years ago. I want to bifurcate my memories of him and place the past half in a box and soak in the present and this weekend and last night's foray in the garden and his room.

I can feel his heart beating faster against mine, both our pulses racing even as we slowly move together to the notes of the song. We're pressing closer and closer to each other, and I'm finding it almost impossible not to tilt my head up toward him and kiss him.

His hand strokes my back, and I flash to last night—to the way his hands danced on my bare skin and made me hum with pleasure. It's exceptionally distracting.

The song stops, but he doesn't stop holding me. We are standing, bodies pressed tight, cheeks touching, unable to look at each other, while the band prepares to play one more song.

"Let's get out of here," he whispers in my ear, and my body shivers at the thought. I practically pull him out of the room, trying to knock all the niggling thoughts out of my mind and instead get back to that cocoon where I can put my body on his and forget everything else in my life.

We try to walk normally as we exit, probably being significantly less smooth than we believe we are being. But as soon as we get outside and onto the path, we are hurrying and stumbling along, grabbing for each other's hands and my bare waist and his silky lapel.

We reach his room, and I can't stop my lips from going onto his while he fumbles in his pocket for his key, desperation pressing both of us onto each other before we tumble into the room.

We undress each other slowly this time—the rushed frenzy of last night having given way to a desire to see everything. I drink in the way he watches me, reverently, staring at every inch of my skin that's exposed to him. His hands make parts of my body I've never considered sexy feel like they're on fire as he glides along them—the right angle of my elbow, the dip of my hip bone, a raised freckle that dots my rib cage, the inside of my index finger. It's like he is cataloging my depths and dimensions.

When I don't think I can take another minute of this slow torture, I push him back onto the bed and climb on top of him, straddling him while he reaches for me and kisses me hungrily. His mouth makes his way across my jawline, dotting every inch of my face until he nibbles on my earlobe, and the sensation makes me press into him.

And then I hear him whisper in my ear, ever so softly, "I still love you, Stella."

CHAPTER

TWENTY-SEVEN

NOVEMBER 24, NINE YEARS AGO

Three days went by in a haze of our entangled bodies and laughter and breakfasts in bed. I ignored everything else around me and instead lazily drank him in for each moment that we were existing in this bubble.

I think my roommates assumed I had joined a cult. They stopped bothering us after feeble introductions and some small talk. I didn't want to share him. I was greedy. And this was a fling to be soaked up between just us, not involving everyone in my life. I didn't need any outside conversationalists asking questions that I didn't have answers to.

The last morning, I woke up and heard him in the shower. I sat up, leisurely looking over at the clock—9:30. He was leaving in an hour for his train. I lay back in bed and looked at the ceiling.

I was not looking forward to saying goodbye. I was not looking forward to whatever this conversation was inevitably going to turn into. My stomach started folding itself into knots.

He came in wearing just a towel, and I looked him up and down.

"Take a picture, it'll last longer," he said, a wry smile taking over his face.

"Sure, just hand me that towel, and then it'll be perfect," I snickered.

He tossed the towel in my face, and I shrieked while he jumped on top of me and planted kisses all over my body. I was wearing his T-shirt, but that didn't stop his hands from going under it and holding on to me.

"So that's a no on the naked pictures then?" I said, kissing the top of his nose.

"Yeah, that's just what I need floating around in your care: dirty photos that you accidentally attach to an email to your professor instead of an essay."

"Who said it would be an accident?"

I grinned when he chuckled, and I felt light as a feather. I lay down and pulled him gingerly on top of me, kissing him softly and then lying on my side, looking at him and drinking him in.

"You'll see me soon enough anyway. Aren't you coming back for Christmas?"

The lightness thudded. My bill had come due.

"Well," I started slowly, "I'll be going home to see my family."

"But you can come to New York for part of the time, right?"

I propped myself up, putting the smallest distance between us so I could say what I needed to say without ruining everything.

"I don't think I can—my family has already started making a lot of plans, and I don't see how I can fit something else in."

"'Something else'?" His voice had gotten colder. It made my whole body cold too.

"You know what I mean."

"No, I really don't."

He stayed silent, not giving me an inch. He was going to make me speak and not hand me over a solution or an indulgence or an out. Whatever ideas he'd been hatching, I had just summarily dashed, and I was going to have to explain myself.

"I didn't realize we had plans," I finally said, weakly.

"You didn't . . . what the fuck, Stella?"

I looked at him, unsure of what to say.

"No, we didn't have *plans*," he said, "but I would assume the next time we are in the same country, you would want to prioritize trying to see me?"

"This is exactly what I was afraid of," I mumbled.

"I'm sorry?"

He looked at me with wide eyes now. I had suspected this wasn't going to be the answer he wanted, but I wasn't expecting him to be so shocked. We had never had any conversations about what came next.

"I'm just saying, you can't expect me to all of a sudden turn my life upside down."

"Who the fuck said anything about turning your life upside down by visiting your boyfriend for a few days over Christmas?"

He never cursed, and now he had done it twice. I was always the asshole dropping f-bombs all over the place. He was mad, but I was taken aback by his anger. I had expected maybe a little lighthearted pushback, but the anger was like a splash of cold water. It made my skin prickle. It made me defensive. The word "boyfriend" made every draw-bridge around my exterior castle come up instantly and close the gates.

"Come on, we have not ever used those words."

"Oh, I'm sorry, does the word 'boyfriend' offend you?"

"You know—you *know* that that is not what I want from you."

"Oh, I know that?"

He stood up and put his pants back on and stood on the other side of the room. It was like he was so disgusted with me he had to put actual physical space between us.

"I have been exceptionally clear with you from the minute I met you, Samuel. I just cannot handle a relationship. This thing between us is great, and I love talking to you and I'm so glad you came to visit, but that doesn't change where I am in my life."

"How can you say that?"

His voice was small. It made me feel physically ill. I wanted to reach out to him, but I was afraid. I was afraid to say this out loud, but I was more afraid to change my mind and take down that barrier and talk about his letter and let everything out of the box I had been hiding it in. That thought was more terrifying than this.

But his defensiveness was giving me a shield too. It allowed me to let exasperation take over all the spots where the terror was otherwise rooted. If I could be mad at him for not listening to me, then I wouldn't have to consider how terrifying letting him actually love me would be.

"Samuel, I am not ready for this."

"You said you weren't sleeping with anyone else. You said that to me the night I arrived. The implication of that is pretty clear as day, and you used that ambiguity to your advantage."

"To my *advantage*?" I was incredulous now.

"You knew this wasn't casual for me. You knew I didn't want to sleep with you if you weren't my girlfriend. You knew that."

"And you deliberately didn't ask. If that was your red line, then surely that was on you to articulate it."

"I did."

"A long time ago," I said, knowing that I sounded like a whiny child who had run out of excuses.

"So you're ready to sleep with anyone that wants to, but God forbid you actually have an emotion about it."

The indignation in his voice was as strong as a slap across the face. "Oh, I'm sorry, have we reached the slut-shaming portion of this conversation?"

Now *I* was mad. Now I was going to let anger fuel me. Now I had a real reason to be angry enough that I could reject him for reasons that I still couldn't quite understand.

"I'm allowed to have sex for whatever casual reasons I want, and I'm not going to be told that that is somehow wrong," I said.

The truth—however marginally I understood it—was now ready to tumble out of me.

"I watched my sister fall in love with someone who told her he'd love her forever. Who married her with those promises. And guess what, Samuel? It *ended* and it *wrecked* her. But more than that, it wrecked everyone around her who loved her *and* loved him. And I couldn't sleep from all the fucking panic attacks and anxiety over not being able to console her enough and guilt over missing the brother he'd become to me. I watched it. I lived it. I'm not ever, ever doing that. I don't *need* to do that. Sex can just be sex. Some of us genuinely *don't want a relationship*. You're not *listening* to me."

He was silent for a moment, momentarily unable to respond to all the previously unsaid bombshells I'd just dropped. He was trying to get himself back to his centered state and was breathing in deeply.

"That's their story, not ours. You don't get to act like I'm making something up. You can't just pretend that the last few months and the last few days are some nothing fling that doesn't mean anything to you."

"I never said that," I whispered.

Maybe it had been selfish to keep pushing reality aside, but wasn't it obvious that this wouldn't last outside our little bubble? Perfect things don't last.

He exhaled again, studying me now, trying to find the cracks in my armor that I was so desperate to hold up.

"I never said you don't mean anything to me. Obviously that's not true," I admitted, my voice quiet. "But that doesn't mean I want to be a girlfriend."

I could see that the calm he was trying so hard to hold on to was slipping. I was sand running through his fingers, and he wasn't ready to stop fighting.

"Damn it, Stella, stop pretending like you don't know exactly what you're doing."

His eyes were blazing, and I flinched because behind my anger and indignation I knew he was right. Of course at this point I knew. I hadn't known it before he arrived, but little by little, over every day and hour and minute he'd stayed here, that knowledge had grown from a tiny seed in the back of my mind into a tree shading every action.

But none of that was the point. It *couldn't* be the point. Deep down he knew who I was. We'd both ignored all the red flags in order to live in a few days of bliss.

"I don't want to be in a relationship with *anyone*," I pleaded, trying to grasp onto another angle.

I wanted him to believe me, so desperately.

I wanted him to let me off the hook.

"Bullshit," he finally said. "You're just afraid."

"I'm telling you exactly how I feel, and you are deliberately ignoring me," I spat out, my anger returning. "*You* feel confident, you feel secure, you have never doubted yourself a moment in your life. Not everyone is like you, Samuel. Everyone can't just cut through the nonsense in their own minds with a clarity of purpose and say whatever the fuck they think and believe it'll all work out. Some of us have seen it *not* work out. Some of us have seen the downsides of love and don't want to engage. You can't just bend the world to your will. You said you knew where I stood. You specifically said you wouldn't pressure me. You *promised* me that."

My voice was cracking, and I was breathing hard from yelling and the effort it was taking not to cry. The allusion to the letter seemed to diminish him, like I'd brought his own words back to haunt him. But I couldn't be sorry I'd said it; I was being as honest as I possibly could, and it was wounding me to see that he did not—could not—believe me. It was like he wanted to believe that his ability to know me so well included an ability to see things that even I had yet to see. And he was wrong.

I could see on his face that he wasn't going to even acknowledge it. Maybe we'd both been deliberately avoiding seeing what was right in front of us.

"I can't fight for both of us. You have to fight for the things you want, too, Stella," he said quietly. "You should fight your own fears and not give in to complacency."

"That's not what I'm doing." I felt unsure of every single word.

"Yes, rejecting me right now, keeping me at arm's length, it's easier for you than having to admit that you might actually love me, and that is scary."

I flinched, and a giant silent chasm broke open between us. I couldn't respond.

He was so right. I knew, in the pit of my stomach, that he was right.

But I wanted easy and I *needed* easy and there was no way for me to say that to him. I didn't have the strength to fight for him *and* to fight my own demons. I was desperate for the easy way. I was too scared to take any other road, too scared that if I didn't stop this now, I would eventually be left loving him long after he'd stopped loving me.

I said the only thing I could. "If you have to fight that hard, then maybe it is too hard."

He stared at me, like a child who won't go to bed even though she is exhausted. His expression was pure frustration and certainty, and I was shrinking.

"You can't have it both ways, you know," he said quietly.

I looked at him quizzically. He was so calm. He'd gotten himself back. The anger had dissipated, and he was now so composed, after all that.

I felt like my guts were on the floor, and I was practically heaving with the weight of everything swimming in my brain, and he was as self-contained as always.

"You can't have me in every way that matters and then pretend like I don't exist and that we aren't in a relationship. You can't have it both ways."

"What happened to not pressuring me?" It came out with venom to hide the desperation.

He sighed and looked away from me. It wasn't possible to shield me from the truth of it all.

"I'm not sure I understood what I was promising," he finally said.

And there it was.

It hung between us.

His guts were out, too, but he had neatly piled them into the corner tidily enough where I hadn't been able to see them through my messy rage and obfuscation. He was wounded and bleeding and he had thought he could handle it, but there was a point where the pain went beyond what he'd expected.

We can read every book and stare at every piece of art about the pain of love, but we never know how much it hurts to be exposed until it's real to us. It's a feeling so foreign to our base state that it is impossible to imagine.

I thought back on the moment when Sophie told me Charlie had left, and the searing pain of realizing everything he'd said to me about being in our life forever was a falsehood. I watched my sister suffer through this exact pain; I had anticipated it now, which was why I had held so tightly to my convictions that I could never let myself shove my insides out of my body and let someone else stomp all over them.

But Samuel hadn't experienced that. All his bravado and confidence and surety had been because he was still shiny and new. He hadn't ever let someone else inside. He hadn't let someone see where he was weird and scared and achy and small and strange. He hadn't felt what it was like to not be able to put that toothpaste back in the tube.

Some small part of me, that couldn't even have admitted it to myself, had wanted to believe he could love me the way he had promised me, that he could contain his feelings for however long it took me to figure out mine. But we don't know what we don't know. And he couldn't have known before then that it was inevitable he would leave.

When the front door slammed, I barely heard it because I was already curled up in a ball under my covers.

Chapter

Twenty-Eight
Saturday, present day

I still love you, Stella.

The sentiment was coursing between both of us. But until this moment I didn't let myself really see it—or rather I've willfully forced myself into repeating the word "fling" enough times that I've made myself believe this man has changed enough to be *capable* of casual.

And now I am too startled and stunned to say anything back. I feel my heart racing from the pit of my stomach, like the anxiety is hammering to get out. I try to tamp it down and breathe slowly, but it's not stopping my body from physically reacting to his words.

"Silence was not the reaction I was hoping for," he says, looking at me, still holding on to me, as I sit frozen, still naked and on top of him and about as vulnerable as I could possibly be in every possible way.

"I really don't know what to say to that."

"You can't be surprised."

I almost roll my eyes at him. It's so *him*. In his world, it would make total sense that I should have intuited this conversation.

"You have literally not spoken to me in nine years," I finally reply. "You have spent three days, sort of, with me now. 'Love' is a strong word for that."

"My feelings on this topic have never changed," he says with a wistful smile, daring me to argue with him.

He is amused and I am dumbfounded.

"Stella, I have been in love with you since we were twenty years old," he finally says quietly. "I called Luca after our first date and told him I was going to marry you someday."

"You can't *possibly* have thought that," I say incredulously.

I'm trying not to get angry, but the absurdity of what he's saying is hitting me; fear is still the dominant feeling clinging to my body, smacking me right in the face, and it is so much stronger than every other emotion.

"We are not the exact same people we were nine years ago," I continue. "I'm not a real person to you—just some figment of a woman you imagine as being perfect, when I am far from it. That isn't reality."

"I don't think you're perfect. But I do know who you are."

"No, you enjoy the chase."

"Oh yeah, I'm truly enjoying this chase," he says with a chuckle. "I thought this many years would really heighten the excitement there."

I ignore his sarcasm.

"Your declaration really doesn't hold much weight, considering if you loved someone so much, you wouldn't give up for nine years."

I see him wince. I've struck a nerve.

"I didn't give up."

So I guess this conversation really *couldn't* be avoided, even in this Italian dreamscape where I've wanted to believe real life could be paused. This fight has been waiting for us beneath all the conversations and banter and flirting. We started it nine years ago and never really ended it. And so here we are again.

"You *left*. You said you loved me, but you didn't love me enough to let me be who I was. You walked away," I reply angrily, climbing off him and wrapping a robe around myself to place a distance between our intimacy.

The anger is fueling me, twisting my anxious heart into something more manageable, something more targeted and controllable. I see his mind is whirring again, trying to come up with how to respond.

"I did. But I was young and stupid and, frankly, in total agony. I thought for sure you would call me or even send me one of your nonchalant emails one day, pretending like nothing happened. But you didn't, and I . . ." He pauses, the memory so clear in front of his face.

He turns away for a moment but then catches my eyes again. "I couldn't face it again. I loved you, but after we slept together, it was all too raw to just keep going on like we had been before. I couldn't hear you reject me again and again and again. You told me I wasn't listening to how you felt—how you couldn't be in a relationship with anyone—so I figured I'd take you at your word. And when you never reached out, I figured you'd never wanted me, really. It was easier to believe that."

"Convenient."

"Really fucking inconvenient, actually," he says, standing up with so much force I am surprised and take a step back. "You don't think I have *tried* to forget about you? I have never been able to maintain a real relationship for longer than a few months, Stella. I have never been able to look at another woman and think, 'I feel even mildly close to being as happy with her as I did when I was just writing a damn email to Stella.' Never. You have hung over me like a ghost on every date and with every woman I've been with."

His words wallop me because I know the feeling. Maybe I haven't let it enter my mind as directly as that, but he has always been the person every man has been measured against. I have always compared and always inevitably found everyone else lacking.

I wrap the robe tighter, as though it can protect me from his words. If his words are true, then I am much less of a controlled mess than I've convinced myself I was. I'm a mess who's always believed it was inevitable that he would leave once he saw the real me. I've believed that my entire adult life. I can't be *that* much of a mess. My chest is tightening, and the anxiety is starting to overtake the anger again.

But he keeps going. "And I spent most of my time studying in law school and then being overly involved in work, so I never really had to face that I was avoiding dealing with it. And in time it became really easy to believe it was just me—that I had idealized you and my memories were heightened and it was all an excuse for me to work all the time and avoid dating. But then you were here, and once we both got over ourselves enough to actually talk again . . . I sat in that poppy field and I couldn't stop myself from feeling the exact same thing. You weren't a mirage, and you weren't something I'd exaggerated. You were you. It's always been you, Stella. There has never been anyone else for me."

He looks so flushed and beautiful. Naked and unafraid. Samuel has never been able to keep something inside or play it cool, and it must be like lifting a weight to finally tell me exactly what he's thinking.

He has spent three days in an unnatural state of not trying to spook me, and now he is clearly done. It's always been our kryptonite—my cautious, anxious, logical mind butting heads with surety, a steamroller in the body of a broad-shouldered, tousled-haired man.

"It's too much for me," I say quietly.

"We're going to do this again?"

My heart is pounding, and nausea is gripping me. Paralysis seems to be tingling up my body because I am terrified and it's making me immovable.

I hear him, and I believe him. I can believe that it's possible I avoided taking any blame for my own part in never really giving us a chance.

But I'm not sure after all those years of hurting that I am capable of throwing myself in front of the proverbial bus. I'm not sure I can take the seeming inevitability of getting hurt by him again. I can't suggest just going on a casual date when we're back in New York and seeing what happens, because he has never allowed me to do that, to be gradual. He couldn't let us do that for even a single day. And if I'm already feeling this anxious from his impulsive need to go at his own pace, then it can't possibly be worth trying to make that work.

"You can't just leap in front of me and then insist I catch up to you," I say quietly. "I am at a different speed."

"You're always waiting to feel comfortable, Stella. You wait and you miss out. You're staying in a job where they don't appreciate you instead of going out on your own and thriving."

I let anger wash back over the fear, like a deal with the devil that I'm heartily accepting. If I can be mad at him, then I don't have to face the fear. I don't have to consider whether he is right. Indignation has always been the easiest way out. It served me with him once before.

"That's not fair. You don't know anything about my job."

"I know that you should have been promoted, and somehow they gave it to someone else. Not because he was better than you, but because he went for it. He put himself out there and gave it everything he had, while you hid in the corner so that when they didn't give it to you, you could just say, 'Oh well, I didn't really want it anyway.'"

"That isn't true."

"Isn't it?"

We are on opposite sides of the room, combatants ready to spar but without anyone making the first move. My body is a bundle of nerves, itching to let him hold me and touch me, but my brain is firing on all cylinders, telling me to escape and avoid.

"You've always held that power," he says. "You just are afraid to use it and get burned. It's why I was so afraid to sleep with you when we first met. You had such a hold on me, but you had no idea how to use it. It's amazing to me that you still don't. It's amazing to me that you are so scared of what would happen if you fail that you won't grab your own happiness with both hands."

"My life is fine without you, Samuel."

"Well, we all should definitely aspire to fine," he says with a sarcastic bite in his voice, and he looks away from me.

It's like the weight of the honesty of everything he has been needing to say has come crashing down on him, and he is done.

He is sad and I can't bear it. I can't bear to have this conversation; it's like enduring thousands of small cuts over every inch of my body. I have to get out of here. I am anxiety personified, and this is too much for me. I can't let myself think about this because I will explode.

My life living with Elena and going to work only gets muddled when I do stupid things like apply for jobs I'm clearly not going to get or sleep with men I used to have strong feelings for. *This* is what I'm always working so hard to avoid.

I *am* fine, and fine is better than scared. Fine is better than letting him in again, only to have him walk out on me once he sees more of the real me. We already did this once before, and he didn't love me enough to have patience. Fine, maybe I pushed him away, too, and maybe I had to ignore my role in everything in order to get over him. But why would this time be any different? I'm still me and I'm still scared and I certainly don't have the capacity to take that risk.

I find my underwear and put it on. I haphazardly pull up my skirt and throw my blouse back over my head. He is watching me, stunned, and I can see that he's trying to find the right words.

"Please don't walk out," he finally says, and it stops me in my tracks.

I was not expecting that. My heart, covered strategically by layers and layers of anger and fear and animus that all think they are a shield against pain, fractures. There is no shield strong enough to enclose every aching part of me.

"I barely survived losing you the first time," he says, taking a few tentative steps toward me. "I can't come after you. I can't do it to myself again."

Fight or flight tastes bitter in my mouth. Is all this just a perception of a few hazy days of one summer and one brief moment of a November that could never live up to the expectations?

Love at first sight is illogical, and his was one sided. It is endorphins and serotonin and dopamine rolled together with lust and hope. It is untrustworthy and unreliable. Our gut feelings are fair-weather friends that want us to believe that we have it all figured out, when we really are so unsure that we're inventing excuses to propel us forward.

If he loved me, he would recognize the pain he caused when he told me I was worth waiting for, only to go back on that promise. If he loved me, he would understand that I have always needed more time than him. If he loved me, he would let me move slowly.

He thinks he knows me, but if he did, he wouldn't have ruined this by acting so rashly, twice. All the evidence I have, the years of missing him whenever I allow myself to think of him, is subsumed by my need in this moment to tell myself that he is wrong. Because however much it is going to hurt to walk away, it would hurt so much more to believe in *this*, only to be rejected *again* whenever he realizes he was wrong.

The years of closing myself off and avoiding and locking my heart away can't be undone in the course of one weekend.

When I walk out, I slam the door harder than I intended to. But I can't look back.

Chapter Twenty-Nine

November 24, nine years ago

From Samuel
To Stella

I love you. I will always love you. But until you decide how you actually feel I just can't do this to myself anymore.

Chapter Thirty
Sunday, present day

There is a soft knock on the door, and Elena gets up to answer it.

I have been curled up in a ball under my covers for hours. My limbs are stiff and my eyes are puffy from silently crying on and off all night. I didn't sleep. But I didn't talk to Elena when she came back to the room last night either.

"Hey, do you know where . . ." I hear Hadley's voice stop. "Stella?"

I poke my head out from under the covers and sit up. It's bright outside and is clearly sometime early in the morning. Elena and Hadley are standing in the door, but Hadley is now looking past her at me. I probably look like complete shit.

I expect Hadley to be furious with me, but her face instead is a ball of confusion when I look at her.

"You're here," she says, not really asking a question but seemingly trying to process why I am in front of her. I am tired and cranky and not in the mood.

"Where else would I be?" I say, looking over at Elena, who also seems a bit surprised.

"I—" She pauses before she says anything else.

I sit up a little straighter, wondering what piece of the puzzle I am missing. Has she not talked to Samuel at all? But if she hasn't, why wouldn't she expect to find me in my own room?

"Where is Samuel?" she finally says.

"How would I know?"

My defensiveness is like a sharp weapon that has sprung up instantly. Hadley narrows her eyes at me in a way that lets me know she is on to me. I look over at Elena, who seems less pissed but no less surprised by this outcome.

"What?" I finally say, unable to stop pretending.

"How dumb do I look?" Hadley says coolly.

I balk. "Am I supposed to answer that?"

I turn to Elena, but she shoots me a pointed look, and I shrug back at her like a sullen teenager.

Hadley clearly isn't in the mood for my nonsense.

"If he is not with you and his room is totally emptied out"—my defensive mask falters, because I'm actually surprised by this information—"then seriously, what the hell did you do?"

I stand up and walk over to her. I'm exhausted from a night of spinning circles inside my brain and my head hurts, but I am completely confused by what she is saying. I have to admit to myself that acting like a brat probably isn't going to get me anywhere.

"What do you mean his room is emptied out?"

Hadley stares at me like I'm an idiot just catching up to the events of the day. She straightens up, and the inches she has on me suddenly feel like a widening gulf.

"What else could 'emptied out' possibly mean? I mean, he's packed all his stuff, and he's no longer in his room. I *assumed* you were with him somewhere, but obviously that assumption put a little bit more faith in you than I should have."

"Hey, hey, that's not fair—" Elena stands protectively in front of me, and my heart leaps at her defense of me. I probably don't deserve it, but I want it nonetheless. I am too tired and cranky to fight this battle alone.

But then Elena turns to me, and I see she is going to press me anyway, even though there is no judgment in her eyes.

"Stella, if Hadley is worried about Samuel, perhaps it might be good to share whatever happened last night."

I look at her incredulously. I don't want to share what happened last night. I don't even want to *think* about what happened last night. I want last night to go sit in the corner with all my other memories of Samuel that I've blockaded from my brain for nearly a decade.

But Hadley's face is filled with anxiety, and I clearly have not fooled anyone. Going back into my bed and pulling the covers over my head is *probably* not going to make anyone believe I have disappeared. There are no good options. I might as well say something. My incredulity falters, and I take a deep breath.

"I don't know where he is," I say honestly, putting both hands on my hips and shrinking into myself. I'm mumbling; I can't bear to say the words out loud. "We sort of had a fight last night, so I haven't seen him since."

Elena and Hadley share a look that annoys me. Clearly there has been some discussion of whatever they both think they know—I have no idea what Samuel has shared with Hadley, but I obviously haven't told Elena anything recently on this topic. So whatever they are thinking is hearsay.

I'm starting to feel indignant again—that old friend that allows me to shove every fear and worry to the side and let anger take over—when Hadley gives me a hug.

What the hell?

"He said too much, didn't he?"

She sits down on one of the elaborate chaise lounges and grabs a bottle of water off the bedside table. I stare at her as she casually drinks it. Well, *this* is unexpected. The room is filled with silence, and Hadley looks between Elena and me and sighs.

"I always sort of suspected there was a reason he didn't date, or at least not anyone seriously," she says. "He skirted around the topic a lot and waved it off as being too busy. To be fair, he always *was* really busy with school or work. For a while I thought maybe he was closeted, and having a lesbian best friend was the easiest beard for him—"

I shoot her a look, and she laughs.

"But I saw the way he looked at women, and I heard him with women because we share a wall"—*ugh*—"so that theory never really seemed to hold water. And he did date, sometimes, although it always seemed to fizzle out before it could really begin."

I'm staring at her, unmoving, because I'm not quite sure where she is going with this. But I am really, really curious how this relates back to me. I think about what Samuel said last night about dating, and I feel a sharp pain.

Hadley drinks more water and keeps going. "When he asked me to come on this trip with him, I knew something was up. So of course I got him drunk and made him share the whole story. He's a real light-weight—he cracked like a nut instantly."

I look over at Elena, who doesn't seem surprised in the least. I feel a pang of guilt—I have never allowed her to know the whole story. I hid it behind all my armored bullshit of casualness, letting her believe Samuel was a fling with no emotional bearing on my life. It all stayed locked away. I *deliberately* locked it away so I wouldn't have to face the rising panic the thought brought to the forefront of my mind.

"At any rate," Hadley continues, "I probably shouldn't have encouraged him as much as I did. It all just seemed *extremely* romantic. I can't imagine focusing on any woman for like a week, let alone pining after her for nine years."

The word "pining" hits me in the gut.

"But no offense," she says. "I saw the way you were looking at him, too, and I thought maybe it was mutual."

"Like a starving person in front of a buffet," Elena retorts, chuckling.

I shoot her daggers from my eyes, and it makes her laugh even more. Hadley is trying not to burst out laughing alongside her. Well, I guess I *really* haven't been fooling anyone.

"It's not that it wasn't mutual . . . ," I say, and Hadley perks up. I sit down on the bed across from her and put my head in my hands. "But yes, he did say too much."

"I knew it." Hadley is shaking her head, amusement and disappointment streaming across her face. "You can't spring that shit on a girl and confess your undying love when that's the thing that scared her off in the first place."

She is rolling her eyes at Samuel in absentia, and I can see why they get along so well. She is as straightforward and brash as he is—and he has always been able to take as well as he gives. It's no surprise he would want someone next to him who would be that balance for him.

"It's normal to think about your exes," I venture, trying to defend him a little bit from the verbal lashing Hadley is clearly planning for him. "I obviously thought about him a lot too."

"You did?" Elena says, surprised, and maybe even a little bit hurt.

All this time, living life next to each other every day, she is only just now realizing her best friend has kept something so basic from her. I now have a new dose of guilt to contend with.

I want to fix it. I have to normalize it.

"No, I mean . . . I compared people to him, whenever I was dating someone. And late at night sometimes, you know, I'd think about him and wonder how he was or what he was doing."

They are both staring at me, and I have no clue what I've just said that is so surprising.

"That's normal, though," I eke out, trying to convince even myself. "Everyone does that."

Elena and Hadley share that look again, and I feel exasperated. They are both shaking their heads.

"No, girl," Hadley finally says. "That's like a few weeks or months. Not nine fucking years later on a constant basis."

I'm desperate to prove her wrong. "Well, it ended so abruptly with us, so maybe it just felt unfinished."

"Would you tell me what actually happened?" Elena says quietly. "The first time? I understand not wanting to tell people at the time, if you were confused about how you felt. But I'd really like to hear what happened from you."

I look over at her, and the weight of keeping this all inside for so long breaks through like a dam. I'm crying and she is holding me and I am stunned by my own stupidity for thinking that ignoring this was going to resolve anything.

Once I start talking I can't stop. I tell them about how that summer I played it off like a fling—because maybe if I said it enough, I would believe it. Even though, undoubtedly, that was never the case. I try to explain the letter, seeing Sophie right after, then ignoring the letter. And after that the daily emails, and how things grew from there. I admit that I let him come to visit, and I share how we both stupidly tried to ignore everything we weren't saying. And the fight. I can barely get through talking about the fight.

But surprisingly, I don't feel that tightness in my chest or the anxiety rising, like I expected it to. I'm sniffling and raw and everything that Samuel has been chipping away at for the last few days is like a giant bruise being poked and prodded. But while it hurts, it doesn't give me the panic I keep thinking is going to creep up.

"I never responded to that last email. I couldn't," I finally finish. "I know I messed up, too, but at the end of the day, after telling me he wouldn't pressure me, he did. And then he walked away and left me with a final missive saying it was up to *me* to fix it? I was not in a place to be in a committed long-distance relationship. Who could be at that age?"

Both Hadley and Elena are nodding with so much vigor that I am feeling some of the guilt I have held inside for so many years start to calm.

I continue. "And I convinced myself it was right, even though I woke up every day and checked my email and hoped I would see something from him. But I was so prideful and young, and I truly believed that if he'd left like that, he was over it. Men always leave eventually anyway."

"Yeah, no, men are idiots. Obviously I'm inclined to agree with that," Hadley says.

Elena snickers. My head hurts, and I rest it in my hands.

There is silence for a moment while none of us seems to know what to say, now that the whole story has been unearthed.

Finally Hadley speaks. "So you moved on."

It surprises me how wrong that feels.

A few days ago, I could have brushed that off and truly thought it was accurate. But the truth is that I have never completely moved on, clearly. I've always just thought, *It'll pass*, and then eventually, when it hurt less, I assumed it had. But it hasn't passed so much as that I've grown accustomed to the loss. It wouldn't have this effect on me after so many years if time could heal this wound. I had just moved *away* from Samuel, running all the time, until nine years later he finally caught up to me and made me slow down enough to face the fact that no one else had ever compared to him.

"But Stella . . . ," Elena says cautiously, clearly afraid to rock the boat. "You keep saying he left . . . but what choice did you give him?"

"He had a choice."

I keep my head in my hands so I don't have to look at Elena.

"I think you've decided to tell yourself that for a long time because the truth was harder. But no, sweetie. He couldn't possibly have left you, because you never let him be yours in the first place."

Her words hang in the air. It is impossible not to feel like she's turned my entire viewpoint of a decade upside down with one simple sentence.

Elena puts her hand on my knee, and I lift my head to look in her eyes. "Why didn't you ever tell us?"

"I didn't think . . ." I stop. I don't really have an answer for her. "I genuinely was trying to not think about him as much as was humanly possible. The anxiety overwhelmed me," I finally mutter.

She pulls me in and hugs me for a long time. I start quietly crying again, and she holds me tighter.

"You don't have to explain it. I get it. Sometimes it's easier to avoid our problems than face the things that scare us. We create the narratives that protect us. And he certainly didn't make it easy for you to move at your own speed."

I nod, so grateful for the lack of judgment and the love she is giving me in this moment where I feel pathetic and weak and like a terrible, concealing friend. But it also feels like a huge weight has been lifted off my shoulders just to tell someone else what happened.

I spent so many years thinking that if I kept it all to myself, it wouldn't have power over me. But its power was actually in trying to push the feelings down without letting them see the light enough to be examined properly. Because allowing other people to examine our story for even a few minutes has exposed how wrong I've allowed myself to be for so many years. I wipe the tears from my eyes and feel like I can breathe again.

I can still see Hadley's meddlesome eyes on me, and I get the sense she has more to say. She is looking at both of us, biding her time until it's appropriate for her to speak again.

"What?" I finally mumble.

She doesn't even pretend to be sheepish. She has to say it.

"So, okay, I get nine years ago. But why did you walk out last night?"

"I already told you," I say wearily.

"No, you said he said too much. Which I would be the first to admit that he certainly does. He pushes and pushes. But . . . is he wrong?"

"Isn't he?"

The glances continue, and I put my head in my hands, unable to ignore my pounding headache any longer.

"I think . . . ," Elena starts and then looks over to Hadley, who nods encouragingly. They are on the same page, even if I am clearly not. "I think fear of failure is not a good reason. I know what happened with Sophie shocked you, but hers isn't the only story. I don't want to diminish your anxiety and the effect that has on you, but it's something to work to resolve, not let it take your life over. You've been able to have casual relationships and sex without it affecting you emotionally, and that's great. Sometimes sex can just be sex, and I totally get that. But *this* isn't that. I think if you have been missing him on some level for nine years and then you see him and everything you feel for him is the same, you owe it to yourself to not walk away."

"It's crazy to just walk away," Hadley concurs.

That touches a nerve.

"We barely know each other!" I shout, trying to stop myself from having to listen to more of Elena's logic and her valid points that are all far, far too close to home.

I'm a short fuse, and I have been shocked too many times in one day. Telling the whole saga has drained me, and I want them to understand me, to understand why it's all too much for me, to feel the weight that comes when the anxiety rises up from the pit of my stomach into my chest. I want them to let me avoid thinking about this anymore so I can go back to not feeling this much pain.

"But you love him," Hadley says, shrugging her shoulders.

My God, she is like a Samuel clone. It is as simple as that for her. She can see it written plain as day on my face, so why not say it like it is.

My heart is tightening because I know what she is saying is true.

I knew it when he said it to me last night.

I do love him.

I have always loved him. I am just so exceptionally scared to let myself believe it.

I am stunned, and Elena sees it and scoots closer to me. She pushes my hair behind my ears, like a mother to her child, and takes my hand.

"This cautious approach to life is not making you happy," she says softly. "Not at work and not in your personal life. You have always been so methodical, and of all people, I get that. Creating order among chaos is the best thing to keep us grounded and avoid getting overwhelmed. Hell, I know we sometimes hold each other back by complacently living and doing everything together. But that's not the *goal*, right? I love you, but I don't want to grow old with someone who definitely doesn't want to have sex with me."

I laugh, even though it's still melding with some tears, probably making me look and sound as unattractive as humanly possible.

But Elena just strokes my hair. "It's okay to be messy sometimes. It's okay to tell people how you're feeling."

"I am sorry for not telling you," I say honestly.

"I wasn't talking about me, but thank you. I know." Her eyes are looking a bit misty. "I'm sorry that you felt like it would be easier for you if you didn't."

I nod, sobbing a little bit again and nestling my face into her shoulder. She strokes my hair a bit more, and I slowly get myself under control.

"It's okay to tell him all of how you feel," she says softly. "The love and the fear, okay? It sounds like he wants all of it."

"He really, truly does," Hadley says, laughing.

I shake my head. "I ruined it. He said he couldn't do this again."

"Yeah, he can't do the part where you're an idiot and pretend like you don't give a shit." I look at Hadley. Damn, that was cold. "Not the part where you finally fucking tell him you love him. That he will do."

I shift uncomfortably. "I'm not sure I can," I say, tearing up again. "I have so much anxiety; sometimes it seems like it's going to swallow me whole. Just saying you love someone isn't enough to make it the right thing for your life. Look at what I said to Sophie—I upset her so much the other day, but I *genuinely* am so afraid for her. I don't want to watch her get hurt again. I want to tell her to go for it and to have hope in the future, but I don't have that hope myself. How can I tell everyone to risk something for love when I'm not even sure I can handle it?"

Elena grips my hand, and Hadley stands up and then kneels right in front of me. She grabs my other hand and looks me right in the eyes.

"Stella, I don't know you very well, and I certainly don't know your sister. But I know Samuel. He has never regretted anything in his life more than not letting you move at your own speed. And he is just such a fucking idiot and so clearly in love with you that I don't think he was able to contain himself from saying what he was feeling. But just *tell* him all of this. Tell him you need to start slowly and not rush. Tell him you are afraid. Tell him what it physically feels like. Give him all the gory details. But you can't give up on letting him love you."

Her sincerity makes me start to bawl. Again. I can't help it. My whole life I thought I had to be the tough person, that going off to school on my own and getting the job I wanted required me to do everything for myself. My parents gave me the space to be whatever I wanted to be, but I always felt like I had to repay that by showing them I was strong enough to handle it. And then I had to be stronger than Sophie so they wouldn't have to worry about *both* daughters. I never took any risks, in case I could stumble off track. I hid from every relationship for the fear that it would knock me off course and tilt my world.

But I realize that *this* feels strong—this, crying in front of my best friend and a new friend and being honest with them. I pushed Samuel away once because of fear. Maybe I need to have real strength this time instead of fake bravado.

Maybe the real strength is risking the fear for the chance of happiness.

"Okay," I finally say tentatively, taking deep breaths and trying to wrap my mind around this change of plans. "Let's get him back."

I look up at them. Hadley jumps up and starts shaking her fists.

"Hell YES. Dramatic airport scene? Getaway car? Confessing your love on the plane? Skywriting? What are we doing? When do you think he left?"

She is getting worked up and pacing around as the ideas spill out of her.

Elena just stands there laughing. "Uh, sorry to burst your bubble, but we have the postwedding brunch to go to."

I stare back at her. Shit.

After being so distracted all weekend and just barely skating by, I could not do anything else to Subrata to make her finally realize how totally crap I've been. Of course the moment I am ready to leap off the building would be the moment that an important obligation would stop me in my tracks.

On the other hand, maybe I need to do this my way.

Maybe it was Samuel's way to run in and say how he felt and press the issue. He would be the person chasing me down at an airport or standing up dramatically. But if Samuel wants me, then he should get *me*. I am not impulsive. I am methodical. I think things through. I need to get my ducks in a row before I make any grand declarations. I need to do this for Samuel, but mostly I want to do this for myself. I have to stop being afraid, and for me that includes thinking a plan through.

Maybe this time slow and steady could win the race.

Chapter
Thirty-One
Monday, present day

Walking into my office this morning is surreal.

Nothing jolts a postvacation, jet-lagged body quite like the static hum of air-conditioned cubicles and fluorescent lighting. No more wisteria vines snaking around ancient columns. No more aperitif-soaked, sunshine-filled lunches with friends.

No more Samuel.

Yesterday at the brunch, I was dutiful, if distracted by Samuel's glaring absence. I tried to shake it all off once I got on the plane by watching some thrillers to get my mind off anything romantic. When I got home yesterday evening, I immediately collapsed onto my bed and conked out. At least this time my suitcase made it back with me.

But today, despite the cognitive dissonance of being back in my office, I feel determined, even if that determination is causing me deep anxiety. I might be a world away from the fantasy of an Italian wedding weekend, but I still know what I need to do. I'm not going to put my head down and play it safe anymore. Not today.

Today I'm going to use my fastidious recipe-writer tendencies to organize my personal life. If talking to Samuel is like cooking the big meal, then today I need to do all the prep work to get myself in order first.

Before I can lose my nerve, I walk right into my boss's office, knocking as I close the door.

"What's up, Stella?" Yoli asks, looking up and giving me her full attention.

"I need to talk about not getting the promotion," I say, sitting down across from her and getting straight to the point.

She nods. I'm frankly surprised at how clearly not surprised she is. "Let's talk then."

I take a deep breath. "My performance reviews have been stellar. I'm a huge asset to this team, and I've already been doing the work that the promotion would have had me do anyway."

"I know that, Stella."

Her eyes are kind and understanding, but I'm still sweating through my shirt. This is so hard for me to articulate. Every fiber in me is screaming to abort, but I'm pushing past it. I *have* to be able to push past it.

"So," I continue, "I get that Reid got this particular promotion, and I'm realistic in understanding that we work in media and budgets are what they are. I know that there's twenty corporate layers in between every choice. But I need to know I'm valued. You said last week I need to start exploding fireworks, but my *work* is *already* the fireworks."

I'm so nervous to see how she's going to react. But all she says in response is, "I appreciate you coming to me like this."

"You do?"

I know I shouldn't sound so shocked, but I haven't really gotten past this part of my little spiel in my head. If I'd actually allowed myself to think about Yoli's potential responses, I probably would have chickened out.

"It's been bothering me, too, honestly," she says with a sigh. "There's a lot of freezes in place—as you say, media being what it is—but it doesn't mean your instincts aren't valid. I know I count on you for so much, and it's time for me to try and make you know you can count on me too."

"So what does that mean exactly?" I say, still a bit stunned.

Yoli laughs a little. "Well, at the moment, nothing. I'm going to run the question up the flagpole of whether there's any room for a title bump or a raise or both. I can't promise anything, and honestly I don't want to get your hopes up. This is not an industry renowned for its allegiance to talent. But I owe it to both of us to try."

Her unanimity has rendered me speechless. I know probably nothing will come of it, but just hearing the words is satisfying. Hell, even knowing I could say what I was thinking without imploding is satisfying.

"Thank you, Yoli. I really appreciate you even trying," I say, standing up.

"You're worth it, Stella," she says with a smile.

And with a nod I walk out and get back to work.

At home, later that evening, my apartment is already filling with the fragrance of garlic and my new stash of lentils when my buzzer goes off. I look at it and am surprised to see Sophie outside my building. I buzz her up and crack the door open. I get back to cooking.

I hear her before I even turn around. The thud of her giant bucket bag—always filled with too many contingency plans—hits my entry table.

"What are we having for dinner?"

I roll my eyes. Presumptuous sister. As though the last time we spoke she didn't practically hang up on me. But if she can avoid for a minute, I can *always* use food to avoid.

"I brought back some lentils from Umbria," I say casually as I keep stirring the pot. "They're famous for them. I got some sausage at the farmers' market before work this morning, so I'm trying to re-create this sausage and artichoke version I had last week. These sausages are a little fennely, so I'm not sure it's replicable."

She comes up next to me and sticks her nose in the pot, smelling the concoction I'm brewing while I swat her away. Laughing, she shifts into a tentative side hug.

I give in and turn to give her the kind of hug I know she really wants—what she used to call my "spider monkey hugs" when I was a kid. The full-grasp, impossible to extricate yourself from, squeezy kind of hug that makes both of us feel placated.

"I'm really sorry, Soph. I was such a bitch on the phone to you last week," I mumble, my face buried into her neck.

"Yes, you were," she says with a small laugh.

I pull back and grab her hand, looking at her new engagement ring. It's so different from the classic solitaire Charlie once gave her. It's gold filigree with a ruby in the center, probably antique: dainty but solid, intricate but not fussy. Bassem found the perfect ring for her. I should have recognized that after so many years she wouldn't have said yes to someone who doesn't truly know her, even if the timing seemed quick.

"I had a lot of time this weekend to think about what you said," I start.

But Sophie waves her hand the way she always does, like it's no big deal. This has been our perennial unspoken problem. We let things go so we won't make each other uncomfortable. The big sister wanting to smooth everything over for the little sister and the little sister having too much adoration to ever question anything the big sister says.

We can't go on like this, though.

"No, Sophie, let me really apologize," I say, a bit more forcefully than my usual tone, and I can tell by the look on her face that she understands I mean it.

"Okay."

"Okay," I reply. "I mean, everything you said was right. We *didn't* ever talk about what happened with you and Charlie, and it did affect me in a major way. It was hard to watch you suffer, and for so long. Of course that affected me. But none of that excuses my reaction to your beautiful news."

She's silent for a moment, letting the sentiment sink in.

"I'm sorry, too, you know," she says. "Not for being sad, because I couldn't help that. But I wish I had talked to you about it more. I couldn't have solved anything for either of us—there isn't some big secret revelation or anything that could explain away his actions and make it all make sense—but we could have leaned on each other more. I didn't want to burden you, but looking back on it now, I don't think that sentiment helped either of us."

I nod, her apology already worming its way into the bruised part of my heart that I know has started healing.

But there's still one difficult question looming; even though I'm afraid of even saying it out loud, I can't help but let it slip through all my crevices.

"Are you worried now? That it will happen again?" I whisper.

She nods slowly.

"I don't think it would be realistic not to be a tiny bit, on some level."

She sits down on a stool at my counter and pours herself a glass from the bottle of grechetto I've already opened. I sit next to her and fill up my abandoned glass too. This conversation needs it, and we both take advantage of the natural silence that fills the room after her admission, enjoying the crispness of the wine in front of us.

"But," she finally says, "I'm not *scared* anymore. I was, for so many years. Before he walked out, I really was happy with Charlie, and I had no idea that he wasn't. Some people *do* just leave. And that's a reality that I can't change. But he's only one person. I look at Mom and Dad—they choose each other every single day. That's real. That's just as strong a data point as me and Charlie. Look at Luca and Subrata. Some people find real, lasting love that never breaks. And then there are also some loves that change too much over time and become broken. We can't know what's going to happen. It took me a long time, but I'm finally recognizing that one experience doesn't automatically determine the next one. We take the information we have, and we have to live fully in each iteration of our lives. Otherwise we're just treading water. I did that for too long, and that's so much worse than living boldly and sometimes getting burned."

I get up from my stool and give her a hug, breathing in her familiar shampoo smell and relishing how damn happy she looks.

"When did you get so wise?" I ask, pinching her cheeks while she bats me away like I did to her earlier.

"Eh, it should've happened sooner. I took way too long to realize I shouldn't ever be afraid to bet on myself."

I lightly pat her hand and then take another sip of wine, the floral nose of the grechetto whisking me back to poppy fields and lopsided grins.

"I think I know what you mean," I sigh.

"Oh yeah?" Sophie says, interest piqued.

"Yeah."

And then I share the whole story of the weekend, knowing that no matter what happens when I finally talk to Samuel, I want Sophie to know all about what's happening in my heart.

I'm betting on myself either way.

On Wednesday, Yoli calls me into her office and asks me to shut the door.

"So, I had a couple of conversations, with a few of the higher-ups and with HR. Everyone was very enthusiastic about your work and you and wants to make something happen to get your role to what it deserves to be. Unfortunately, it's not going to be right now. There's no budget, and any title promotion would usually also come with a salary increase, so it's impossible to do any of that at the moment. *But*, I'm going to keep pushing on it, and they said to bring it up again in a few months and we can revisit. So, I know it's not what you want to hear, but hopefully at some point—now that you've brought it up—we can make something happen. It may not be this year, but at least it's on their agenda."

Yoli looks so uncomfortable that I find myself starting to say, *It's totally fine*, but I stop myself before the words can come out. A week ago, that would have been my response. It *was* my response to so many things.

Instead I say, "Thank you for letting me know. And seriously, thank you for trying."

I get up and walk out, heading to the test kitchen to start tinkering on a recipe I'm working on for a version of the chocolate walnut cake I had last week.

I've been trying to get the ratio of melted chocolate to cocoa powder right to ensure the right level of chocolatiness. I lose myself in the process that I love—tinkering with a recipe, making sure it's approachable and easy for anyone to execute, testing the time and temperature to get just the right texture on the cake.

But no matter how much I try to focus on baking, my mind keeps coming back to Yoli. Before, I would have kicked the thoughts away, reminding myself how lucky I am to have this job. I'm standing in a kitchen eating cake for a living! Who wouldn't be grateful for that?

But . . . it's as though the whole world has been given a new context.

Samuel's voice dances in my head. *You are so scared of what would happen if you fail that you won't grab your own happiness with both hands.*

Samuel's words are joined by Elena's. *You're strong enough to take some leaps, Stel.*

I have to trust in my own worth.

I know now what I need to do.

Chapter Thirty-Two

Thursday

I'm finally ready to go talk to Samuel. Everything with work and Sophie has merely been a warm-up for this conversation.

Hadley has given me her and Samuel's address (her pleas for a public flash mob in Times Square on the red steps were quickly shot down), and she promised me that he is "lame enough that he will be home if you show up after work any day of the week." I don't want a public spectacle. I want to do the thing that is actually the hardest for me and the thing Samuel deserves the most.

I walk into the lobby and ask the doorman to buzz Samuel.

"Who should I say is here?" he asks.

"Tell him Stella has come after him for once."

The doorman looks confused but dials. He speaks quietly into the phone and then looks at me.

"You can go up," he says, uninterested now.

I thank him and get in the elevator. My stomach feels like a swarm of butterflies has taken up residence, but I try to breathe through it. No getting spooked now.

Samuel's door is open when I step out of the elevator. He is standing there in a gray T-shirt and shorts, stubble unkempt on his face, his perfect hair a messy pile on his head. He looks at me with no expression, and my heart pounds in my chest. I can't read him, and it instantly unsettles me. Maybe I really have already blown it? Maybe this is a horrendous idea.

He waves me in with his hand and still says nothing. I walk into the apartment and go into the living room. The whole look of the room is metallic and black and modern—I wonder if that aesthetic is Samuel or Hadley, or maybe their similarities also extend to their decorative choices. I am suddenly desperate to avoid having this conversation, and I start looking around as though maybe a photo or piece of art could distract me.

But Samuel is standing in the doorway with his arms crossed, and I know I have to say what I came here to say. He might not want me anymore, but he also hasn't thrown me out. And I certainly owe him an explanation. He deserves that. So that's where I will find my opening.

"I owe you an explanation," I say lamely, my voice high pitched and nervous.

This isn't a good start.

"Can I grab a glass of water, actually?" I ask, walking over to the sink in the kitchen, which is in the same giant room as the living room. He nods at me and I find a glass, fill it, and down it all in one go. Shit, I'm really skittish. I need to pull myself together. I have to simply start talking.

"I am not good at recognizing and demanding the things I need," I finally say, not quite sure where to begin. I'm fidgeting, but I try to make myself stop. "I think most kids have to push against their parents to get what they want, and I never really did, so it made me deferential.

It made me independent, and that was great, but it also made me scared
to say what I need when it's uncomfortable. I let nervousness—or really
the *fear* of nervousness and panic—stop me from moving forward."

I can feel my pulse getting contained a little bit. Now that I've
begun, I'm on a roll, and it's getting easier. "So I quit my job yesterday."

His eyebrows lift. I should have segued into that a little better, but
now I need to barrel forward and get it all out. At least I definitely have
his attention.

"I got back from Italy and knew I needed to make some changes. I
talked to my boss about the lack of promotion, and she said she would
try to see if something could be done. Budgets being what they are, she
couldn't. I sat on it for a bit and decided that I have had enough of being
scared. I am worth more, and I'm worth trying to see if I can write what
I want and freelance and take that on. So I told my boss how much I
appreciate everything she's done for me, but that I had to quit. And I
have you to thank for seeing through my bullshit and telling me I was
wrong to be so complacent. I need to challenge myself, and I need to
not let fear dictate my happiness."

At that his eyebrows raise again. His arms are still crossed, though,
and he isn't going to give me an inch until I get to the real crux of why
I am here. I am dancing around the point, but it's hopefully becoming
clearer. I tap my fingers on a table and try to keep building the courage
to say what I actually came here to say. I take another sip of water and
try to calm my nerves.

"But that's not really the thing I wanted to tell you. I mean, I also
wanted to tell you that, because I think you deserve some credit for it,
and also it will make me happy and you probably would be interested
in that, but it's not why I'm here."

I am babbling. It is hard to breathe, but I have to push through it.
He is looking at me so intently that I feel like he's going to burn a hole
in me. It's impossible to read what the feeling is behind his eyes, though,

and it makes me exceptionally nervous. But it isn't his job to make me comfortable—I have to stand up for myself.

I continue. "You said to me once that I had to fight my own fears to be able to fight for you. It was easier for me to be complacent than work on my own issues, and you were totally right about that. I knew it in the moment, even when you said it to me. But it was too scary. My life was *fine* where I was, and I couldn't go back to not being fine. So I panicked. Twice."

His expression is getting lighter as I'm talking, and it makes me fill with hope. Maybe, just *maybe*, he can forgive me. He is standing so still that he is like a sphinx, inscrutable to the end.

"But I made the wrong choice, Samuel. Also, twice," I say with a chuckle. "I have anxiety, a real honest-to-God problem with it, and I have let the fear of it and the fear of my sister's past rule me for too long. I was so wrong to push you away because I was terrified. And I have to be honest with you and say that I am *still* extremely terrified. I am so terrified and anxious that I'm honestly sort of shocked I haven't spontaneously combusted right in front of you. On this really pretty carpet."

I look down at his white fluffy carpet and imagine what it would look like if I just melted into it right now in order to avoid finishing these sentences. But I have to have the courage. I have to face my fears. I've let them rule me for too long.

"I am so terrified that I will tell you how I really feel and you will say it's too late. I am terrified you will say yes and then realize in a few weeks that you are sick of me. I am terrified that months or years down the road, you could crush me and I would never get over it and it would ruin my life. But you have always been honest with me no matter how much it scares you—if anything scares you—and I owe you the same. So yes, I am completely terrified of all of those things, and I kind of am a bit worried I might pass out right now from a panic attack."

My heart is beating so hard I worry it is going to fly out of my chest. But I have to finish. I need to tell him. I can't keep avoiding this, or I will never be able to look myself in the eye and know I am able to fight for myself.

"But I love you."

His eyes go wide. I can see that I have shocked him, but I can't tell if it's good or bad. He hasn't moved at all or come toward me, and it's making it so hard to keep going, but I have to.

"I didn't get there as fast as you. I didn't see it the first night we met or after our first date—which, yes, was a date—"

He cracks a small smile, and the effect on my body is like a tidal wave crashing down. Hope is now beating out of me.

"I tried not to realize it or even think about it when you wrote me your letter. Even after all those emails and waking up smiling every day, knowing you would be there in my inbox, I wouldn't even consider it. I didn't let myself realize it because I was so determined not to get hurt in a way that was irreparable. But it didn't make it any less true or less real. When you walked out the door that day, after you told me that I was afraid to admit that I loved you . . . I knew it then. I pushed it away, but that was the moment that I really knew, and it was also the only moment where you put the ball in my court.

"And I failed you because I couldn't handle it. So I wasted nine years because I convinced myself that if you were able to leave then, that you would always leave eventually. And I've lived too safely ever since, allowing myself to get more and more stuck in the most cautious directions, because that hurt of losing you was too much for me. And I didn't want to ever feel that way again."

I pause. He wants me to finish. I can see him willing me to say my piece. Whatever his decision is, I have to see this through.

"When I saw you in Italy, it was like nothing had changed. Time hadn't dulled a single piece of you for me, and that really shocked me. So again, I tried to ignore it."

I get braver. I walk up to him, and he sharply draws in breath. I put my hand in his hair and tuck a small piece behind his ear.

"I have to work on myself and figure out why I get so scared. Beyond quitting my job, I've also made my first therapy appointment. I have anxiety, and I need to face that and deal with it and learn how to actually cope with it in a productive way. Because I need to get comfortable not hiding from the things in my life that are hard. If you are ever going to trust me and believe me that I really do love you and accept this totally absurd and very poorly phrased apology, then I am going to do everything I can to show you—"

"Stop, Stella."

He puts a finger to my lips, and I see tears welling up in his eyes, and my heart sinks. I can't help but feel like this is the moment where he tells me he can't listen to this nonsense anymore. That I've ruined it by pushing him too far. That he can't be with someone as emotionally damaged and afraid as me. That he can't go through this again with me. That maybe he loves me, but I'm too much.

But then he smiles. His whole body has shifted, and he is lit from the inside, and suddenly I realize that maybe, just maybe, being brave is everything he's been telling me all along.

"You don't have to say any of this," he says finally, his voice a whisper and his fingers still on my lips. "I told you that night we first went out—I've loved you since you told me to overorder pierogi. I always wanted to hear you say it, too, so I think maybe I let you babble on a little too long—"

I laugh and now my eyes are welling up, too, because he has always had me pegged completely.

"But I have always been yours, Stella. Even when I left, I was still yours. I have regretted that for so many years. But I promised you I would always love you, and I always have."

Tears are now starting to fall down my cheeks, and I am delirious. He wipes them away and cups my face in his hands.

"But I owe you an apology too. I didn't believe you when you said what you needed, and in that regard I failed you. I told you I would wait until you were ready and that I wouldn't bring it up again until you were. I should have heard you and stopped being so selfish. I didn't realize how much anxiety was affecting you—I just believed I inherently knew everything about you, and that's obviously not how life works. I was impatient and I needed you, and I wrecked it for both of us."

I'm laughing now through the tears, and I probably look insane. But I can't stop myself from kissing him all over now like a deranged kissing addict. I'm kissing his cheeks, his earlobes, his eyelashes, everything I can get my lips on. I feel so light and free from the burden of keeping myself from him that now I want everything all at once, and I don't even know where to begin.

"You didn't wreck anything," I say finally. "I just needed a bit of time to catch up to you."

"But now you have," he replies, a smoldering look crossing his eyes as he grabs me around the waist and pulls me closer.

"Now I have. Thank you for your letter. I know I'm nine years late in responding, but I love you too."

"You're worth the wait," he says and then he kisses me, lifts me off my feet, and carries me toward his bedroom and a lifetime of allowing myself to be loved.

EPILOGUE
ONE YEAR LATER

"Aha!" I exclaim, pulling out a bottle of hair spray from the back of the medicine cabinet. "Hadley is always on my side, leaving me all the womanly things I need."

"Or she is simply a lazy roommate who never cleaned out properly when she left."

I see Samuel come up behind me wrapping a towel around his waist but still dripping from the shower. He puts his arms around me as I shriek.

"You're all wet!"

He laughs and kisses my neck.

"And now I have to change again," I say, scolding him as he pulls away and looks at the giant wet splotch on my dress.

"Hm, it looks like *you* are all wet now. And I like how that sounds."

I roll my eyes at him, but the giddy look on his face is impossible to resist, and I pull him up close to me and kiss him softly.

"Well, if you're going to ruin my outfit and make dirty jokes in my face, I guess I am powerless against your charm," I say sarcastically while still somehow succumbing to him.

His hands grab my butt, and he pulls me in. I'm about to get lost and my mind is buzzing when he pulls back.

"Listen, little horny toad, don't take advantage of me when I'm trying to take you out to brunch." He gives me a quick kiss on the nose. "We're going to be late."

I sigh and watch him as he takes the towel off from his waist and uses it to dry his hair, giving me quite the view.

"Take a picture, it'll last longer," he says, smirking as he watches me from the mirror.

"I tried to do that once, and this very stubborn man wouldn't let me."

"Yeah, well, I know someone who was a lot more stubborn," he says with a smile. He kisses my cheek, then wanders away to get dressed as I make a point to stare at his backside as he leaves the bathroom.

I finish my hair and makeup and go to my closet for a change of clothes.

I have no idea whether we are still on time or not when we leave because Samuel hasn't told me anything about this particular plan. I was surprised we were doing something on a weekend morning—he's been working so much at his law firm lately that usually when he finally gets to sleep in, he relishes it.

And since I moved in last month, it's made the weekends more relaxing for both of us—no more fumbling around to remember clothes or deciding whose apartment we're going to be in or which person already has groceries. I've been working from home on my freelance writing, a ghostwriting cookbook project and a few corporate recipe clients, which was making swapping apartments constantly a huge hassle from my end.

Logistically, we probably should have moved in sooner, yet, true to his word, Samuel kept his promise to let me go at my own speed. But when I finally mentioned it might be easier if we just moved in together over Chinese takeout one night, Samuel got so excited he knocked noodles all over his white carpet.

And luckily, my favorite part of dating Samuel didn't change when we started cohabitating. On his train to work every morning, he still writes me an email. Even though I've usually been with him the night before and he doesn't have much new to report on, I love getting his little notes about the morning news, what's upcoming in his day, and what crazy outfits he sees on the subway.

We arrive in front of Veselka, and he stops, turns to me, and beams. "Okay, we're here!"

"We're having brunch at Veselka?"

"Not just brunch at Veselka," he says, grinning as we walk up to a table already full of people. Subrata, Elena, and Cat beam at me. Sophie and Bassem are clearly giddy with surprising me. Hadley stands up and starts clapping.

Oh, shit.

What is everyone doing here?

"Now, before you start to epically freak out," Samuel says, sensing my defenses immediately going up, "this is not about to be me proposing or springing anything on you that we have not discussed, because naturally that would be a total betrayal of every promise I've ever made to you."

He is looking at me seriously now, catching my eyes with his and seeing right into me. He takes my hand gingerly into his and rubs my thumb in a comforting way. Damn, he really has worked on his listening. But then the serious face goes away, and that smirk I love so much is back.

"But," he continues, "I am surprising you somewhat because you kept a pretty big secret from me, and as such I get to pay you back in whatever method I deem fit." I scan my brain, trying to understand what he's talking about. "I saw the letter you got from the *Best American Food Writing* book editor for this year—I'm so proud of you that your essay is being included!"

Ohhhhh. My heart leaps. I *haven't* told Samuel about it—my editor at the magazine where it was originally published submitted my essay about a favorite restaurant I grew up with, and I was so shocked at the inclusion that I almost blocked the entire thing from my mind. It seemed unreal that something I had written right after I quit my job and took the jump into freelancing would be recognized in that way. I guess I still had to work on my avoidance skills in some areas.

"So, since you are completely terrible at celebrating yourself and recognizing your own brilliance—"

At this Elena and Hadley start whooping and tapping their forks to their glasses, making enough noise that I am sure a waiter is going to come and shush us.

"—I figured we should have some pierogi and pancakes in your honor at the one place I was certain you wouldn't get mad at me for springing a surprise on you."

He looks at me with that adorable nervousness behind his eyes, desperate to have done the right thing, and I pull him so fast into a kiss that he's startled.

"Thank you," I whisper. "Thank you for making me so much less afraid in every part of my life."

I give him another kiss and then go to kiss everyone on their cheeks—and rub Subrata's growing belly for good measure.

"I'm so excited for all the food! We need to order some appetizers, ASAP," Subrata exclaims, staring more at the menu than anything else.

Somehow her cream-colored maternity jumpsuit is still making her the chicest woman in the room.

"I'm definitely never going to be pregnant, but I think that sentiment makes me relate to all pregnant women," Hadley quips while flagging down a server and ordering a heaping pile of potato pancakes and pierogi to get us started. "I feel like I could eat all of that myself."

"I am definitely on board," Elena agrees, scanning the rest of the menu to figure out what we're missing.

"Oh yes, eat everything now so you can be all dainty on your date later," Hadley snorts and Elena blushes.

"Who is your date with?" I say, surprised to be so out of the loop.

The only part I hate about living with Samuel is not getting to see Elena every single day anymore.

"Hadley has set me up with her brother," she mutters, matter-of-factly.

I tilt my head.

"Uh, you're going to have hooked up with siblings?" I say, and Elena turns an even deeper red.

It became exceptionally clear after Subrata's wedding that Elena and Hadley had also been sneaking off during the festivities, but it fizzled out once we all got back to New York, and now they've become close friends.

When I asked Elena how they'd made such a seamless transition, she laughed and replied, "Because Hadley is too insane for me to be in an actual relationship with, but she makes for an extremely entertaining friend. Great in bed, though."

When I relayed this to Samuel, he laughed and said that Hadley's response to the same question was, "She's not gay enough for me. We are way better as friends. Great in bed, though." So at least everyone was on the same page.

"I'm mostly just desperate to know which of us has the bigger dick," Hadley responds, wiggling her eyebrows as Elena facetiously puts her head in her hands.

Cat looks up from trying to secretly respond to work emails under the table. "I'm sorry?" she says, confused by the sudden inclusion of salty words as Hadley and Elena cackle like pervy teenagers and Subrata mutters about the sanctity of her wedding memories.

"It's not our fault you brought us all to the most romantic place on earth," Samuel points out to Subrata, and she laughs.

"True. Umbria has its own brand of magic."

"Yeah, my brother is going to have to compete with that," Hadley giggles as Elena elbows her sharply under the table.

"You know I'm not telling you anything about your brother's anatomy, right?"

"Please not to me either," Samuel replies jokingly as steaming plates of pierogi and latkes get dropped unceremoniously on the table.

Everyone instantly starts piling them onto their plates to get started eating. I can't help but smile as Sophie gingerly lifts a giant pierogi and tries to stuff the whole thing into Bassem's mouth. *God, they're annoyingly cute. And thank goodness.*

"Hey," I say to Samuel under my breath as Cat starts a new conversation reminiscing about which meals in Umbria were the best, while Subrata starts encouraging Sophie and Bassem to go on their own trip there. "Thank you for doing this. I can't think of a better celebration."

Samuel beams. "I was worried I was going to scare the crap out of you with a surprise, so I'm sorry if I rushed through the explanation a little too much."

"No, that was actually my favorite part. Thank you for knowing me well enough to know it was necessary."

I put a reassuring hand on his knee and squeeze.

"I also want to make it extremely clear that I *would* propose to you and marry you in about one second if you ever told me that was what you wanted. But just so you know, I'm going to wait until you explicitly tell me to do it because I am never planning to scare you off again. Not for anything in this world."

I take his face in my hands and softly caress his cheeks. He really has nothing to worry about. "Thank you," I reply, trying to eke out every ounce of sincerity for his thoughtfulness.

Although his sweet declaration does make it extremely hard to contain my giddiness for the plan I already have to surprise him with a proposal back at Veselka next week.

RECIPES FOR AN UMBRIAN-INSPIRED DINNER

This book is the culmination of a dream to write rom-coms, but in my other work-life I'm typically dreaming up recipes. So it seemed necessary to take both of my dreams and bring them together with a dinner plan for an Umbrian evening inspired by this book.

Recipe for Second Chances is a love letter to Umbria as much as it is to love, and it's mostly because I wholeheartedly believe the region should get more attention from non-Italian audiences. Even as an Italy fanatic, when I went, I figured my seafood-loving self would never fall quite so hard for this meat-heavy, decadently truffle-obsessed region. But I came to discover that, like so much of Italy, the stereotypes are only the surface, and the variety and vibrancy of Umbrian food are among the country's best-kept secrets to outsiders.

If you want to learn more about the rustic joys of Umbrian food, I would highly recommend following or reading anything by Elizabeth Minchilli—she is one of my favorite English-language Italian food writers, and she just happens to live my dream life straddled between Rome and her gorgeous home in Umbria. That will get you much more traditional recipes, since what follows here are my own interpretations based on feelings and ingredients and not exact replicas.

I also want to note that a few of the businesses mentioned in the book are very real. Palazzo Seneca is a gorgeous historical hotel in Norcia. Villa Amati is not real, but much of its visuals are based on a hotel called Borgo Dei Conti, outside Perugia. And if you want that pistachio gelato (which truly did win a "best in the world" designation), go to Gelateria Crispini in Spoleto.

But if you want to travel from home, let Stella and Samuel live with you a little longer by getting a taste of the magic they found in Umbria. You can make one recipe or make them all as a spectacular (but quite easy to actually execute) dinner party—and yes, in honor of Stella, I've included two desserts.

Umbrian Lentils with Sausage and Artichoke

Umbrians give the humble lentil new life in Umbria. They grow exceptional varietals, but even if you can't get your hands on the beloved Castelluccio version, any green lentil with this firepower of flavors will make for a full meal in a bowl (or an excellent starter to a dinner party). Serves 4 as an entrée (serves 8 as an appetizer).

Ingredients

2 tablespoons olive oil

1 large onion, diced

8 cloves minced garlic

2 cups cherry tomatoes

4 large Italian-style sausages, removed from their casings and crumbled

2 cups green lentils (Italian, and specifically Castelluccio, preferred)

6 cups water or stock

1 teaspoon salt, plus additional as needed

14 ounces (or one can) artichoke hearts, chopped
1 1/2 cups kale, finely chopped

In a large pot over medium-high heat, add the olive oil, onion, and garlic and stir gently for a few minutes until the onions start to soften. Add the tomatoes and sausages and cook for another 5 minutes. Add the lentils and stir to fully coat, cooking for an additional minute. Add the water and salt and bring to a boil, stirring occasionally. Lower the heat to a heavy simmer and cover for 15–25 minutes or until the lentils are tender. Add the artichoke hearts and kale, cook for another 3 minutes, taste to see if additional salt is needed, and then serve.

Note: You can make this ahead and reheat in a microwave or on the stovetop as needed.

Fettuccine con la Ricotta

This fettuccine delights in its simplicity—Umbrians love their sheep-milk cheeses, and ricotta and pecorino are two of the most beloved. But with simplicity comes an importance of ingredients. Buy a nice ricotta and see if you can find a high-quality pasta, or even a fresh one (but make sure to reduce the cooking time in that case). You'll have a dish that is as irresistible as it is simple.

Serves 4 as an entrée (serves 8 as an appetizer).

Ingredients

1 pound fettuccine
16 ounces ricotta
1 lemon
Dash of salt and pepper
1/2 cup grated pecorino
Chopped soft herbs like parsley, mint, or basil (optional)

Bring a pot of salted water to a boil and add the fettuccine. Cook for 8 to 10 minutes, or until al dente, as directed by your particular brand of pasta.

While the fettuccine is cooking, add the ricotta to a bowl and zest the lemon into the bowl (make sure to only get the yellow peel and stop at the white pith). Then squeeze the juice into the bowl as well. Add a few tablespoons of pasta water to the bowl if the ricotta you are using is not very wet.

Once the pasta is ready, drain it and add the ricotta mixture, along with a dash of salt and pepper. When serving, top the pasta with the pecorino. If you have fresh soft herbs such as parsley, mint, or basil, you could always add those as well, if you want a bit of color, and you can also zest more lemon.

Umbrian Pesto Lamb Chops

The classic pesto we are familiar with—with basil and pine nuts—hails from the seaside region of Liguria. But this recipe is a pesto in homage to the flavors of Umbria. And it pairs perfectly with meaty dishes like lamb chops. I know, I know—the mayo is decidedly un-Italian, but that's my twist to keep the chops moist. Trust me, you'll get the taste of the region but with the easiest, quickest version of lamb chops around.

Serves 4 (or 8 as a small course).

Ingredients

2 tablespoons fresh oregano
2 tablespoons fresh thyme
Juice of 1 lemon
1/4 cup mayonnaise
3 cloves garlic
1/4 cup walnuts
1/4 cup grated Parmigiano Reggiano cheese

1 teaspoon kosher salt

8 small lamb chops (around 3 pounds total)

Place an oven rack close to the top of your oven and turn on the broiler. Line a baking sheet with aluminum foil. In a blender, combine the oregano, thyme, lemon, mayonnaise, garlic, walnuts, cheese, and salt. Spread the mixture across both sides of the lamb chops and place them on the baking sheet.

Put the chops in the oven under the broiler for 3 to 4 minutes, then flip the chops to the other side. Cook for an additional 3 to 4 minutes and then remove and serve.

Hazelnut Miso Cookies

Hazelnuts are ubiquitous across Umbria, which grows a fair share of Italy's bounty. While we might be most familiar with Italian hazelnuts for the much-beloved Nutella, this recipe actually uses hazelnuts to make a twist on the classic Italian pignoli cookie, which typically uses pine nuts. I think the hazelnuts add a delectable depth that gets an extra assist from the decidedly un-Italian miso paste. It's a simple light cookie that everyone will fall in love with.

Makes 12–16 cookies.

Ingredients

1 1/2 cups roasted hazelnuts
2/3 cup sugar
2 tablespoons white miso paste
2 large egg whites
1/2 teaspoon salt

Preheat the oven to 325°F and line a baking sheet with parchment paper. Blend the hazelnuts in a blender with the sugar and miso paste.

Using an electric mixer (or whisk if you have the stamina), beat the egg whites and salt in a bowl until the mixture has fluffed up and holds stiff peaks. Gently add the nut-and-sugar mixture and combine.

Place spoon-size dollops onto the sheet, making sure to place the cookies far apart, since they do spread and flatten. Bake the cookies until golden, about 12 to 13 minutes. Remove from the oven and allow the cookies to cool.

Chocolate Cake with Walnuts

Rustic cakes are a staple in Umbria, and this recipe tries to live up to that simplicity. With the no-fail solution of chocolate, as well as the omnipresent walnuts, you get a cake that can be served for dessert or saved for breakfast the next morning.

Makes 1 cake.

Ingredients

1 1/2 cups walnuts, divided
2/3 cup dark chocolate chips
3 large eggs
3/4 cup sugar
1/2 cup olive oil
1/3 cup cocoa powder
1 cup all-purpose flour
1/2 teaspoon kosher salt, plus additional
2 teaspoons baking powder

Preheat the oven to 350°F and oil a 9-inch cake tin. Chop the walnuts so they're small but still have texture. Melt the chocolate chips in a microwave, stirring every 30 seconds until smooth. In a large bowl, combine the eggs with the sugar (using a mixer is preferred to fully incorporate). Add the oil, cocoa powder, and melted chocolate. Stir again to combine. Add in the flour, salt, and baking powder and lightly combine. Add in 1 cup of the walnuts and stir. Transfer the batter to the tin. Sprinkle the remaining walnuts and additional salt on top (flaky sea salt if you have it). Bake for 24–30 minutes, or until an inserted skewer or toothpick comes out clean. (You can start checking at 20 minutes if your oven runs hot.) Let the cake cool before serving.

Acknowledgments

Recipe for Second Chances started as a secret project, just for me, to see if my suspicion that I would love writing fiction as much as I loved writing recipes was true. It's only in your hands now because along the way I allowed a few other people inside, and they believed in me and this book. I am more grateful to them than words can express, but I'm going to try.

I have to start with the person who truly made this book happen: my agent, Wendy Sherman. She is the kind of champion who believes in her clients so deeply but also pulls no punches to tell you what you need to hear. I never dreamed I'd have an agent who speaks my language so perfectly. I know I'll keep telling you this more times than you want to hear, but I'm putting it in print too: thank you.

Thank you, Lauren Plude, for being the editor who said MINE and then immediately convinced me you were the only person who could shepherd this book properly (you had me at data). Thank you, Lindsey Faber—your discerning insight is as perfect as advertised. If we could monetize enthusiasm, the three of us would have a real gold mine on our hands! Bill Siever, thank you for copyediting with humor, meticulous skill, and endless patience for my time/tense jumping. Kyra Wojdyla, thanks for keeping the trains running on time and making everything so seamless! Jenna Justice, for the thorough proofread, and Angela Vimuttinan, for the precise cold read. And to Katrina Escudero for believing that this little story could and should be more.

To my uproariously funny, laser-sharp, insightful pen pal and now friend, Mary Kuczkir. The world knows her as the bajillion-times best-selling author Fern Michaels, but I know her as the person who agreed to take time out of her incredibly busy schedule not only to read my book but also to rip it to shreds with me and insist I make it a thousand times better. I'll try to write as fearlessly as you do and achieve all the goals you've brazenly set for me. Thank you for everything.

This book is a romance, but it is also an ode to friendships that lift you up and champion you, even when you aren't sure you can champion yourself. I am so lucky to have friends like that, and a few of them were instrumental in making this book a reality. I trusted Molly Aronica to edit the very first draft, when I was scared to even tell a single other person I'd written it. Thank you, Molly, for giving me the encouragement to believe this could be real. Matthew Kane is a phenomenal writer, but more importantly he's been a beloved secret-keeper and advice-giver for a quarter century. Thank you for reading (multiple times!) before this was anything. Thank you, Charlotte Druckman, for our walks (a.k.a. listening to every winding stage of this journey and cheering me on). Thank you, Yasmin Fahr, for all the commiseration and championing (and now please come back to New York, ha-ha). Thank you, Adriana Herrera, Alana Rush, Nicole Campoy Jackson, and Jane Bruce for reading at points when I really needed the encouragement and feedback. And thank you to all my other closest friends who didn't slap me when I told them I'd sold a novel that I'd written in secret and hadn't told them about, and understood it was only because I was too scared to get my hopes up. (You all know who you are, and I hope you all see the flashes of yourselves across this book. I'm so grateful to have the best friends a girl could dream of.)

I'm so lucky to have family always in my corner: Annie, Will, Jon, Skye, Yehuda, Natalie, Aaron (and always missing Rachel).

Thanks most importantly to my mom for being my champion my entire life. It's the greatest gift a kid could have. And to my dad for bestowing the writing gene on me, even if you will never ever (please never) read this book. I love you both so much.

To Guy, Joy, and Rae—thank you for being the lights of my life.

Finally, to Daniel. I believe in true love—real, joyous, messy, sexy, mundane, fun, often infuriating, continuously surprising love—because of every single day belonging to you. We are lucky people.

ABOUT THE AUTHOR

Photo © 2022 Melanie Dunea

Ali Rosen is the author of *Recipe for Second Chances*, a novel about which *New York Times* bestselling author Fern Michaels said she "couldn't turn the pages fast enough."

Aside from loving escaping into fictional worlds, Ali is also the Emmy- and James Beard Award–nominated host of *Potluck with Ali Rosen* on NYC Life as well as the author of cookbooks, including the bestselling Amazon Editor's pick *Modern Freezer Meals* and the upcoming *15 Minute Meals*. She has been featured on shows like the *Today* show and Food Network's *The Kitchen* and has written for publications including *Bon Appétit*, the *Washington Post*, and *New York Magazine*.

She is originally from Charleston, South Carolina, but now lives in New York City with her husband and three kids and can usually be found wandering the Union Square Greenmarket or curled up in a chair reading a romance novel. Connect with Ali online at www.ali-rosen. com and find her on Instagram and Twitter: @Ali_Rosen.